A collection of stories centered around Christmas cookies.

Eight Nights of Apricot Cookies by Roni Denholtz

Shortbread Shakedown by Sofia Aves

Oh, Gingersnap! by Sonja N. Griffing

Drizzle with Caramel

by

Roni Denholtz
Sofia Aves
Sonja N. Griffing

Drizzle with Caramel

Cover Art by *The Wild Rose Press, Inc.*

The Wild Rose Press, Inc.
PO Box 708
Adams Basin, NY 14410-0708
Visit us at www.thewildrosepress.com

Publishing History
First Edition, 2022
Trade Paperback ISBN 978-1-5092-4510-9

Published in the United States of America

Eight Nights of Apricot Cookies

by

Roni Denholtz

Christmas Cookies

Dedication

In Loving Memory
Of My Two Grandmothers

Ada Radel Rosenthal
and
Rebecca Oberfield Paitchel
You both baked the best cookies!

A note from the author...

Dear Readers,

Sugar cookies in Hanukkah shapes and Rugelach are the most popular types of Hanukkah cookies. My grandmothers, Ada and Rebecca, made both. But my grandmother Ada also made apricot cookies, which were a favorite of mine. I liked them so much she made them at other times of the year too.

Sadly, Ada never wrote down most of her recipes, since they were in her head. So the secret to the apricot cookies was lost. My mother found a recipe that sounded similar, and I tried it out, but it came out too mushy. So, I went on a quest while I was writing this book to find a recipe that tasted like my grandmother Ada's.

I finally found one, and after experimenting and making some changes, it tasted pretty close to the original recipe. I'm including it for all my readers!

Happy Holidays!
~Roni Denholtz

Chapter I

Erica sat back on the yellow and orange linoleum kitchen floor, blowing out a breath in frustration. Where on earth had her grandmother hidden her favorite recipes?

She'd already gone through the two dozen or so marked-up cookbooks her grandmother had collected, and they were now toppled on the floor. Now she'd expanded the search to Grandma Franny's stash of papers in the kitchen. But she hadn't yet found her most treasured recipes. Including the one she was most eager to find: the apricot cookies. The ones Grandma made for Hanukkah, plus other times of the year, because they were such a favorite.

The ones she, Erica, wanted so badly to try to make. She wanted to continue Grandma Franny's traditions.

"No luck?" Erica's cousin Alyssa entered the kitchen.

"No." Erica shook her head. Alyssa was not just her cousin but her best friend. She was only six months older than Erica—Erica's mom Joan was the younger sister of Alyssa's mother Jenny—and they'd grown up in the same neighborhood here in Union, New Jersey, just minutes from their grandmother's house.

"How about you?" Erica asked Alyssa, dropping down beside her.

Erica gazed at Alyssa's brown eyes—so much like

her own—and their grandmother's. Although her hair was a deep brown and Alyssa's a much lighter brown shade, there was no mistaking they were related.

Alyssa placed a sympathetic hand on Erica's shoulder. "Our moms have almost finished packing up Grandma's clothes to donate. And we found the jewelry box with all her costume jewelry. But we still can't find her good jewelry collection and all the necklaces, bracelets, and pins she wanted us to have. I just got through looking in the downstairs bedroom."

Erica sighed. "She was so good at hiding things. I don't know why she was afraid of being robbed; this is a very safe neighborhood, and nothing like that happened to her, ever."

"My mom said one of Grandma's closest friends was robbed years ago, back when everyone lived in Newark." Alyssa shrugged. "It must have made her cautious."

"Yeah, that's very probable," Erica agreed. She stared down at the floor where she sat. The floor's pattern had always fascinated her as a child; the geometric squares and rectangles in varying shades form yellow to pale orange to a deeper orange tone.

"Are you okay, cuz?" Alyssa asked.

Catching the concerned note in her cousin's voice, Erica looked up.

"I'm okay."

Alyssa pressed her lips together, her expression anxious.

Erica sighed. Everyone was worried about her.

Not only had their wonderful grandmother died two weeks ago, leaving them all horribly sad; but last week Erica had learned that Lance, her former, two-timing boyfriend, had gotten engaged. And it had brought their history to the forefront of her mind. When she thought of him, a searing pain hit her middle.

She could still barely believe it. A little over a year ago, she'd been doing laundry in her apartment early in the evening, including jeans and a couple of T-shirts Lance left at her place on a regular basis. They'd been going steadily for nearly two years. That evening, automatically going through the pockets of his pants for loose change, she'd felt something silky.

And pulled out a black thong.

She'd frozen. She didn't care for thongs and never wore them.

So whose thong was it?

She had been furious by the time he came over an hour later. They'd had an argument, which escalated when he admitted yeah, he'd had a "little fling" with Jordana, but it wasn't a big deal. According to him he'd never promised Erica he would be exclusive, even though they acted that way; and didn't she want some variety too? No, she didn't, and had told him so in no uncertain terms. When he refused to see it as cheating, that had been the end of their relationship.

She hadn't dated anyone since then. Not even when her well-meaning friends and relatives offered to set her up. Thinking of how he'd cheated on her always made her angry and sad.

The news that Lance had committed to his current girlfriend—Jordana—on top of her grandmother's death, had left Erica feeling depressed. Nothing was going right.

Tears sprang to her eyes now, as she recalled the devastation she'd felt last year, and again last week when she'd heard he was engaged.

"It's okay, cuz," Alyssa said softly. "You did the right thing to break up with him. Who wants a man who cheats?"

"I know, but—after two years? And—I had no idea at the time!" How could she have been so stupid not to see the signs? They were there when she thought back. Her naiveness had hurt, too. She grit her teeth as the frustration rose up in her for the hundredth time.

Alyssa hugged her. "I can imagine how difficult hearing that news was. He's a total idiot. You'll find someone better in no time."

Of course, her cousin was an optimist. She was in love, newly engaged to her boyfriend Matt—who was devoted to her—and Alyssa had stars in her eyes.

"I'm not ready for another relationship. I don't know if I'll ever be," Erica said darkly. How could she trust another guy?

They heard footsteps coming down the stairs of the cape cod house where her grandmother had raised her three children—Jenny, Joan, and their brother Barry.

"How are you girls doing?" Erica's mom Joan called out.

"No success yet." Erica sighed.

"I was all over the guest room down here," Alyssa said. During the last three years, their grandmother had taken to using the downstairs bedroom—originally Joan and Jenny's room and then a guest room—to sleep in, since she had more and more trouble going up the stairs. Since there was a full bathroom on the first floor, this made total sense and her family had pushed her toward that decision. "I really thought she might have put the good jewelry down here near her bed," Alyssa finished.

"We couldn't find anything in her original bedroom, either." Her mom shook her head. She zeroed in on Erica. "Are you okay, honey?"

"I'm fine." Erica tried to smile to soften her words. "Sorry, I didn't mean to snap." Her whole family was worried about her. She knew they cared, but she preferred not to discuss the news about Lance any further.

She stood up. As she had before, she could swear she caught a whiff of her grandmother's favorite perfume, Chanel No. Five

It gave her comfort—as if Grandma Franny was still there.

"I still have a little more searching to do in here—" she waved at the kitchen—"and then I'll try the dining room and living room."

"Ok. We have all the clothes packed up." Aunt Jenny pointed upstairs. "Your dads will come over this weekend and help us bring them to the charity drop-off location. Do you need anything else?"

"We're okay," Erica said. She didn't want her mother and aunt hovering around her, checking to see if she was all right. They looked stressed themselves. Grandma's death from a heart attack had been sudden. Everyone was missing her sunny personality.

She walked over to hug her mother, then her aunt. "This has been difficult for you. Go home and get some rest."

Aunt Jenny sniffled, and Erica's mom wiped at her eyes. "Yes," Joan said, her voice sad. "But your grandmother lived to be eighty-eight, and she had a good life. Dying in her sleep was the best way to go. She probably never even felt the heart attack."

"True." Alyssa hugged them both, too. "You go ahead. We'll lock up."

They left, and Alyssa asked," want to spend more time searching? Or do you want to leave too?"

"Maybe another fifteen or twenty minutes." Erica glanced at her cousin. "Is that all right?"

"Okay."

They searched the upper kitchen cabinets since Erica had already combed through the bottom ones. But besides dishes and glasses, the only thing they found was an advertisement for a new cookbook from 2006.

"She must have been planning to order it," Erica concluded.

"Yes. Are you going to keep these dishes when you move in?" Alyssa asked.

Erica shook her head. "No. Aaron needs a set, so he's going to take them." Her brother had been using an old, chipped set that originally was her parents'. "When I moved into my apartment, I got a new set so I'm okay. Don't forget you're getting Grandma's fine china."

"I won't forget. I always liked the pattern," Alyssa said.

Erica felt discouraged when they finished ten minutes later. "Well, I guess we'll have to come back again another day."

"Yeah." Alyssa sighed. "I can't get here for a couple of days, though."

Erica was about to answer when a sudden rapping on the front door startled her.

"Hello?" A masculine voice called out.

"Hello?" she and Alyssa responded.

Alyssa was nearest to the door, so she moved over and opened it. An attractive man of about thirty stood outside. He had brown wavy hair, and dark eyes.

"I'm Noah Zelman, your neighbor next door," he stated. "I came to say how sorry I was to hear about Franny's passing."

"C'mon in," Alyssa invited.

She opened the door all the way and he stepped inside, bringing a gust of chilly November air with him.

The man was tall, and his medium-brown hair glinted with some red under the hall light. His face had classic, handsome features, and Erica sucked in her breath as she got a good look at him. Broad shoulders and a kind expression made him look very appealing.

Too appealing.

Alyssa sized him up. "You must be Sonia's grandson. We heard you moved into your grandmother's house last year after she passed."

"Yes." He gave each of them a sad smile. "She left the house to be sold, and I was the only one in the family who wanted it, so I bought it from her estate."

Now Erica realized she had seen him around when she'd visited her grandmother during the last year, but they'd never actually spoken. Sonia and Franny had been close friends.

"I've seen you with some construction people," she said. "I thought Sonia's family was going to sell the house."

"I wanted to live here," Noah said.

"I'm Alyssa, and this is my cousin Erica," Alyssa said hastily. "That's exactly what Erica's going to do— buy the house and live here." She sent Erica a speculative look.

Erica tensed. She could guess what her cousin was thinking. She wasn't happy that Alyssa appeared to be playing matchmaker.

"I'm sorry I couldn't attend the shivah service," Noah continued. "The night you had it here, I had to work."

"Where do you work?" Alyssa asked. Trust her cousin to get the info.

"At the local pharmacy on Route twenty-two. I'm one of the pharmacists there."

"Oh. That must be a difficult job. Lots of people get sick at this time of year."

"Yes."

It was near the end of November, and Erica knew it was true. Her cousin, a history teacher, was always telling her about the many kids who came to school sick during the winter.

"That's an important job," Erica stated.

"I like to think so." He turned to focus on Erica, his eyes assessing. "We try to keep our customers healthy. Getting back to your grandmother, I'm really sorry I missed the shivah service. I liked your grandmother a lot." He appeared sincere.

"Franny felt close to Sonia," Erica said. "I know she missed her since she passed."

"Yes. As a matter of fact, your grandmother used to bake me some of her apricot cookies. I missed my grandmother's cooking and baking, and she knew my grandma loved those cookies, too, so she'd make them for me sometimes. I was looking forward to getting more cookies from her. She promised me some for Hanukkah just a couple of months ago." His expression turned sad.

Erica leaned forward. "Speaking of her cookies—we've been searching for the recipe all over. Do you have any idea where she might have stored it?"

He shook his head. "Sorry, no. I thought she made them from memory."

"Yes," Alyssa said, "but she did tell us she had her favorite recipes written down. We've been looking for them all evening."

"Oh, that's too bad. Listen, I have tomorrow off. I could meet you here and help you search."

His expression was one of entreaty, as if he truly wanted to help them look. Erica was tempted. But did she really want to spend time with a handsome man? Although he appeared to be kind—

"I'm sure my cousin would appreciate the help." Alyssa sent Erica a look that clearly said "take advantage of the help. He's eligible."

Erica resisted the impulse to grit her teeth. Did her cousin feel obligated to try to find romance for her? She wasn't interested. At least not right now.

"I'd be happy to help," Noah added.

Erica repressed a sigh. "I don't want to inconvenience you."

"It's not a problem, really." He actually looked hopeful.

"Oh-kay," she agreed. "I can get here by around six thirty, after work."

"Where do you work?" he asked her.

She was surprised that he sounded so interested. "I work at a marketing firm in Elizabeth," she answered.

He grinned. "Okay, I'll see you tomorrow. Bye."

The minute Alyssa had closed the door behind him, Erica cleared her throat. Loudly.

Alyssa turned, an innocent expression on her face.

Erica tsked. "You know I'm not interested in meeting new men right now." Erica shook her head.

"But he's offering to help, and you could use the assistance," Alyssa said, flushing. "Really, I'm just trying to help. Grandma Franny always said he was a nice guy. I suggested she try to get him together with you, but she said it was too soon since you'd just broken up with Lance."

"It's still too soon," Erica retorted.

"It's been a year," Alyssa protested. "You can't avoid men forever. You always said you wanted to get married and have a family."

"I'm not ready yet."

"Well, maybe a little harmless flirtation will get you more ready," Alyssa suggested.

"I doubt it," Erica stated.

"Why don't you at least give him a chance? If you don't like him, you don't have to see him again. Grandma thought highly of him, and he was a good neighbor to her. What harm is there in spending one evening with him?"

Put like that, it did sound reasonable. Erica swallowed. "All right. I'll give it a try."

"Great." Alyssa reached out and pulled her into a tight hug. "If nothing else, it will get you into the social whirl again."

Erica hoped she'd feel comfortable doing so.

****

As Noah walked back to his house, he mulled over meeting the two young women.

It seemed obvious the one named Alyssa, who wore a flashing diamond ring, was trying to set him up with her cousin Erica.

Not that he had an objection. Erica had soft-looking, shiny brown hair, a classically beautiful face, and a sweet expression. Except when she glared at her cousin. Or looked at him with doubt in her eyes.

Did she not want to meet him? Did she perhaps have a boyfriend already, maybe one her family didn't know about?

That thought only reminded him of Tema. The woman who had kept a big secret from him—that she had another boyfriend.

He should have realized from the way she was never available for a whole weekend—she'd spend Friday or Saturday with him, but never both—that something was going on. But no, he'd been naïve, newly in love, and had thought they had a future together. She was bright and fun and easy to be with.

Unfortunately, someone else thought the same, too.

And when his best friend had told him he'd seen her with another guy—he'd been quick to deny it.

Until things all started to add up.

He'd confronted her and told her she had to choose. They'd been dating over six months by then.

She'd chosen all right—the stockbroker who was making tons of money. More than a plain old pharmacist made.

That had been over a year ago, and he was just now feeling like he was ready to dive into the dating pool again.

His friends, his family, even Franny Liposky next door had urged him to start seeing women again.

And the photos of her granddaughters had intrigued him. Especially the one with the sweet face. She was smiling up at the camera, her dark hair waving in a breeze as someone caught her happy expression in front of Franny's house.

Franny had said the photo of the young woman with the sweet face was a *very* special picture.

He learned that photo was of Erica.

Now, he got the definite feeling Erica was not interested in getting to know him better.

Which was too bad. Because when he'd looked at her, something had clicked inside him.

Something—decidedly like attraction to a good-looking woman.

A woman who seemed interesting, too.

Well, he'd just have to see how their meet-up tomorrow went.

Besides, if they found that cookie recipe, he wanted to sample them.

Chapter II

Erica left work on time, fought the usual traffic, and went to her grandmother's home. On the way, she stopped at a sandwich shop near the house, bought a turkey sandwich and soda, and continued to the house.

Once there, she ate, then freshened up before Noah got there, spending more time than necessary combing her hair.

While she waited for him, she pulled out her iPad and listed the rooms she'd already checked for the recipe, then the ones she still had to go through. The kitchen and all the bedrooms had been done. That left the dining room, living room, and the small bedroom Franny had used as a home office/den.

The basement was unfinished, and she doubted it would hold the recipes, but added that to the list. Along with the laundry room and basement, though they were doubtful, too.

She swept her gaze around the house. She'd be officially buying it in a few months, but in the meantime, her family agreed she could move in soon so the house wasn't vacant.

On one hand, it might be weird living in the home her grandmother had occupied for sixty some odd years. On the other hand, she wanted to live where she'd had so many good memories. Her relatives were happy she wanted to keep it in the family too. At first, she'd wondered about Alyssa wanting to live here, but then learned her cousin was excited about moving into a sleek, modern condo with her fiancé. The only question was, would Erica be able to live on a tight budget even if the family was going to give her a break on the price?

This weekend, her family members were going to go through the furniture—her brothers and cousins wanted a few pieces, and so did her mom and aunt and uncle—and they'd start moving things out.

She was contemplating room colors when a knock sounded on the door.

She opened it and found Noah standing outside.

"Hi, Erica," he greeted.

"C'mon in."

He entered, and she noticed he had a bottle of wine in his hand. "I thought we might have some wine while we're looking."

"That was thoughtful of you," she said and took the bottle. "I'll get some glasses."

"So, when are you moving in?" he asked as she moved to the kitchen and took glasses out of a cabinet.

"The Wednesday before Thanksgiving. I'm taking Monday off to do some painting, and I figure it will dry Tuesday."

"How much do you expect to paint in one day?" he asked, furrowing his brow.

"Just the kitchen and master bedroom. My dad is coming over to help and he said he'd also do the living room." She waved at that room. "The rest of the house will have to wait."

He nodded.

"Can you open the bottle?" she asked, grabbing a corkscrew from a drawer. He'd brought red wine. She didn't know too much about wines, but the label said it was a merlot.

"Sure." He did so easily.

She poured some into each glass, then handed him one.

He raised his glass. "Cheers."

She met his eyes. For a moment she couldn't breathe.

His expression was one of a man interested in a woman. She sucked in a noisy breath. "Cheers," she echoed, her voice slightly raspy.

He touched his glass to hers, and a loud clink reverberated in the small kitchen.

She bent her head and sipped the wine. It was mellow, smooth, and fruity. Looking up again, she saw him take a sip from his glass.

"I like this brand," he said.

"It's good," she agreed, wondering why her voice now sounded breathless.

There was an awkward silence. "So…tell me what this recipe might look like," he said.

"I remember my grandma had some recipes on lined white paper, the kind that came from a pad of paper. I don't remember if the cardboard backing was still attached."

"And where have you looked?" He sipped some more.

"We've already been all over the kitchen, the two bedrooms upstairs, and the bedroom down here." She sighed. "I want to try the dining room—all the cabinets—and the living room. And we have to look in the little den—her office—and maybe the basement if we don't find it in one of the other rooms." She frowned.

"We don't know why she hid the recipes."

"Could she have been experiencing some dementia?" he asked.

"No, she was pretty sharp till the end," Erica protested.

"The reason I ask," he said calmly, "was that the last time I was here for coffee and some of those delicious apricot cookies, she said she was worried since there was a robbery in the neighborhood. But that was a couple of months ago."

"There was a robbery?" Erica felt astonishment. "She never told me."

"Maybe because the last one I heard of was over four years ago, and it was the next development, not this one. Turned out it was a kid looking for drugs in his uncle's house."

"Oh." She blew out a breath. "So it wasn't even this neighborhood, or a random thing."

"No. The kid and a friend targeted that house specifically." He regarded her. "I think that maybe she got mixed up. Not that it indicates dementia—anyone her age could get confused."

"Yes...and if she was thinking about it, she may have decided to be super cautious. Which explains why she hid the recipes she treasured—and some of her jewelry, too."

"Yes." He nodded.

"Ok, let's start with the dining room," Erica said. She pointed to the small dining room adjacent to the kitchen and living rooms. "Why don't you start with that china cabinet and I'll work on the sideboard."

"Okay." He followed her into the room. The wood table still had a pair of silver candlesticks on it, placed on top of a brown and gold autumnal table runner. She placed her glass on the table runner, and he followed suit.

"If you find a box of any kind, open it up and look inside," she directed. "She did keep some things in boxes."

"Of course." He opened one of the hutch's glass doors and began to move some china, searching behind the pieces there.

"My cousin Alyssa is getting that good china," Erica said, feeling she should make conversation.

"It looks old and valuable." He stared at the gravy boat he was holding. "Are you getting any of these things?"

"Another cousin is getting the crystal glasses," Erica said, opening up the drawer at the top of the sideboard. "I'm getting the good silver." She waved at the silver chest sitting on the sideboard. "It's an old, popular pattern I always admired."

"How did your relatives handle the fact that you wanted to buy the house?" He placed the gravy boat back in the hutch and looked behind a platter.

Erica began lifting things from the drawer. Shabbat candles, some linen napkins, and an old ash tray that belonged to her great grandfather were the only items there. "They were okay with it," she said. "I'm buying it for a fair price. My married cousins live mostly in south Jersey, and one in western New Jersey, and another in North Carolina. Alyssa and her fiancé are buying a newer condo. And one of my brothers lives in Jersey City and the other's still in college." She omitted the fact that her mother and aunt worried about her moving into a mostly "family" neighborhood. "How will she meet any men there?" she'd heard her Aunt Jenny whisper to her mom just the other day.

She was not going to worry about meeting men. "How did your family react when you bought your grandmother's house?" She gestured toward his house next door.

"They were fine with it. My parents had retired to Florida, and my older sister and her husband had bought my parent's house in East Brunswick." He placed the platter back on the shelf and took out the sugar bowl and creamer. "I only have two cousins on this side of the family, and one lives in Massachusetts and the other in Texas. So everyone was happy when I bought it and moved in." He grinned. "Of course, I had to have some remodeling done. I got rid of the shag carpets from the 70s, renovated the bathrooms etc."

"That's what I'll be doing here," Erica said, "but slowly." Knowing her grandmother's penchant for placing things in boxes to keep them in good condition, she decided to look inside the first one. Lifting it, she heard a metallic sound.

"Hmm," she murmured, opening the box.

Inside lay two white candles…and a pile of jewelry.

"I found her good jewelry!" Excitement swept through her entire body. "This is where she hid the pieces."

She slid the items onto the table runner. "We've been looking for these."

Noah approached. Glancing at the box, he chuckled. "She hid her jewelry in with the Shabbat candles?"

"Yes!" Erica sifted through the pieces. Only a few were in small boxes. Franny's favorite emerald necklace and matching earrings; a sapphire pin and matching bracelet; her double strand of pearls and a topaz pin were the ones she remembered most. There were two other bracelets and another brooch as well. "I'll have to let my mother know," she said. "She and my aunt were looking all over for these."

"Great job," he said, returning to the hutch. He'd finished going through the top, and now crouched down to open the doors of the bottom. "Maybe I'll find something here." He removed the first china protector holder and began going through the plates. The occasional clink of china echoed in the room.

Erica plopped down on the old, gold-colored carpet and opened the doors on the bottom of the sideboard. Slowly and methodically, she went through the items there—crystal glasses in lined protective holders, a crystal pitcher, and a couple of board games.

There were no recipes in any of the boxes, games, or sitting loose on the shelves inside.

She sighed. "Nothing else unexpected here."

"Or here," Noah said.

She got up slowly, suppressing a yawn. "Well, I think I'll save the living room for tomorrow."

"I'll help."

She raised her eyebrows. "You really don't have to."

"I'm volunteering," he said. "I'll bring another bottle of wine. And I can pick up pizza for dinner. What kind do you like?"

He was being so nice. Too bad she didn't trust him, a little voice in the back of her head said. Lance had seemed really nice at first, too. "Plain is fine. That's nice of you."

"You got it. As long as I'm helping out—I have a favor to ask."

Caution rose up inside her. "What kind of favor?"

Lance used to ask her to help with his laundry on occasion—not that she minded when they saw so much of each other—but sometimes he wanted her to do errands too.

"When we do find the recipe—can you bake those cookies for me?"

Chapter III

Friday, Erica spent the majority of her time during lunch surfing the internet, looking for recipes for apricot cookies.

Noah was being so nice and accommodating and helpful. She'd decided on her drive home last night that even if she didn't find her grandmother's recipe, she should at least make him some similar cookies. She intended to also look through her few cookbooks and her grandmother's and mother's collection, in case she found something there which she could adapt.

Of course, with everyone moving furniture this weekend she wouldn't have a chance immediately.

She drove to her grandmother's house, and moments after she entered, the doorbell chimed. She looked through the peephole and saw Noah standing outside. He held a pizza box, wine, and a large bottle of cola.

"Come in," she invited, swinging the door open.

As if on cue, her stomach grumbled.

"I'm hungry too," he said with a smile. "I had this delivered not five minutes ago."

"That's perfect! How much do I owe you?" She reached for her purse as he shut the door.

"My treat," he declared. He strode into the kitchen and set down the box and beverages.

She trailed after him. "You're spoiling me,"

"What sweet, beautiful lady shouldn't be spoiled

occasionally?" He raised his eyebrows, studying her.

She felt herself flushing. Lance had never thought *she* should be spoiled. She doubted he spoiled his new fiancé, either.

It was nice, to feel that *someone* thought she was worth that "spoiling". "Thank you," she murmured.

He shrugged off his jacket and placed it on an empty chair. He wore a brown and tan flannel shirt and faded jeans. She guessed he had changed after work.

She, on the other hand, was wearing gray slacks, a white shirt, and a forest green vest. Her black flat shoes didn't add to her height, so he towered over her.

She brought out paper plates and napkins. "My grandma Franny always lit Shabbat candles every Friday night for the beginning of the Sabbath. Do you mind if I do?" She had explained to her friend Krista at work, just that afternoon, that the Jewish day began in the evening; so the Sabbath officially began on Friday night.

"Of course not. I remember her doing that once when I was over on a Friday," he said. "My grandmother wasn't as religious, and only lit them rarely—except on holidays."

Erica went into the dining room, found the candles in the sideboard, and placed them in the silver candle holders. Once she lit them, she began reciting the traditional prayer.

Noah chimed in, his voice a pleasing baritone.

"Shabbat Shalom," she said when they finished. "Good Sabbath."

"Shabbat Shalom," he echoed.

They sat down to eat. Heat rolled off the pizza when he opened the box, and the smell of cheese, tomato sauce, and spices was invigorating. Erica blew on her slice, then bit into it carefully.

She chewed, enjoying the tastes of cheese, garlic, and tomatoes. "This is delicious."

"It's from DeRosa's," he said, naming a place she had passed many times.

Over dinner they discussed the towns where they'd grown up—Noah in East Brunswick, Erica here in Union. They talked about their first apartments, too. Noah had rented a condo in East Brunswick until he moved here; Erica lived in an apartment now in West Orange. She was happy that her commute to work would be shorter once she moved into Franny's house.

When they finished, they commenced searching for the recipes in the living room. Noah began with the upper shelves in the wall unit. Erica began with the lower, closed cabinets.

They worked silently for a few minutes. Noah shook each book out in case the recipe was stuck in a page, he told her. Erica removed all the items in the first section of the cabinet, and then slowly went through the boxes of wine glasses; a box containing some old photos of Jenny, Joan, and Barry; and a box of ashtrays which her grandfather had used when he was alive. Erica could smell the faintest trace of cigarettes.

Once she was done, she moved to the second cabinet.

Surprisingly, several of the items there had sticky notes.

"Look at this," she said. "This vase is labeled "For Abby—she's a cousin of mine—I believe she always liked this one." It was a beautiful, cut-crystal vase that had been a favorite of Grandma's. "And this Lenox platter is labeled 'For Jenny'—my aunt. And—" she stopped.

Grandma's old brass Hanukkah menorah was labeled "For Erica."

She stared at it a moment, then burst into tears. "She remembered!"

Noah placed the book he was holding on the coffee table and dropped down on the rug beside her. "What is it?".

"My—grandma—re-remembered," she cried. "I always loved her menorah and—and she left it—for me!" Another sob escaped her.

Noah pulled her into his arms. She cried against his shoulder as he held her tenderly. stroking her hair repeatedly.

The brass menorah was inlaid with different painted colors on a stand. As a child, Erica had been fascinated by it. As an adult, she realized it was one of the prettiest she'd ever seen.

She knew she was getting Noah's shirt wet, but she couldn't help it. "I'm so—so touched she remembered how much I liked it!"

"I'm sure that's why she left it for you," he said, his voice soothing. "She wanted you to have something you really liked." He hugged her gently.

His warm embrace felt good. Comforting. She burrowed into him.

After a few minutes, her tears slowed. She sniffled. "I'm—so sorry—I got your shirt wet."

"It's no problem. I think maybe you needed a good cry after losing your Grandma." He stroked her hair.

"You're right." She straightened, leaning back to put some space between them. "I need a tissue." She scrambled up, embarrassment overtaking her. He probably thought she was a hysterical female. That's what Lance would have said about her show of emotion. "I'm sorry I let loose like that."

"Don't be sorry!" he exclaimed. "There's nothing wrong with giving into your grief. When my grandmother died, I shed a lot of tears, too."

She walked over to the piano, where one of her relatives had placed a box of tissues. She grabbed one and blew her nose.

"I don't usually cry in front of people," she added.

He stood up and took her hand. His warm one surrounded her cold one, and she was startled to realize how good it felt. As good as being held by him while she cried.

Which was awkward. She wasn't used to this. Especially with a man she hardly knew.

He's more sympathetic than Lance, a little voice in her brain whispered.

She pulled her hand back and reached for another tissue. The last thing she wanted now was to get involved with a man, even a sympathetic one.

But…oh, it had felt good to have someone to lean on, even for a short time!

He was studying her. "How about some water?"

"Good—good idea." Her voice still sounded shaky, and her legs felt that way too as she moved into the kitchen.

She took a water bottle out of the refrigerator and offered him one.

"Thank you again for your—understanding," she said, her voice low.

He raised his eyebrows. "Of course. Any friend would understand."

Is that what they were, friends?

"Well, let's get back to searching." She tried to sound light. Once back in the living room, she took the menorah and carefully placed it on the dining room table. "I'll clean it so it's ready for Hanukkah."

They continued their search, but after an hour they finished with no success. They hadn't discovered the recipes in the living room.

Erica blew out a breath. "I won't have time to search when I'm moving in next week. I guess after I move, I'll try again." She glanced around the rooms, almost as if she hoped the answer would jump out of her.

"I'd still like to help. I'm working this weekend. What day did you say you're moving?"

"Next Wednesday, the day before Thanksgiving. This weekend my family will be moving stuff out and my dad will help me paint a few rooms."

"Wednesday I'm working a long day since they gave me Thursday off for the holiday. I won't be able to help you."

"Oh, thanks, but I have some family members who'll be here to help," Erica said. "And my brothers and a cousin will load the van at my apartment before they come over here."

"Well, I'll stop in after work to see how you're doing," he said.

"That's sweet of you." She paused. He was being nice and helpful. Was he always this way? she couldn't help wondering. He was so different than Lance. At least, it appeared he was. Or was she misjudging him the way she'd been wrong about Lance? She took a deep breath. Maybe she should find out.

"Listen, I looked up cookie recipes while I was on

my lunch break today," she told him in a rush. His head tilted slightly as he watched her. She was aware he was listening closely. "I'm going to experiment with them and see if I can find one which tastes like Grandma Franny's cookies. I thought I'd try them out each night of Hanukkah." She swallowed. "Would you like to come over and help me taste test them? We can start on the first night of Hanukkah."

He broke out in a smile that looked, to her, like sunshine after a gray day. "I'd love to!" he declared. "I'd enjoy being your taste-tester."

Erica found herself grinning at his enthusiastic response. "Okay," she said.

"It's a date! I'll see you Sunday night for the first night of Hanukkah—the first experiment!" His voice had a lilt in it.

They left the house together a few minutes later. As she drove back to her apartment, his words echoed in her head.

"It's a date!"

It sounded a lot like it was.

And oddly, she was looking forward to it.

Chapter IV

The weekend sped by. Erica showed up on Saturday to help her cousins pack up things like the fine china and other smaller items, while her brothers Aaron and Scott and cousins Dave and Jay moved an old, badly worn couch to the curb for pick-up by the garbage men; and took several chairs, a coffee table, the kitchen table, and the good couch to the moving van. They were dividing up most of the furniture. Erica was keeping the dining room set and one bed in the guestroom for visitors.

By four o'clock everyone was gone. She went back to her own apartment and put her feet up.

Sunday, she met her parents at the house, and they prepared the rooms for painting with painter's tape.

Monday she and her dad painted the kitchen and bedroom. Tuesday her parents were kind enough to return while she was at work and do the living and dining rooms.

On Wednesday, her move went smoothly. She didn't have a whole lot of furniture—basically just a bedroom set, living room furniture, and a kitchen table—although she had a lot of tschokas and books. Once her brothers and cousins brought everything into Grandma's house—it was still hard to think of the cape cod house as hers—she got them pizza and sodas and beer. When they left around 2 o'clock, she started the difficult job of unpacking.

Alyssa surprised her and showed up, being that she'd only worked a half day since it was the day before Thanksgiving. Together, they were able to unpack all her dishes, pots and pans, and get her kitchen set up.

Noah called and said he had to work late, unexpectedly, and wouldn't be able to stop by. She reassured him that it wasn't necessary, and she'd see him soon.

By nine thirty Erica was alone and crawled into bed with a good book. She wouldn't have cable and internet until Saturday. She heard a car pull in next door about ten o'clock as she was switching off the nightstand lamp. Noah must have worked *really* late.

Thanksgiving Day was spent with her family at her Aunt Jenny's house. She enjoyed seeing everyone, but seeing how happy Alyssa and her fiancé were, and her cousin Jay and his wife, and Aaron with his girlfriend made her feel particularly alone. When she got home, she spent the evening reading and doing a little more unpacking. She also used painter's tape on the smallest bedroom downstairs which had been Grandma's TV room. It was going to be her home office.

Friday, she tackled painting her home office and the downstairs bedroom, with the help of her parents.

Saturday, she was up by seven o'clock and heard a car next door. Noah must have arrived home late last night since she hadn't seen him, or his car around. It appeared he was heading to work early.

Alyssa and their cousin Abby came over and helped her finish unpacking. After they left, Erica surveyed her home. Only a little more painting to do, replacing a few curtains and carpets, and it would be the home she'd always wanted.

Sunday morning, she took out the first cookie recipe she intended to try and got out the ingredients.

After baking the cookies, she heard her cellphone ping. Checking it, she saw she had a text from Noah.

"Is 6:30 okay for me to come over? I'm bringing something from the deli for supper."

Wow, he certainly was being helpful. She texted back "Yes! And thank you!"

She took a quick shower once the cookies were done and cooling. She dressed casually, though. By 6:30 she was placing candles in Grandma's menorah when her doorbell rang.

She peeked through the peephole. Noah stood outside, a bag in his hands.

Her heart rate increased.

Chapter V

The First Night of Hanukkah

She swung the door open. "Hi."

The minute he entered, she could smell delectable aromas. "What did you bring?" she asked eagerly. "It smells delicious!"

He held up the bag, grinning. "The local deli makes their own brisket and potato latkes. I brought enough for tonight and tomorrow."

"Yum!" she said, taking the bag. "That was so thoughtful of you!" And it was. She remembered her last Hanukkah with Lance, when he had told her to cook him a nice dinner. Told her, not asked her.

She would have volunteered, naturally. She was a decent cook and enjoyed it. But being told by her then-boyfriend that she should cook him a meal had set her on edge.

She'd set the dining room table today and put out placemats she'd bought a few years ago, which were decorated with Hanukkah motifs. Now she placed the brisket and sauce on a large dish. The potato pancakes looked and smelled fantastic, and Noah had even brought a jar of applesauce to slather on the latkes.

"This is perfect!" she exclaimed.

"I hope you're hungry." He glanced around. "I see you've painted the rooms. You must have been working hard."

"My parents and cousins helped me paint and unpack," she told him as she brought out some wine that her Mom had brought over. She filled two glasses and set them beside glasses full of cold water.

She saw him observing the "Happy Hanukkah" sign in the living room, the snowmen she had put on the wall unit and coffee table, and the accordion paper dreidel in the middle of the table.

"Nice decorations," he said approvingly.

"Thanks. I thought we'd use Grandma Franny's menorah." She indicated the menorah on the sideboard.

"Perfect."

She picked up the box of matches and struck one. Her hand trembled slightly. "This—this is the first time someone other than Grandma Franny is lighting these candles." She touched the match to the *shamash*, the "helper" candle, which sat in the tallest holder on the menorah. When it caught fire, she shook out the match, then picked up the *shamash* and lit the first candle. Since it was the first night of Hanukkah, this was the only candle besides the *shamash* that she would light.

Noah began chanting the traditional prayer, and she joined in.

"Baruch atah Adonoi…"

When they finished, she placed the shamash back in its holder, and for a moment, they stared silently at the menorah. She blinked back tears as she thought of her grandmother, wishing so much she was here.

"Happy Hanukkah," she whispered.

He reached out, placed an arm around her shoulders, and hugged her to him. "Happy Hanukkah, Erica."

She smiled up at him, then moved back, and waved

at the table. She still felt a little choked up as thoughts of Grandma Franny bombarded her. "Let's eat."

They started in on dinner, and for a minute, they were silent.

"This is delicious," Erica said after she'd chewed some of the brisket in a savory sauce. "I taste mushrooms and onions…it tastes kind of like my other Grandmother's brisket. My grandmother Esther died when I was in high school."

"It reminds me of Sonia's brisket," Noah said, cutting another piece of meat. "This is the way she made it. That's why I always buy it from Irving's Deli."

Erica liberally spread applesauce on top of the two latkes she'd placed on her plate, then sampled a slice of one. "Ohh…" She closed her eyes in delight. "Nice and crispy! Just the way I like it."

When she opened her eyes, she found Noah staring at her. "What?" she asked. "Don't you like them that way?"

"I do," he said. "It was just…when you had your eyes closed, you looked positively…" his voice drifted off.

"Positively…?" she prompted.

He grinned. "I was going to say…orgasmic."

She stared at him. Orgasmic? A sudden, shocking awareness of Noah skimmed up her spine. She could imagine that a considerate guy like him would know how to please a woman and know exactly what that woman's smile would look like while making love.

She felt her face flame. Grabbing her glass of cold water, she took a big gulp.

"I hope I didn't offend you by saying that," he said hastily.

"Not—not at all." But her voice trembled.

He continued to regard her. She met his eyes, trying to look carefree and innocent. Like she wasn't thinking about sex and orgasms. And his long-fingered hands, and what they would feel like caressing her skin.

"I really appreciate your bringing over dinner," she said, striving to keep her voice level. She almost succeeded.

"There's enough food for tomorrow, too," he reminded her.

"I know. So why don't you come over again tomorrow and we'll try a second recipe if this one isn't right?"

"That's a great idea!" He smiled again.

She switched the topic, asking him about some of his favorite foods. He told her that he liked Italian food a lot. Since she did too, she decided to cook something Italian for him one night. "I have some of my friend's family recipes. I'll make you dinner on—" she thought rapidly—"how about this Friday?"

"I'd love it."

"Do you cook?" she asked him.

"A little. I'm not really very versatile at cooking. I can make steak and baked potatoes and a few other things. That's why I picked up take-out," he admitted.

When they finished eating, they cleared the table and wrapped up the food for tomorrow's dinner.

Then she brought out the first batch of cookies. "Okay, here's experiment number one," she said, cutting the bar cookies and placing two on plates. She continued to strive to keep her voice light and cheery.

And avoid any thoughts of sex.

"Cheers. Maybe this one will be the right recipe."

He raised his wine glass.

She raised hers as well. "Cheers." She took a sip. "We need to clear our palates first," she joked, "as they say on the food shows." She placed the wineglass down and lifted her water glass, taking a drink.

He followed suit. Then he placed his glass back on the table, reached for his cookie, and bit in.

She watched him carefully as he chewed.

After minute he swallowed, then shook his head. "No, this isn't it."

Disappointment pinged inside of her. She took a bite of her cookie, too, as she watched him.

The minute she did, she had to agree. After swallowing, she took another sip of water. "You're right. This cookie is not as sweet as Grandma Franny's were." The cookie, while not bad, was definitely not as sweet as the ones she recalled.

"That's right. But they're okay." He reached for another one from the baking pan. "I'll still eat them!"

"I'll give you some to take to work," she said. "You can have them with your lunch tomorrow."

"You should do the same."

"I will. Well, it will be on to recipe number two tomorrow," she said. "And…we can continue each night of Hanukkah until we find the right one." She hoped she found the correct recipe.

"I'm looking forward to more taste-testing." His eyes twinkled.

Surprisingly, she found herself looking forward to tomorrow's cookie test, too.

Chapter VI

The Second Night of Hanukkah

After a busy Monday at work, Erica rushed to get out on time, glad her commute had been shortened by her move.

Once home, she took out the second recipe. She followed it carefully and baked the cookies. They were ready before Noah got to her house.

When he arrived, they lit the Hanukkah candles and recited the prayer. Then she reheated the food from yesterday. He practically devoured it.

"You're hungry," she observed.

"Yes. I barely had time for a sandwich today," he said. "The pharmacy was so busy. Apparently a lot of kids are sick with strep throat and bronchitis. We had a run on antibiotics. And I don't like to keep them waiting, so we were filling prescriptions as fast as safely possible."

"You really care about customers," she remarked. "You're dedicated."

He shrugged. "A good pharmacist should care about his or her patients."

She smiled at him. "Well, eat as much as you want. There's plenty!"

"I will." He returned her smile.

"It's just as good as yesterday—maybe even better,

now that's it's rested in the sauce overnight," she added.

He nodded. "I think so, too."

She asked him the question she was curious about. "What made you go into pharmacy?"

He took a sip of water, then set down his glass. "I always liked biology and chemistry. And whenever I would get sick and go to the doctor, I was more interested in what medicine he was giving me than in his diagnosing me. And I like being helpful—I used to tutor other kids in chemistry. So, I decided to become a pharmacist since it seemed to combine all my interests."

"That's cool. What about hobbies? Do you have any?" She sipped her own water.

"I like to ski. And I love photography, especially photos of nature."

"Oh, that's great! There's plenty of skiing up in northern New Jersey during the winter. And photography is fascinating."

"You'll have to come over and see some of my photos. I've enlarged quite a few and they're hanging on the walls in my house." He cut more brisket. "What about you?" he asked, switching the focus to her. "What made you chose your career?"

She chewed her delicious, crispy potato latke and swallowed. "I liked writing but didn't want to go into journalism and cover the news. So, I went into marketing. The company I work for specializes in small businesses in the county."

"Do you get to do a lot of writing?"

"Yes. I do their weekly email newsletter; and I do all kinds of social media for them. I also write some advertising copy and try to get the businesses featured in local papers and magazines."

"Any hobbies?" he asked.

They'd finished their supper, so he helped her clean up as they continued to talk. She noticed again how helpful he was. She really could understand why someone like him went into pharmacy.

She made coffee, and he put out dessert plates and mugs.

"Yes, I do have a couple of hobbies," she said as they worked together. "I do needlepoint—I find it relaxing. I'm making something to frame for a friend's baby right now."

He glanced around. "Do you have anything you've done recently on display??"

"Yes. I'll show you." She went into the living room and lifted one of two identical pillows. She'd needlepointed the designs to go with her gray couch and the green accents in the room. "I love to read, too." She waved at the books standing in the wall unit.

He studied the pillow. "Nice work! My mom does needlepoint, too."

She returned the pillow and then poured coffee in mugs for them. He took the mugs from her and carried them to the table, the roasted coffee bean aroma wafting from them.

She placed a cookie on each of their plates, and they took seats opposite each other.

"Ready?" she joked.

"Ready."

"Dig in."

He did, and she watched as he chewed. Then, she took a taste.

Ugh. The cookie was dry and fell apart as she bit into it.

"This isn't it," she said after swallowing.

"Right. It's too—crumbly."

"Exactly. I agree," she said. "No, this recipe is nothing like my grandma's."

"True. But I'll eat one more anyway," he said and reached for an additional cookie.

She sighed. Two recipes down, six to go. "I really hope that one of these recipes turns out to be just like my Grandma Franny's."

"I do too." He met her eyes. "Thursday, I have a day off. Why don't you come over for supper and I'll cook?"

Her heart jumped. Go over to his place? It sounded—almost like a date, she thought.

"Okay." She took a slow breath. Although, she didn't know if she was ready to actually go on a date with Noah.

It's not really a date, her brain argued. *You're simply going over to his house for a meal. And bringing cookies which you made.*

He smiled at her. "And you'll bring the cookies?"

"I won't forget," she said. "I'll bring some wine, too. And remember, I'll make dinner for us on Friday."

"Perfect."

She figured it would be nice, since he was so helpful, to bring Hanukkah candy to his home Thursday. The drug store near where she worked carried it. She could pick up some during her lunch hour.

"Is there any place you want to search tonight, for the recipe?" he asked as he reached for his coffee cup.

She shook her head. "I think I need a break from looking. Maybe I'll get an idea and we can search more in a couple of days." She hoped she'd get an idea of where on earth the recipes could be.

They finished, and Noah helped her stack the dishwasher, then left. "How is six thirty again for tomorrow?" he asked. "To taste the cookies?"

"That should be fine," she said. "I'll have enough time to make the third recipe for the apricot cookies."

"Great. Thanks." He pulled on his jacket.

When he left, she shut the door, and blew out a breath.

She enjoyed Noah's company. But—she wasn't sure if she wanted to have this relationship go any further than friendly neighbors.

But going to *his* house for dinner sounded like something more.

She couldn't help recalling what he'd said yesterday about her expression being orgasmic.

Just remembering his words sent tingles all through her body.

Chapter VII

The Third Night of Hanukkah

During her lunch hour, Erica dashed out to the pharmacy which was a block from her office.

It was chock full of people, all busily selecting items from gift bags to cold medicines. She found the display of Hanukkah items—wrapping paper and cards; dreidels; the chocolate coin-shaped Hanukkah candies called *gelt;* and even plastic electric menorahs like the one she'd used in her apartment.

She really should take it out and put it on the windowsill, as was traditionally done. Now that she had her grandmother's menorah, she hadn't thought about using her old one; but you were supposed to display it in the window if you could do so safely. She decided to do that once she was home.

Now, she selected some gelt and a couple of Christmas gift bags for friends' gifts. Staring at the Hanukkah display again, she picked up a box of wooden dreidels in different colors. She had a bunch of dreidels she'd had for years, but it would be nice to bring some to Noah, even if he had a few already.

She was near the prescription department, and as she passed, she glanced over, to see Noah talking to a middle-aged woman standing by the "consultation" counter.

"Make sure you take this with your meals," he said. "And not on an empty stomach." He handed her the bag, then moved to the register. "That's very important."

Startled, Erica stared at him. She hadn't known he worked at this pharmacy. She rarely came into this location, since there had been one closer to her old apartment.

She paused, and when the woman paid, thanked him, and left, he must have sensed someone was looking at him. He looked up and caught sight of her.

"Erica!" A smile lit up his face. He moved back to the counter. "How are you? I hope you're not sick."

"No." She shook her head. "Just shopping on my lunch hour. I didn't know you worked here."

"Actually, I usually work at the location near our homes. But this branch was short-handed since someone had a death in the family. And it's a really busy store, so they asked me to fill in today. They do that sometimes."

"They do seem really busy." Catching sight of a man standing right behind her, she said, "I don't want to take up your time. I'll see you tonight." She smiled and moved aside.

"See you then." He focused on the man who was waiting. "Can I help you?"

Erica spent a few minutes wandering around the store. She could see the pharmacy department was swamped. Yet any time she glanced at Noah, he appeared unruffled and pleasant, patiently answering questions.

He really was a nice guy.

The kind a girl could easily fall for.

The kind *she* could fall for, if she wasn't careful.

****

Noah had been surprised but pleased to see Erica at the store today. He wished he'd had at least a little time to speak to her, but it had been a hectic day. He drove home, planning to put his feet up for a few minutes before grabbing a bite to eat. Then he'd head to Erica's house.

The more he saw her, the more he was struck by the fact that she was not only a beautiful woman, but sweet.

Which made him wonder why she didn't have a boyfriend or fiancé in the background.

Maybe he'd bring up the topic.

Once home, he changed into jeans and a flannel shirt, then poured himself a soda and plopped down on his favorite chair in the living room. Turning on the TV, he surfed a couple of news channels before turning it off. He didn't want to hear more about economic problems and international unrest.

He was due to go over to Erica's at six thirty. He made himself a sandwich, then ate while watching The Weather Channel. With a little time to unwind, he decided to call his best friend, Todd.

Todd answered on the first ring. "Hey, bro."

They caught up during the next half hour. Todd was engaged to a woman he'd met last year, and Noah was going to be a groomsman at the wedding. They discussed the planned bachelor weekend in Key West in January and talked about some mutual friends.

"So what's new with you?" Todd asked.

"Well…I met someone. I like her a lot." Noah went on to describe Erica, including the fact that she seemed hesitant around him.

"Maybe she's been burned by a previous boyfriend," Todd remarked.

"I thought of that," Noah said.

"Why don't you ask her?" Todd suggested.

"I just might do that," Noah answered.

They spoke a little longer, then he got ready to go to Erica's, bringing along another bottle of wine.

She didn't answer the door right away, and when she did, she said, "Sorry. I was in the basement. I'm still trying to find the recipe."

He entered, sniffing the air. He could smell something. "The cookies smell good. Maybe this recipe will be the one."

"I hope so."

"Why don't we spend a little time looking for the recipe over the weekend, if the next few night's cookies don't seem right?" he asked.

"Thanks. Maybe we can," she said, sounding unsure.

"Here." He gave her the bottle of wine.

"You're spoiling me," she said lightly.

He opened the wine for them, and she poured it into glasses. He noticed she'd put a plastic menorah in the window. "Did you get that at the pharmacy?" he asked as she prepared to light her grandmother's menorah.

"No, I've had it for a few years. I forgot to take it out since I had Grandma's, but seeing them in the pharmacy reminded me," she told him.

They lit her grandmother's menorah, then the plastic one, which "lit up" when you screwed the small bulbs in tightly.

"Let's try tonight's recipe," she said, and took a platter from the kitchen, placing it on the dining room table. The platter was blue and decorated with snowmen.

He smiled at her and took a seat.

Erica inclined her head, catching a whiff of his citrusy aftershave. It was lighter than the scent Lance had always preferred.

She had to stop thinking of Lance. And comparing a nice guy like Noah to her traitorous ex.

"So I saw how busy you were today," she said, lifting the cookie. "You must be tired."

"Yes, but I have Thursday off, so I can sleep in then." He took a bite and chewed.

She did the same.

She knew at once it wasn't the right recipe. "This isn't right," she declared.

"You're right. The apricot taste is too strong," he said.

"Right. In Grandma's cookies, it's more subtle."

"Yup." He reached for another one. "But I'll eat one more. It's pretty good."

Typical guy. Food was always important to them. Although Lance had never been very complimentary about her cooking or baking.

She sighed. "I was hoping this would be the right one."

"Me too." He sent her a sympathetic look. "But thank you for trying. Listen, over the weekend, I'm working Saturday morning but not the rest of the day. Why don't you let me help you bake?"

"You want to bake?" She was astonished. Lance had never, ever been interested in helping her with domestic chores, not even enjoyable ones she thought were fun, like cooking together.

"Sure. Why not?"

"Okay!" She sucked in a breath. This might be fun! "I'll be happy to let you help." She smiled. "In my experience, most men don't like helping in the kitchen."

He raised his eyebrows. "Did you have a former boyfriend who didn't? And while we're on the topic, how come a beautiful and friendly woman like you doesn't have a significant other?"

She looked away as she felt her insides squeeze. Then, after a few beats of silence, she turned her head and met his eyes.

He was studying her. "Am I being too nosy?"

She took a deep breath. "No, I—it's just—painful. I did have a boyfriend for a couple of years," she said, then reached for her coffee. "Last year I found evidence that he was cheating on me. I broke it off." Her voice was strained as she said the words. The usual punch to her stomach that would follow her words wasn't quite as piercing as it used to be. Was time helping to heal her wound? She sipped her hot beverage.

He scowled. "The guy must have been a *schmuck*." The derogatory Yiddish word—which she'd heard her grandmothers use only sparingly—sounded loud and adamant as he said it. "Anyone who would cheat on a partner—especially one as sweet and kind as you—is a total, complete ass." He set his mug down with a loud thump on the table.

"Thanks." She tried to lighten the mood. "Grandma Franny would scold me if she heard me say that word, she almost never used it. But it's actually appropriate." She tried to smile but knew it came out faltering. She decided to turn the tables and ask him the same question. "How come a nice, handsome guy like you doesn't have a girlfriend?"

"Like you, I had a girlfriend until a year or so ago."

"What happened?" She made her voice gentle.

He sighed loudly. "I started dating Tema after we met at a party. She was friendly and fun to be around. I thought she was a nice person." He made a face. "I didn't know she was a status-seeking, money conscious person. It turns out she met another guy a few months after me, and she was seeing us both—not that either of us knew. When I found out, I gave her an ultimatum: it's me or him." He frowned. "She chose him. He was a stockbroker, living in Jersey City, making a ton of money. She told me she liked his lifestyle better." Now resentment crept into his voice.

Indignation on his behalf rose up in Erica. "What a jerk! But if money is what is most important to her, good riddance. You don't need a woman like that in your life. You should have a woman who cares about you for yourself, for your character. Any woman who had you as a boyfriend would be lucky!"

He smiled at her rant. "Thank you. It took a while, but I realized I'm better off without someone like that in my life."

"It's true," she said adamantly. If he was her boyfriend, she'd appreciate him—

Whoa. Where had that errant thought come from? If he was her boyfriend—sure, she would appreciate him. *But he wasn't her boyfriend.*

And she didn't want him to be.

Are you sure about that? A little voice at the back of her brain asked.

Yes, she was sure.

Almost sure.

Chapter VIII

The Fourth Night of Hanukkah

Erica worked through her lunchtime on Wednesday to get the newsletter ready to send out as usual on Friday. She wanted to get home promptly and not work late as she often did when working on the newsletter. She'd purposefully baked the fourth recipe's cookies last night, to save time. So she arrived home earlier than usual.

She had about an hour to spare when she got home. She used the time to continue looking in the basement for the recipes.

Most of the old furniture in the basement had been donated, except for a side table that went to her cousin Abby. What was left was a few boxes, a bookcase with some books that didn't fit into the shelves upstairs, and some gardening supplies.

She went through one large box. It contained some old family photos she knew her mom, aunt, and uncle should have. But no recipes.

Glancing at her watch, she realized Noah would arrive in half an hour. She brought the box upstairs to bring to her mother's, knowing she'd divide up the photos. It had been fun going through them, but now her work clothes were dusty. She took a quick shower and changed to jeans and a purple sweater.

She took out the candles for the menorah as she

waited for Noah, anticipation curling inside her. A feeling she was reluctant to admit. Did she want to get more involved?

It wasn't whether she wanted to get involved. She was afraid she already was.

****

Noah had just pulled into his garage when he heard the familiar ping of his phone.

He glanced at the text message when he turned off the car.

Tema.

Ugh! Why was his old girlfriend—who'd dumped him—texting him?

He grit his teeth and read the message.

Hi honey, he read. *I've been thinking about you a lot. Give me a call so we can make plans to get together, ok?*

It was followed by the heart emoji.

What the heck?

Did she really expect that after choosing what's-his-face, the rich stockbroker over him, that he'd want anything to do with her? And what the hell happened to what's-his-face anyway?

Maybe, he thought smugly, the guy had dumped Tema.

Served her right if he did.

But that didn't mean that he, Noah, wanted anything to do with her. Hell, no.

He texted back tersely, *No.*

By the time he'd emerged from his car, clicked the garage door shut, and went inside to freshen up, his phone pinged again.

You don't mean that, honey.

Oh, yes he did!

He decided ignoring her was the best way to go. He didn't want to waste any more time on that woman.

As he headed over to Erica's, his phone rang. He glanced at the read out and saw Tema was calling.

He let the call go to voicemail and silenced his phone. He didn't want to have calls interrupting the evening with a woman he liked, and respected; and who seemed to feel the same about him.

Erica answered the door almost immediately. He entered her home, and shrugged out of his jacket, sniffing the warm smell of vanilla and fruit.

"Hi," she greeted him, sounding a little breathless.

She looked so pretty. She wore a purple sweater and jeans which showed off her trim yet curvy figure. Gold earrings shaped like snowflakes dangled from her ears.

"Sorry we couldn't eat dinner together," he said.

"No problem! I understand your schedule can change day to day," she said lightly.

Unlike Tema, who demanded to see him when *she* wanted.

So she could see the other guy as well.

He felt his phone vibrate in his pocket. Tema must have left a voicemail. It was annoying. Apparently, she had trouble taking no for an answer.

He didn't want to even think about his ex-girlfriend when he was with Erica. "Come on, let's try out those cookies," he told Erica, smiling.

"Okay. Let's light the menorah, first," she suggested.

They chanted the prayer together as she lit the shamash, then four other candles. When she placed the *shamash* back in its holder, she turned and met his eyes.

The attraction he felt for her slammed into him. Along with something else.

Caring. He cared about Erica's feelings.

She gave him a mug of hot cocoa and they sat at the dining room table, the candles glowing nearby. Erica had already sliced up the cookies and placed them on a platter decorated with snowflake motifs.

He eagerly bit into tonight's cookie.

Not it.

She must have read his disappointed expression because her own face dropped. She took a delicate bite of hers.

"This is too crunchy. I was afraid of that," she admitted, frowning. "I wanted to try this recipe, which includes oatmeal, but I didn't think Grandma Franny used oatmeal in hers."

"It was worth a try," he said. "They're not bad; they're just not Franny's."

"Yes." And she sighed as if deeply disappointed.

He wondered if she was getting tired of feeding him.

"Don't forget, tomorrow I'm making dinner," he reminded her.

She flashed a smile, just as he felt the phone vibrating again. He was glad he'd turned it to silent. Next, he would turn it off completely.

"I'm looking forward to it," Erica said.

So was he. He was looking forward to seeing Erica again tomorrow, in his own home...a lot.

Chapter IX

The Fifth Night of Hanukkah

Thursday, Erica quickly re-applied lip gloss and brushed her hair till it shone. Then she pulled on her coat and went next door, carrying her presents and the latest apricot cookie experiment.

When Noah opened his door, a delectable, spicy smell greeted her.

"Something smells good." She handed him the gift-wrapped Hanukkah *gelt* and dreidels she'd brought over, along with a bottle of wine.

"Thank you," he said. "I'll open these after we light the candles. Want a tour first? The chili has to cook for a few more minutes."

"That would be nice." She inhaled the yummy aroma coming from the kitchen.

Noah's home was a typical bilevel. The living room, dining room, and kitchen were all painted cream. He had a large brown sectional sofa, a simple dining room table and chairs, and a few older accent tables which she suspected were from his grandmother. The kitchen had newer-looking cabinets and a smaller table, and a new granite counter in earth tones.

Also upstairs were three bedrooms and two full baths. The smallest bedroom was a guestroom, and he'd turned the mid-sized one into a home office. A large computer stood on the desk, and his bookcase was full. She recognized the names of several popular mystery and suspense writers.

His bedroom had a king-sized bed, and she couldn't help wondering how many women had shared it with him. The room was surprisingly cozy, painted blue with a navy comforter on the bed. The rest of his furniture was modern and plain.

Downstairs was a nice-sized family room with a large TV, another sectional sofa, and side tables. There was a laundry, half bath, and the fourth bedroom, which he was using for storage at the moment. There was a door leading to a two-car garage. "It's really nice to have a garage in the winter," he said.

"I wish I had one," she admitted. "But I'm happy to get out of that noisy apartment complex."

He'd decorated the whole house with a lot of his own photos, and she stopped to gaze at them as they walked through his home. She especially liked some pictures he'd taken at Yellowstone National Park, and at the Grand Canyon.

"They're gorgeous," she said more than once. She stared for a long time at a beautiful view of the Grand Canyon. "Especially this one."

"Thanks," he said. "I really enjoy capturing the beauty of nature with my camera." He looked around the room. "I've been thinking of getting a dog. My family's always had dogs, and there are so many in shelters who need homes."

"I have been too!" Erica declared. "I love dogs, and my family's always had them, too. Of course, since I work a full day, I'd have to get a dog walker to walk him or her a couple of times during the day."

"That's not a problem," he said. "There's a mother three doors down who has a pet sitting and walking business. I see her outside and she seems very nice and takes good care of the dogs."

"Good to know." Another thing they had in common, Erica thought. They both liked dogs.

They returned upstairs, and he checked on the simmering chili, then turned off the stove. "Shall we light the candles?"

His menorah was a sleek, stainless steel one. "My mother took my grandmother's old sterling silver menorah," he explained as he took out matches. "I found this one online."

"It goes with your décor," she said, glancing at his sleek furnishings.

He lit the shamash, then the five candles. They recited the prayer together.

"Open the gifts," she urged when they finished.

He opened the bright blue bag first. It contained a red merlot wine. "Thanks," he said. "Although I bought some beer for us to go with the chili. We can have our choice."

"You can always use the wine another night," she suggested.

"Yes," he agreed.

"Chili's perfect for a cold night like this," she added.

"I didn't bake cornbread; but I picked up corn muffins to go with the chili. The beer is a craft beer from a brewery in western New Jersey that I went to this summer with some friends."

"Sounds great. Can I help with anything?" she asked. As she observed what he'd cooked, smelling the savory food, she realized he'd gone to a lot of trouble to make her dinner. Her insides softened.

He indicated his simple dining room table, which held placemats and dishes. "I already set the table. Since it was my day off, I had plenty of time to do all this. You relax, and I'll open the other two presents."

He smiled at the chocolate candy *gelt*. "We can have this with the cookies for dessert."

"Or use it with the next gift," she suggested.

He raised his eyebrows and proceeded to tear the blue Hanukkah wrapping paper off the box holding the set of four dreidels, each a different color.

"Perfect," he said. He met her eyes. "You do know how to play the dreidel game?"

"Yes, although I haven't played in years."

"Why don't we play after we have our dessert?"

She agreed, and Noah took out the beer, and they sat down to supper. Erica blew on the hot chili and tasted it. The pop of subtle yet delicious spices hit her tongue. "This is good!" she told him. "Spicy but not ridiculously so. You're a good cook."

"I admit, I made it from a packaged mix," he said. "But I added onions and green pepper myself."

"Well, you did a good job," she praised, taking another bite with some of the corn muffin. "This is a great meal. As they say in those food programs, the sweet corn balances the spices of the chili.".

He smiled and nodded. "I agree." He seemed pleased by her enthusiasm. "In this weather, I'm glad I don't have to work outdoors."

"Although I have to walk several blocks from the parking garage to my office," she said. "But I don't mind the cold; I just wear a hat and gloves with my coat."

"How do you like your co-workers?" he asked,

lifting another forkful of chili.

Erica chewed. The muffin was sweet, contrasting nicely with the spice of the chili. She savored it for a moment. "They're nice people. I've become friends with Krista, who works with me. I went to her wedding in September." She scooped up more chili. "What about you? Are you close to any of your co-workers?"

"Yeah. I got friendly with Tim Miyakowa, who works a lot of the same shifts as I do. It's pretty interesting learning about Japanese food and culture from him. I'd love to travel to Japan someday."

She asked him about traveling he'd done and learned that he'd been to California, England, and Spain with his family. "And I've been to the Bahamas, and Italy, with friends," he said, drinking some of his beer, "as well as the Grand Canyon and Yellowstone National Park with my friend Todd."

She sampled the beer. It had an earthy taste, slightly bitter, with a tang of coffee.

"The beer's coffee-flavored," he said.

"I thought so. I'm not a big beer drinker, but it's not bad." She took another sip.

"So where have you traveled?" he asked.

"New Mexico and Arizona with my cousin Alyssa—she's my best friend. Like you, out to California with my family, and also the Bahamas and Puerto Rico and Florida. And I traveled to Canada with a couple of college friends after graduation."

They polished off dinner, speaking about favorite places they'd seen on their travels. Erica helped Noah clean up, and then he placed the dreidels and chocolate coins on the dining room table. Then, they had coffee and sampled the cookies.

She recognized at once this recipe wasn't the right one, either, and sighed. "It's too salty." Although bakers used some salt when making cookies and other baked goods, this was definitely too much.

"You're right." He swallowed his bite. "But, it's not bad."

She appreciated that he tried to always compliment her baking. "Thanks. I'm sorry none of these have been the correct recipe."

"Nothing to be sorry about." He smiled again. "I'm enjoying the taste-testing, and your company, a lot."

Well. That was interesting. She felt herself flush as warmth flowed through her body.

He looked at her expectantly.

"I'm enjoying your company, too," she admitted. And it struck her: she was enjoying every one of the evenings she'd spent with him.

He chose the dreidel which was blue and put it in the center of the table. After counting out four chocolate coins and placing them in the middle of the table, he divided the rest up between them. "We used to play for real money when I was young," he told her. "Pennies at first; then we graduated to quarters. My mother would scold my dad, telling him he was teaching us to gamble."

"Well, it is a gambling-type game," Erica said. "We played for chocolate kisses."

He met her eyes, and a mischievous grin lit his face. "We could always play for *real* kisses."

Her face grew hot. "Real kisses?" she squeaked.

"Well, how about this," he said. "We play for this gelt, and the winner—" he waggled his brows—"gets to kiss the loser."

"On—on the lips?" Shoot, she sounded like a preteen. She reached for her coffee and took a gulp.

He watched her, that grin still hovering around his mouth. "However that person wants to kiss the loser."

Her muscles had tensed at his suggestion, but now they relaxed. If she won, she could give him a brief kiss. Or a simple peck on the cheek.

But if he won—

She couldn't help it: excitement flared inside her, like a flame on the Hanukkah candles.

"All right," she agreed, striving to sound calm and collected. Not like someone who hadn't been kissed for over a year.

"You're the guest; you go first," he said.

She spun the dreidel. "Nun." The Hebrew letter meant she won nothing and paid nothing. "My family would play for half an hour—my mother timed us—and whoever had the most chocolate kisses won."

"In our house, we played until the whole pot was gone. But we didn't play where a Gimmel got the whole pot; we played the person who got Gimmel got two pennies, and the person who spun Hey got one."

"I've played that way, too. There's so many variations," she added. "Okay, let's do it the way your family always played," Erica said.

He spun the dreidel. "Hey." He took one coin.

She spun again. "Shin." She paid, putting one coin in the middle, joining the pile there.

He sipped his coffee, then spun. "Gimmel." He took two coins.

On her next turn, she spun a Hey, taking one chocolate coin. Then he spun a Hey, taking one coin.

They continued, sipping their coffee, and eating one more cookie. Erica tried not to look too disappointed about the flavor. She still had three more recipes to try.

And she found she was enjoying herself, actually relaxing as she played the game with Noah.

But as the minutes wore on, he had a growing pile, and hers was rapidly diminishing.

Uh oh. Was he going to win, and kiss her? And—how intimately?

She finished the last of her coffee. "Can I get some water?"

"I'll get it." He stood up. "Now, don't go changing the piles of candy," he teased.

"Of course not."

He returned with two glasses of cold water. She sipped hers, the thought of kissing him heating her whole body. And as she watched his long fingers spin the dreidel, she couldn't help wondering how those fingers would feel stroking her skin.

She took a bigger sip of the cool water, trying to quell the heat she was feeling in every part of her body.

She spun a hey and took one candy. He spun Nun and didn't take or get any, but next turn she spun a Shin.

"You're down to one chocolate," he observed, spinning the dreidel. "Gimmel." He took two.

She concentrated on the dreidel. "C'mon, Gimmel. Or Hey."

She held her breath, and spun.

The top spun rapidly, and then suddenly keeled over.

Shin.

Shit. That was her last chance.

Her heart thudded as she placed her sole chocolate coin in the middle.

"I'm out. You won." She tried to sound lighthearted.

But as she met his eyes, her heart rate increased.

Nice, kind Noah had a predatory gleam in his eyes now.

"I won." He sounded triumphant. His chair scraped back and he stood. Walking around the table, he extended his hand to her.

Slowly, she put hers in his.

He pulled her up. They stood close, and she could feel his breath skim over her cheek. He reached out and gently cupped her chin.

"Erica," he whispered.

His lips touched hers, tenderly. His lips were warm and softer than she expected. Automatically, she closed her eyes as he pressed his lips more firmly against hers.

And then a slow flame, bright as the flames on the Hanukkah candles, began to burn inside her, deep down.

As if he knew, he pressed his lips harder against hers. She breathed in his crisp aftershave, felt the slight stubble on his cheek move against her skin as he tilted his head.

It felt better than she'd imagined.

Without thinking, her lips parted on a breath. And his tongue slid into her mouth, tasting slightly of coffee and chocolate.

Their tongues danced, and his hand left her chin and he pulled her against him. Pressing her close.

Her hands moved around his neck as if they had a will of their own. She clung to him, and he pulled her even closer, his tongue dueling with hers.

Someone moaned.

Oh, God. It was her!

Because the kiss was hot and enticing, and suddenly

she was feeling things she hadn't felt in ages—maybe ever. Flames licked her inside, and she wanted more and more of his kisses.

Wanted Noah.

That thought startled her enough to cause her to pull back, breathless.

"Noah…"

"Erica." His eyes looked dazed as he stared at her.

"I—" she couldn't think of anything to say.

He gave her a lopsided grin. "If I knew how good it felt to kiss you, I wouldn't have waited till I won the dreidel game."

Her entire body grew hotter.

"I—" she couldn't say what she was thinking.

I wouldn't have waited, either.

Chapter X

Sixth Night of Hanukkah

Erica was afraid she would hit Friday evening traffic, but she was lucky and the ride home was smooth and quicker than normal. Maybe lots of people had left their jobs early, she mused. The radio was already playing holiday music, and she listened to classics like "Rockin' Around the Christmas Tree" and "White Christmas" as she drove. Many houses were already decorated for Christmas with glowing lights, and quite a few had Hanukkah menorahs in the windows. Across the street from her house, her neighbors had an inflatable snowman standing in the front yard.

She'd gotten up a little earlier than usual, so she could put the ingredients for her friend Krista's chicken cacciatore in her crockpot. She'd stopped at a bakery on her way to work and picked up a freshly-baked *Challah*, the traditional Jewish Sabbath bread, instead of the garlic bread she usually served with this dish.

Once home, she readied the menorah with six candles plus the shamash. She quickly made the sixth batch of apricot cookies. Would these be the correct ones? She was having doubts. It seemed these included a lot of coconut, more than she guessed was appropriate for the cookie. But the recipe she'd found online had a photo which looked like Grandma's cookies.

She tossed a salad, then went to check her make-up and spritz herself with more cologne.

The thought of seeing Noah had her heart hammering, much more so than usual.

She'd be spending more time with him—kissing him? she wondered.

She didn't know for sure if they would kiss again. But…they'd both enjoyed the embrace. She'd practically melted.

Why was she acting like a teenager, obsessed by one kiss?

Even though it had been earthquake-inducing.

Afraid that after dinner they would have nothing to do but end up in each other's arms—and unsure if she was ready for more of that—she went online to see if there were any activities that looked interesting for the evening, that they could join locally. She found the closest synagogue was having an outdoor, giant Menorah-lighting after the Friday night services, and snacks afterward for a singles' gathering—ages twenty to forty.

Well, it didn't say you couldn't attend *with* someone. She'd suggest it to Noah.

She pulled the cookies from the oven when they were ready. Promptly at six thirty, when she was finishing the spaghetti, her doorbell rang. She smoothed her hands down her black pants, then went to answer the door.

Noah stood outside, a wrapped package in his hand.

"C'mon in," she invited.

Cold air accompanied him as he entered. She noted the blue and white Hanukkah gift wrap featuring dreidels.

"This is for you," he said, handing her the present.

He was really thoughtful. "You didn't have to do that! Thanks," she said. She couldn't help thinking that most women would be glad to have someone who brought them a Hanukkah gift like this. If only she wasn't so hesitant because of Lance's shabby treatment of her.

Noah shrugged out of his coat. "You've been baking for me all week. It's the least I can do. Open it!" He sounded eager.

As he placed his navy winter coat in the closet, she ripped the paper off, inelegantly, in her haste.

Inside was a small white box with the logo of a nearby jewelry store.

Her throat went dry suddenly. Jewelry? They hardly knew each other!

She thought rapidly back to the few times Lance had ever given her jewelry. A silver bracelet for her birthday last year. He'd given her perfume for their first Hanukkah when they were dating, and an unoriginal gift card to a department store their second Hanukkah. She'd known then that Lance put no thought into her presents. She, on the other hand, had spent hours looking for the right sweater for him.

She gingerly opened the box from Noah. Cute silver dreidel earrings sat nestled inside.

"Oh how cool!" she exclaimed. "I'll put them on right now!" She unfastened the simple gold hoops she wore often and put the dreidels on. "Thank you, Noah! This is so sweet of you."

Once they were in her ears, she moved to the mirror over the dining room buffet. He followed her, standing behind her.

He placed his hands on her shoulders. "They look pretty on you."

She met his eyes in the mirror, and her breath caught. He was looking at her with—longing.

And she felt an answering urge deep inside. The desire to turn and hug him, be held by him, to kiss him again.

She swallowed. If they did that, they'd never get to dinner. Or to her idea for the evening.

She wanted to be in his arms—she admitted it to herself. But she was still fearful. What if, despite his kindness, despite the thoughtful gift, he was like Lance? How could she trust another guy?

As if sensing her hesitancy, he stepped back. She saw a flash of disappointment on his face before his expression became neutral. "Something smells good."

"It's ready," she said quickly. "I made chicken cacciatore since you said you liked Italian food."

"Yes."

They lit the six candles plus the shamash.

"I remember coming over just last year on a Friday night and lighting the candles with Grandma Franny." Her voice shook slightly. "It was kind of nice, just the two of us, without any other relatives here. Like we— shared a special moment."

"You did," he said, his voice soft.

She glanced at him. She caught the sympathy in his face.

Erica wiped away a tear. "I miss her so much."

"I know." He placed a hand on her shoulder and squeezed gently before letting go.

She waved at the table and they were soon sitting down to eat.

Noah praised her cooking as they ate, and Erica had to admit the chicken had turned out pretty good.

"This is just the thing for a cold night," he said, ladling more onto his plate.

She brought up the topic of the Menorah lighting. He agreed it would be fun to go. Although, when she mentioned the snacks and deserts they were serving for "singles" his expression dimmed.

"I don't mind going, as long as we're together," he said.

"Of course," she agreed hastily. Did Noah want to appear as a couple? A glad feeling wove through her.

Once they'd finished dinner and he'd helped her put away the leftovers, he asked her, "How about if I take you out tomorrow for dinner?"

That sounded an awful lot like a date. She glanced at him.

His expression looked eager, now.

"That sounds good," she agreed. "And we can come back here for dessert. More cookies, unless tonight's is the right recipe."

It wasn't, though. She'd been correct—there was way too much coconut in this recipe.

"It's more like a coconut cookie, not an apricot cookie," she said, sighing.

"Still, I like the taste," he said, picking up another one. "I like coconut."

After dessert, they cleared the table. She marveled at how he didn't have to be asked to chip in, the way she'd had to prod Lance. Perhaps Noah's parents had taught him that everyone pitched in to clear the table.

Shortly afterward, they bundled up in coats, hats, and gloves, and Noah drove them to the nearby temple.

There was already a crowd there, although the menorah lighting didn't start for another ten minutes. When they emerged from the parked car, wind blew scattered snowflakes in their faces.

Noah took her hand and led her closer to the giant menorah. It appeared to be electric, with wires running into the building. They stood nearby as conversations buzzed around them.

"So I told him I quit!"

"My grandfather's health is going downhill."

"Did you hear? She's pregnant again!"

Normal conversations on a normal night at a temple. But standing beside Noah, small and feminine next to his height, she felt surrounded by his warm presence. As if he was taking care of her, looking out for her.

She liked the feeling.

Two men and a woman ascended a podium near the menorah. "We're going to begin," one of the men said. "Before our Rabbi says the prayer for Hanukkah, I have a couple of announcements to make…" He went on to announce the snacks afterward, for anyone present, but they were hoping the single young people would stay and introduce themselves and meet others. There would be a breakfast Sunday morning for the women's club…as he droned on, Erica glanced around.

She caught sight of an attractive blond woman, staring hard at Noah.

Noah seemed oblivious. He was zeroed in on the group at the podium.

The announcements over, the Rabbi said the traditional prayer, and the woman, who'd been introduced as the president of the sisterhood, plugged in the "candles" for the shamash and the six nights.

The Rabbi began singing "Oh Hanukkah, Oh Hanukkah, come light the menorah…" and the crowd joined in.

A cold wind blew, but squeezed next to Noah, and with her heavy coat, hat and gloves, Erica didn't mind the December weather. The cheerful voices and festive atmosphere made her feel good. Noah slid his arm around her, and she automatically leaned into him. It felt wonderful being close to him.

Almost like he was her boyfriend. She'd missed this kind of affection. Not that Lance had been very affectionate, but—there had been moments when they shared that comfy feeling. And she'd always appreciated it.

After the song, the Rabbi invited everyone into the temple.

As they moved with the crowd, Noah smiled down at her. "It was a good idea to come here."

Once inside, they left their coats and hats in the coat closet and joined the other people in the social hall. She'd spotted a sign that said: "Coffee & Tea & Hot Cocoa."

There were plenty of tables in the room, but a lot of people, as well. "I'll grab us seats," she said.

"Okay. I'll get us drinks. What do you want?"

She asked for cocoa, and he wound his way around tables, moving toward the hot drinks.

She was heading toward a group of round tables when she saw the woman who'd been staring at Noah earlier sidle up to him. She had obviously bleached blonde hair and a wide smile. She placed a possessive hand on his arm.

He turned to look at the attractive blonde. As Erica

watched, Noah's smile froze.

Erica grit her teeth. Who was the woman? She wore a blue cocktail dress with a plunging neckline, much too fancy for a night at the synagogue, and a black leather jacket that looked like it provided little warmth. She probably wanted a guy to warm her up, Erica thought cynically.

The woman, sleek and sexy, stared up at Noah adoringly. She actually blinked her eyes at him, and then slid her hand up his arm.

Did Noah have another girlfriend?

Erica shook her head. He'd said he didn't. Oh God, what if he was like Lance—

Her stomach tightened at the thought.

Could she believe Noah? Lance had cheated, and she'd been totally ignorant of his other girlfriend. Until she found the evidence.

Noah stepped back. He said something to the woman, then turned and headed toward the hot drinks. His mouth was set in a grim line.

The woman stood, staring after Noah, her mouth open.

Erica watched as he got two cocoas s and made his way to the table where she stood.

"I'm going to get some desserts," she told him.

"Wait." He stopped her with an outstretched arm.

She raised her eyebrows.

"That woman you saw me with—that was my old girlfriend, Tema."

Erica dropped down into the chair next to him.

He sat beside her, meeting Erica's look. "You know that wealthy boyfriend she dumped me for? He just dumped *her*. Now, she's prowling for a new guy." He twisted his mouth in a grimace.

Gladness engulfed Erica. So, he wasn't reciprocating the woman's obvious flirtation. In fact, he sounded annoyed. Maybe even disgusted.

She reached out and placed her hand on his arm without a second's thought. "I'm glad you're not—interested in her, any longer."

He covered her hand with his. The warmth from it seeped into hers with satisfying pressure. "I'm not. The only one here I'm interested in, is *you*." He emphasized the last word.

She felt her cheeks warm.

"Hey Noah!"

A young man, probably in his early twenties, strode up to them, balancing a plate piled with cookies.

"Hey, Brian," Noah said. He turned to Erica. "Erica, this is my cousin—second cousin—Brian. He lives not too far from here. Brian, this is Erica Fine. She just moved in next door to me."

"Nice to meet you." She smiled at the young man.

Brian grinned. "You too," he said.

"What brings you here?" Noah asked.

"I had nothing to do tonight, and my buddy Cole suggested we come here. Maybe meet some girls." Brian winked.

"Ahh," Noah said.

Brian gave them both a sweeping look. "Looks like you don't need help in that department." He grinned again. "Nice to see you guys. Noah, I guess I'll see you at Aunt Ellen's next week."

"Yes," Noah replied.

Brian moved toward another table where a few young people were sitting.

"He seems nice and friendly," Erica said, sipping her sweet cocoa.

"Yeah, he's a good guy. He just graduated college in May so he's still pretty young," Noah said. "His mother is my mother's cousin."

They chatted a bit about their families, and then Erica went to get cookies for both of them since the line was shorter. Noah remained at the table, watching her.

She was turning to go back to their table, a filled plate in her hand, when someone stepped in front of her. "Hi, Erica."

She caught her breath. "Lance?" What the hell was he doing at a singles event? "What the hell are you doing at a singles event?"

He made a sour face. "I'm single again."

She gasped. "What happened to—" what was her name? "Jordana?"

He sighed heavily. "I realized she wasn't for me. She was too—" His face grew red. "Too—money hungry. Grasping. I was nothing but a credit card to her." He actually sounded embarrassed.

"And she was nothing but a meal ticket to you," Erica snapped. She'd heard that the woman came from Old Money. Then she thought better of herself. That sounded crass.

And she was at a singles event, too, with someone. She shouldn't be a hypocrite.

"Not like you." He touched her with one finger, sliding it up the sleeve of her pink top. "You were never a money-conscious person."

She stepped back, shrugging him off.

"I understand why you may be angry with me," he said. "But that nerdy guy you're with—he's not for you,

Erica."

"That guy happens to be a very nice person," she said hotly. "And he treats me well."

"Just look at his clothes, Erica. I wear designer suits—" he indicated the black one he wore—"and he's in jeans and a flannel shirt. You know the old saying—clothes make the man."

"Yeah, they make him conceited," she retorted. "He happens to be one of the nicest guys I've ever met."

"I can be nice."

"Only when you want to be. Listen, Lance, I'm sorry things didn't work out with your *girlfriend*,"—she said the word in a deliberately sarcastic manner—" but you and I are done."

"You won't give me another chance?" Astonishment rang through his voice.

"Nope." Her word was firm. "And, once a cheater, always a cheater—another old saying." She gave him a wide smile, wheeled around, and walked away.

It felt good to have the final word. The last time she'd been with Lance, and he'd finally admitted he'd had another girlfriend on the side, she'd been in tears, and yelled at him to get out. Which he did, but his last sight of Erica had probably been her with tears streaming down her face.

It felt good to walk away now, with her head held high,

When she sat down next to Noah, he eyed her cautiously.

"Someone you know?" he asked.

"My ex-boyfriend, Lance. If I had realized what a snob he was earlier, I would never have dated him so long." She was happy to have realized that, and to have had the last word.

Noah looked relieved. "Looks like a night for running into exes," he observed. "And—his name sounds snooty." He gave a short laugh.

"I wasn't any more impressed by my ex than you were by yours just now," she said, winking.

She hoped he wasn't impressed by Tema. She certainly wasn't.

He winked back, then glanced at the door. "Let's get out of here."

"Great idea," she responded.

They retrieved their coats and headed out. Once they were in the car, she turned to Noah. "I'm sorry. When I suggested this, I never dreamed we'd run into our exes."

"It was a nice idea anyway," he said and reaching over, squeezed her hand. "I enjoyed the menorah lighting."

"Me too."

He pulled out of the parking lot, and drove through neighborhoods, taking a shortcut to their street. Erica focused on the houses, already decorated with blue and white Hanukkah motifs, and multi-colored Christmas lights, and icicle decorations.

"I love seeing the houses all decorated," she said. "All the neighborhoods look so festive."

"Yeah," he agreed. "We had neighbors who used to decorate to the hilt when I was growing up. All the lights on the house were bright and warm."

They reached his driveway and parked. "I'll walk you to your door."

"Do you want to come in?" she asked. She didn't want the evening to end with their exit from the temple.

He hesitated. "Yes, I'd like that."

"Okay." Suddenly she was breathless. What would they do when they entered? Butterflies flew in her middle. Kiss?

Her heart beat erratically as she unlocked the door and they stepped inside.

He shrugged out of his coat, and she did the same.

"Are you up for another game of dreidel?" he asked, quirking his eyebrows.

"Sure."

As they played for candy, she wondered why he didn't suggest playing for a kiss.

They played for about a half hour. Then, despite his coffee, she saw him hiding a yawn behind his hand.

"You're tired," she said. "I know you've been working hard, on your feet all day."

"Yes, sorry. I'll get going," he said. "I really did have a nice evening—despite running into Tema. Tomorrow, I'll call you around noon and we can bake."

She hadn't forgotten he'd offered to help. "That sounds good."

She walked him to the door. When he pulled on his coat, he hesitated. Then he brushed her lips with a soft kiss. When he drew back, she sensed caution in his stance.

"Goodnight, Erica."

"Goodnight." She watched as he walked over to his house, up the driveway, and toward his front steps. When he stepped inside his house, she shut her door and locked it, then leaned against it.

She hadn't been sure what kind of kiss to expect from him—if any—or what kind she even wanted.

But that light one had been disappointing.

She actually yearned for more.

Chapter XI

The Seventh Night of Hanukkah

Saturday morning was always busy at the pharmacy. Especially at this time of year. Between winter colds and flu, and people buying gifts and wrapping paper, there was a steady stream of customers.

Noah had felt unsettled last night after leaving Erica's home. He'd wanted to spend time with her—hell, he'd wanted to wrap her in his arms and kiss her for hours—but the peculiar meetings they'd had with their exes had put a strange damper on the evening.

He had mixed feelings about seeing Tema. On one hand, he felt a certain satisfaction that the fancy boyfriend she'd thrown him over for had now dumped her. Served her right.

On the other hand, she'd been flirting outrageously, and he kind of felt sorry for her. There's been a desperate edge to her. As if she was lonely, or depressed.

Not that it had anything to do with him at this point. He definitely didn't want to renew *that* romance.

And as far as Erica's old boyfriend—he'd noted the guy was sophisticated, slick looking. And had a conceited air that Noah could sense from several yards away. Lance seemed just *too* cool.

He was probably a player, and if Erica ended up giving him another chance, he'd break her heart again.

Glad to have only a half day's work today, since he was going out with Erica tonight, he left the pharmacy at noon. He passed many of the same sparkly houses on his way home, noting that since it was a cloudy day, some of them were lit up in the daytime. Erica's car was not in the driveway when he reached their street. She must be out.

Hopefully, not with that jerk Lance.

What about the cookie baking? He reached for his cellphone.

****

Erica met Alyssa at a nearby mall that morning to finish their Hanukkah and Christmas shopping. Erica needed gifts for her brothers and a Secret Santa present for work. She got her brothers gift cards to a favorite gaming store so they could pick up whatever games they wanted; and bought a large candle and plate for Louise, the middle-aged woman whose name she'd drawn. When Alyssa had completed her shopping, they headed to the food court.

"So tell me what's going on with Noah?" Alyssa asked over her salad. "How do you *feel* about him?"

Erica sighed. "I'm not sure. On one hand, I like him. A lot. Maybe even—" she stopped.

"Maybe…" Alyssa prompted.

She'd been tempted to say she may be falling in love with Noah. But she wasn't ready to voice the thought.

Her cousin guessed. "Maybe even…love him?" she whispered, leaning forward, her palm out in an entreaty.

"On the other hand, I'm afraid, and I don't trust him," Erica said quickly, cutting off thoughts of love.

"Why?"

"Because of what happened with Lance." Erica

frowned and stabbed a cherry tomato with her fork.

"Taking a chance on love is worth it," Alyssa urged.

Erica shot her a glance. "You say that because things worked out well for you."

"It was worth it," Alyssa repeated, getting that starry-eyed look she always wore when she spoke about her fiancé. "Think about it, Erica. If you pass this chance by, you may always be sorry that you didn't explore these feelings, and see where they could lead."

"You're an optimist," Erica accused. "What if Noah doesn't feel the same—or if he's like Lance?"

"You won't know if you don't try," Alyssa pointed out. "Listen, if you remember, I was hurt by a former boyfriend, too."

Erica did recall that. "But that was different. Your old boyfriend turned out to be an alcoholic."

"Yeah, and I didn't recognize the signs." Alyssa sighed. "Just like you didn't recognize the signs that Lance was cheating."

"That's true," Erica admitted slowly.

Her cellphone rang. She took it out, looking at the screen. Noah. Her heart gave a little leap. "Oh, this is Noah," she told her cousin. "Hi," she said into the phone, her voice sounding breathless to her own ears.

He asked about baking, and they agreed to meet at her place in an hour to try baking tonight's cookie.

When she got off, she met her cousin's eyes. Alyssa wore a decidedly sentimental smile.

"We're just baking cookies," Erica said quickly.

"Uh-huh." Alyssa continued to smile as they finished their meal.

Were they just baking cookies? Or was she—like Alyssa suggested—falling in love with Noah?

As she drove home, she pondered that thought.

****

When Noah arrived at Erica's house, she opened the door. "I'm just taking things out now." She led him back to the kitchen, and removed her wooden spoon and measuring spoons from a drawer. She grabbed her mixing bowl, and the baking dish the dough would go into. "Can you get the vanilla?" She pointed to it on a shelf.

He reached for it, and she took a moment to admire his muscles underneath the plaid shirt.

She was really looking forward to baking with him. She watched as he rolled up his shirtsleeves, revealing those muscles even more. Her mouth nearly watered., then she turned on the oven to pre-heat it.

"Now, with baking, you have to measure exactly," she cautioned him, picking up a measuring spoon.

"Okay, just tell me what to measure," he said, looking at the array of measuring cups and spoons she'd placed on the counter along with flour, and more items.

She told him how much flour they needed, then went to the refrigerator to remove the sugar and butter.

Turning slightly, she saw him holding the measuring cup of flour, studying it as he tapped it.

"I see you're being precise," she said. "That's good."

He raised his eyes to meet hers. "Pharmacists have to be precise. We measure medicines and those measurements have to be accurate," he said. "We're very careful so people get the right doses.

"I should have realized," she said, smiling. She could just imagine how he would concentrate while pouring a medicine. "Of course, you're dealing with life-threatening conditions with some clients."

A sudden flash of him concentrating in another area—stroking her skin—blew through her mind, and she sucked in a breath.

He would probably be a very considerate lover, bringing a woman to the peak with as much care as he showed right now in her kitchen.

She swallowed, feeling her face flame. Oblivious to her discomfort, he shook the measuring cup to settle the flour, then smiled. "Ok, here's the flour."

She looked away, hoping he wouldn't notice her red face.

They finished mixing the ingredients while she tried to act as normal as possible.

They agreed to sample the cookies after their dinner. Noah went back to his house to change, and she took the opportunity to change also, while the cookies cooled.

And tried not to keep imagining his hands touching her, stroking her…

****

Noah planned to take Erica to his favorite Chinese restaurant, a place that also served some Japanese and Thai dishes. Instead of wearing one of his favorite comfortable flannel shirts, he chose a blue-striped business shirt and a navy vest to wear with his slacks.

He wanted to look nicer. Like her ex-boyfriend.

Well, almost. At least she had called Lance a snob, and sounded disgusted about it.

When Erica opened the door, he saw she'd dressed up more than usual, too. She wore a dark green dress and black boots that almost reached her knees.

Sexy. She looked damned sexy.

Impulsively, he leaned down and gave her a quick

kiss.

She looked surprised, and her cheeks grew rosy as he regarded her.

"Hi." Her voice was breathless.

He handed her the bouquet of mixed, colorful flowers he'd picked up for her earlier today. "Happy Hanukkah."

"Thank you!" she said. "That's so thoughtful."

He followed her into the living room, where she retrieved a vase from the wall unit.

"Let me put the flowers in here and we can go," she said and proceeded into the kitchen to fill the vase with water.

"I made reservations at Eastern Palace," he said. "I hope you like Chinese food."

"What Jewish person doesn't?" That was a standard joke; it seemed every Jewish person loved Chinese food. "Their food is great." Since it was nearby, she'd eaten there with her family a few times.

"It's my favorite."

Once she'd arranged the flowers in the vase and placed it on the dining room table, she looked up at him. "I'm ready to go."

He helped her with her coat, then took her hand as they walked outside into the chilly air.

They spoke about the Hanukkah gifts they'd bought for family members, and soon arrived at the restaurant. A cold wind accompanied them as they walked to the front door. Once inside, the clink of china and savory smells greeted them. The restaurant was warm and although busy, the booth they were shown to was nice and cozy.

He regarded Erica as she picked up the menu. "You

look really pretty." Boy, that sounded sophisticated, he chastised himself.

She met his eyes. "Thank you," she said softly. "I think you look handsome."

He smiled. "Thanks." Picking up his menu, he opened it.

He knew it almost by heart already, since he liked to take out food from here, too. He watched as she studied the lists, biting her lip.

"Everything on the menu is good," he told her. He scanned the entrees. He decided on one of his favorites, the pepper steak.

She ordered the sweet and sour chicken. Starting with the crispy noodles and then wonton soups, they ate while chatting about cuisines they liked. They both liked Italian and Chinese foods. He liked sushi but she didn't. And she loved Greek food, which he wasn't familiar with.

He ate with gusto, enjoying the meal and her company. The meat was spicy and the vegetables fresh in their sauce.

She told him she thought the food was delicious and would recommend it. They were going back to her place for dessert, and he suggested watching a movie afterward.

"Do you like *Elf*?" she asked. "I know it's a Christmas movie, but I've always thought it was so funny and sweet."

"Sure," he said. "I haven't watched it for a few years, and I always enjoyed it, too."

Once they returned to her house, they went into the dining room and she picked up the box of matches.

He placed a hand on her shoulder and felt a tremor

go through her.

Was she nervous?

She lit the shamash, and then touched it to each candle as he joined her in the prayer.

When they finished, she set the helper candle in its holder and turned to regard him.

"Happy Hanukkah," she said, her voice low.

"Happy Hanukkah." He was tempted to pull her into his arms, but he saw some hesitancy in her eyes. Why? He wondered. Why was she afraid?

Instead, he gave her a quick kiss.

"I'll get the cookies," she said. "Unless you want to wait until after the movie?"

"Let's wait," he suggested. "I'm actually stuffed after dinner."

"Okay." She led the way to her living room and rummaged through a bunch of DVDs on her wall unit. She swayed slightly, and in her dress, her body looked tempting. He swallowed suddenly. She really was a beautiful woman.

Looking for a distraction, he focused on the wall unit, then on the photo of Erica, the one her grandmother always called "special."

"Your grandmother always loved that photo," he said. "She kept saying it was very special."

"I know. I'm not sure why she liked it so much," Erica said, glancing at the picture. "Maybe because it showed me at a special moment, graduating from college." The photo was a close-up. Erica looked beautiful and happy.

She withdrew the *Elf* movie. "Here it is."

She met his eyes, and longing wove through him. For her. And not just a physical reaction.

He wanted to hold her, hug her, make her forget all about that two-timing guy Lance.

And that's when he realized that he really had feelings for this woman.

He recognized the strength of them. It was more than simple desire. He cared for her—a lot.

Maybe he was falling in love with her.

****

After her conversation with Alyssa, Erica wondered if she might be falling in love with Noah. He was so considerate, so caring, and also fun to be with.

But when she'd met his eyes after lighting the candles—that's when she *knew*.

Yes.

She was falling in love with this man. A good man, a caring man. At least, he seemed to be.

She hoped she was correct. She hoped she wasn't mistaken, like she had been with Lance.

Because she cared about Noah…a lot.

Loved him.

They sat on the couch and watched the movie together. After a few minutes, he placed his arm around her shoulders and pulled her close.

It felt good. No, it felt great.

She relaxed her body into his and enjoyed the movie while snuggling with him. They laughed at the funny parts, and when everyone began to sing near the end, she blinked back tears.

He turned to regard her.

"This part always gets to me," she said, her voice trembling.

He kissed her, gently. "That's because you're a caring person."

When the movie ended, she turned to look at him. He was smiling.

"I do love happy endings," she said. She wiped away a tear.

"Me too."

"I'll get the cookies." She scampered into the kitchen, returning with a plastic container. She brought them over to the couch with some napkins and sat back down next to him.

She opened the container and they each took one.

She bit into hers. It was very, very mushy. She chewed and swallowed. "Nope. Not the right texture. It's too mushy."

He swallowed his morsel. "Agreed."

She sighed deeply. "I only have one more night to get this right." *And one more night to spend with you.* The thought pierced her, hard.

She gazed at him as they finished their cookies.

"Maybe tomorrow's will be the right one," he said hopefully.

"You can take a few home," she said.

"I think I'll do that. Maybe I'll have them for breakfast," he joked.

She took two out of the container and gave him the rest which were nestled inside. "You can bring back the container tomorrow." Would it be their last time together? she wondered, her stomach clenching.

"Okay." He regarded her with a serious expression, then leaning forward, kissed her gently. He paused, put the container down, and then gathered her into his arms.

It felt so good to be held by him. Without another thought, she slid her hands around his neck and pulled him closer.

The kiss ignited, and she grew hot. Noah pressed her closer.

"Erica, Erica." His whispered words were entreating. "I want you. So much."

"I want you too." Her words were breathless.

"Let me make love to you." He kissed her cheeks, her brow, her ear, before swooping back to her lips.

"Yes," she answered. There was no question in her mind. A tiny doubt wiggled its way forward. "But I'm not on the pill—" It had been over a year since she'd had sex, and she hadn't thought about protection.

"I have protection," he said. He stood and pulled her gently up. He guided her to her bedroom.

It didn't take them long to shed their clothes. They toppled onto her bed, and Noah proved what she'd suspected. His clever hands stroked her, bringing her to the brink of ecstasy. When he thrust into her, she screamed her release.

He followed a moment later, shouting "Erica!"

Slowly, they drifted back to earth. Erica cuddled into him.

"Want to stay here tonight?" she asked, sleepiness edging her voice.

"I'd love to." He held her close.

As she drifted off, she thought how wonderful it felt to lie here next to him...

But what would tomorrow bring? It was the last night of Hanukkah.

She snuggled closer, not wanting to think about it yet.

Chapter XII

Eighth Night of Hanukkah

Sunday morning Erica woke up earlier than usual, but being entwined in Noah's arms was worth it. She lay still for a few minutes. Then he woke, and they made slow, sweet love.

"I need to go home and shower and change," he said. "How about if I come back in a couple of hours? I'm on call for work and I have to check that they don't need me. If they do, I'll let you know—but it would only be for part of the day. We can spend the rest of the day together."

"Okay," she agreed, as happiness washed over her. He wanted to spend the day with her!

Once he left, she showered quickly, put on jeans and a nice sweater, and baked the last batch of cookies. As they were cooling, she finished wrapping the Hanukkah gifts for her family's party next week, and the Christmas gifts she'd bought for her friends and co-workers.

She felt restless and edgy, knowing that after tonight, the only times she might see Noah was as a neighbor. Could she finagle continuing their relationship? After making love, would they take it to the next level?

Because she *wanted* to. She wanted to take a chance on a relationship with a guy who seemed trustworthy and honest.

And as a lover, he was everything she'd dreamed of. She was right, those long-fingered hands were clever and this considerate man knew how to please a woman.

Erica didn't want to just pace inside her house. She needed to get out for a while. She texted Noah that she was going shopping for a short time, then grabbed her coat. As she locked her door, wind buffeted her, nearly blowing off her hat. It was going to be a cold day.

Noah texted her when she was starting her car. *Still waiting to hear from my boss. I'll be in touch when I do.*

She went to a local shopping plaza that had a couple of stores she liked. She bought another holiday candle in case she needed an extra, last-minute gift; and then strolled around a discount store before buying herself a bright blue sweater she liked. Maybe she'd wear it when Noah came over.

On the way home, she clicked on the radio, listening to a local New Jersey station that was playing some popular holiday hits. She recognized "Jingle Bell Rock" immediately and turned up the volume on the popular tune, humming along.

She noticed a small red car parked by Noah's house when she pulled into her driveway. She turned off her car and was getting out when she heard someone yell.

"Goodbye, lover!"

Startled, Erica looked toward Noah's house.

Tema—his old girlfriend—was rushing down the steps of his house, yelling over her shoulder.

Erica froze. His old girlfriend in Noah's house—calling him lover! A frigid wave welled up in her.

Noah appeared at the doorway and said something, but with the wind whistling loudly she couldn't hear him.

Erica stood by her car, her legs trembling. Noah's old girlfriend—at his house. The woman's coat was open and she appeared to be in another sexy dress, this time in bright yellow.

Tears stung Erica's eyes. She'd thought she and Noah had something good going between them. She'd even slept with him. But it was obvious he was still involved with Tema. The woman's words indicated a physical relationship. Tema certainly looked sexy enough in her dress to tempt any guy.

Tema caught sight of Erica standing there.

"He's mine, and always will be!" Tema screamed at her. "He'll never be yours!"

Erica's legs could barely carry her to her front door. Tears stung her eyes as she fumbled with her keys, all the while feeling like a block of ice had settled inside her. She choked back a sob as she flung open the door.

Inside, she slammed it shut, threw off her coat, and ran over to the couch, burying her face in a pillow.

She faintly heard the screech of Tema's car driving away as the tears fell.

Noah—he was just like Lance. He was seeing her and Tema at the same time.

Of course, Noah had never said that he and Erica had a relationship. Certainly not an exclusive one.

Worse yet, he'd told her Tema was out of his life now.

Another sob escaped her. She'd fallen in love with Noah—and he'd turned out to be just like Lance!

Noise cut through her sobs, and she became aware that someone was pounding at her front door.

"Erica! Erica!" Noah called.

She tried ignoring him, but when he continued to

knock, she wailed "Go away!"

"Let me in! Please, I can explain!"

She buried her face further into the pillow and sobbed harder.

He stopped pounding, and relieved, she curled up in a ball. She felt as if she'd been punched in the stomach.

Two minutes later, she heard the scrape of a key.

"Erica!" Her door flew open.

She gasped, and dropped the pillow, getting to her feet. "How—how—" she could barely speak.

"Your grandmother gave me a key in case of emergencies." His voice was grim, and he closed the door behind him and strode forward. "This is an emergency as far as I'm concerned. Erica, please let me speak. Tema is a witch, and I can just imagine what that scene looked like to you."

"She-she said you were lovers, and you would always be—always be her boyfriend!" she choked out.

"She lied. Tema came over with the express purpose of trying to seduce me. When I refused, she got angry. I told her she would never be my girlfriend again, ever. Look." He thrust out his phone.

She read the texts, from just two minutes ago.

Tema: *You'll be sorry you don't want me!*

Noah: *No. I'm in love with someone else!*

Erica's mouth dropped open. "You're—" she couldn't say another word.

"I'm in love with someone else," he said firmly. He moved closer and grasped her arms. "You. I'm in love with you, Erica. I wanted to tell you tonight."

"You're in love with me?" Her voice was so shaky she could barely speak.

"Yes." Now he cupped her face with his hands. "I've

fallen in love with you. And I think you care for me."

"I—I do, Noah," she whispered. "I was afraid that after tonight, I wouldn't see you anymore, since we had only said we would spend the eight nights of Hanukkah together. And we never agreed to—anything more."

He sighed. "I thought I was making it clear that I wanted more. I want to keep seeing you, Erica, even after Hanukkah is over. I want to spend time with you and get to know you better. I love you, and I think we could have a great relationship." He took a breath. "A permanent one."

As she listened to his words, something stirred inside of her. Hope. Joy. All the feelings the season was supposed to bring.

"I think we could too," she whispered.

He pulled her into his arms and kissed her.

It was not gentle. It was a possessive kiss, the kind that told her she was his. That he loved her, and desired her, as a woman.

She pulled back for a second. "I'm in love with you, too, Noah. I realized it yesterday."

He kissed her again. "I love you."

They gazed at each other. "Everything is wonderful," she said, amazement weaving through her voice. "If we could only find the recipes—" She glanced around the room.

He did, too.

He paused.

She looked to see what he was staring at.

The photo of her. Grandma Franny's favorite.

They both let out exclamations at the same instant.

"The photo of me—"

"Franny's favorite photo—"

They disentangled and hurried over to the photo on the wall unit. Erica picked it up.

"She always said it was very special," he said hoarsely. "She talked about it often."

"Let's see what's in the frame," she whispered.

With trembling hands, she worked the back off the frame and then pulled out the cardboard inside. Wedged between the photo and the cardboard were several papers. She gasped.

She pulled them out. Turning them over, she exclaimed, "Oh my God!" There, in her grandma's neat cursive handwriting, were two pages labeled "favorite recipes." Erica scanned them. "It's her brisket recipe and her apricot cookies!" She tilted her head up to regard his beloved face. "Let's make the cookies for tonight!"

"Not quite yet." He took the papers gently, placed them on the coffee table, and then pulled her back into his arms. "Not until I've totally convinced you that I love you."

And his lips came down on hers as he crushed her close.

Epilogue

First Night of Hanukkah, One Year Later

Erica was just finishing putting the candles in the menorah when she heard the garage door opening and Noah's car pulling in. Moments later he opened the door downstairs and called up, "Hi, sweetheart!"

He pounded up the stairs to the main level. The two dogs they'd adopted ran to meet him.

She smiled and ran into his arms to give him a kiss and hug. He gave her a thorough kiss, then bent to pet the dogs. "Hi, guys. Ready for your new Hanukkah bones?"

They wagged their tails as if they knew what he was talking about.

Erica and Noah had gotten married just a month ago, in November, and she'd moved into his home. Her brother Aaron and his girlfriend Jill had moved into Grandma Franny's house, so it had also been kept in the family.

She'd never been as happy as she was married to Noah. He was truly caring and considerate, and trustworthy. All the things she'd wanted and thought she'd never find.

"Let's light the candles before we have dinner," she said. "And the cookies should be about ready."

She took them from the oven, then left them to cool.

They'd have them for dessert—she'd made enough for the next few nights.

They lit the menorah together, chanting the prayer, and then Noah pulled her into his arms again.

"Should we exchange presents now or later?" he asked.

"It's up to you." She smiled at him, knowing her smile was loving. "The greatest gift I ever got was your love. And all because you helped me with some cookies."

"I'd say it was a fair trade," he said, grinning. "I got your love in *and* delicious cookies.

They laughed together, and he bent down to give her another loving kiss.

Shortbread Shakedown

by

Sofia Aves

Christmas Cookies

Dedication

As a thank you to veterans everywhere,
this is my shortbread cookie for you.

Chapter One

I stood outside the customs exit, the airport buzzing with people fussing over their excess luggage. Carols blared over the cacophony of holiday travelers milling in a controlled frenzy, anxious to locate friends and kin. Festive trees lined the large floor-to-ceiling windows that overlooked the streetscape, wound in bunting, their fairy lights twinkling merrily even during daylight hours.

The crowd that cluttered LAX's International terminal circled me to greet friends and welcome family, but none of them were for me. I scanned above the sea of heads for a placard reading *Dominic Cage*, groping at my hip with a long-honed instinct for an absent sidearm, despite wearing full dress uniform for the flight.

The place where my holster should rest against my leg lay empty, my uniform incomplete without it. People jostled me, bumps coming from all directions. The constant roar in my head blocked out everything else, even the activity around me.

Focus. It's just home. You're home.

But after so many months existing in a tent, transiting back and forth between the two countries, I was no longer certain I could call either *home*.

Living in the desert on and off over so many years meant I only had my bed in the barracks or a tent in the pink dust. Here, I'd be assigned a building that put sufficient distance between me and everyone else. Months of wishing to be back on US soil warped into a bittersweet desire to turn tail and run back to the pink sand that had coated my gritty existence for the past eighteen months.

Grains dusted my hand as I turned, regardless that I had washed my hair before I left the desert. The stuff got everywhere. After the long flight, I appreciated the chance to walk. The comfort offered by a commercial aircraft didn't go unnoticed either—the seats had a lot more padding than the canvas webbing of a Herc. The constant drone of the military aircraft was loud, and exhausting, despite the earmuffs I'd packed. I never wanted to see another red seat again in my life.

Two long weeks had been spent in transit waiting for aircraft that sat on the tarmac. Repairs halted while parts were shipped in, and I spent my wasted hours convincing myself I wanted to be back on US soil. Now, that small, air-conditioned tent in the middle of the desert looked appealing.

A tiny woman with a head of gray hair jostled me. I stepped back and bumped into another body. Movement surrounded me as I mumbled apologies, my shoulders tightening. I stood a head taller than most, which gave me a constant supply of fresh air, and combat boots helped me see over the masses. I refused to part with the boots, despite that they weren't technically part of my dress uniform. Those boots had taken me across so many deployments and brought me back from each one, safe.

Home.

There was that word again.

I picked out the soldier hoisting a sign at chest level in a perfunctory manner, my name printed across it. He'd chosen a good, clear position, highly visible from the customs exit. Either he had arrived very early or wiggled his way into the area to find me. Good man. I made a mental note to praise him to his ranking officer.

I raised my hand to signal to him as a body barreled into me at chest height. Bouncy, honey-blonde curls tangled around my hands—not the sort that came out of a salon, but a true, soft beachy blonde that tumbled over my arms in luxurious waves. The sort of sweet luxury I wanted to hold against my chest when I woke each morning.

Whoa. Where the hell did that come from?

A hardened soldier doesn't deserve the pleasures of a regular home with a beautiful woman. We're too screwed up inside for that.

"Mwffl-axx. Soood eeeooo."

I couldn't make out a single word with her voice muffled between my shirt and her hair.

Swearing under my breath but grinning at the same time, I straightened her, apologies curling my tongue. People bumped us again, a distance growing as the jostling receded from my consciousness. The buzzing between my ears quietened.

In a sliver of a second, I glimpsed deep brown eyes ringed with purple as the terminal fell away. She launched into me, wrapping her arms around my neck to cut off my stunted mumbles—and my airway.

A shock shivered over me in a feverish rush. I wound my arms around her curvy frame in a familiar response, though I wasn't expecting anyone to greet me, other than the soldier I had already noted. I certainly didn't recognize the woman clutching at me as her lifeline.

The scent of something sweet swirled around me. Butterscotch? Her curls sank into my hands as I cupped the back of her head, my breath hitching. Her body curved to fit against mine in all the right places. I hardened at her touch, the thin, white knit sweater and my dress shirt forming the only barrier between my skin and hers.

She smells so damn good. I can't breathe around her.

The thoughts tore through my oxygen-starved brain, tangling together. She was too close, too soft. I gathered the soft material of her sweater in my fist, desperate for skin-on-skin contact.

Reality hit me, or maybe it was the random piece of luggage the size of a small elephant bruising my back. Shuffling forward to avoid banging into people, I managed to step into the unknown girl in my arms. I squeezed her back once more, the shape of her seared into my palms.

She didn't release me, her cheek pressed over my erratic heart.

Warmth and safety draped over me in a heavy blanket. I closed my eyes, stealing a moment that wasn't mine to take. This girl wasn't here for me; I had no family or home left to meet an old grunt coming off his last tour.

Just to be practical, I tugged at her arms wrapped around my throat. They loosened, and I got a breath in right before it sucked from my lungs as I caught a glimpse of her face. I stared, not caring if it came off as rude.

Those luminous eyes stared right back, framed by an oval face with rounded cheekbones. The purple halo around her iris drew me in until weightlessness unbalanced me.

A dimple adorned her smile that had no right being that cute. She might have been in her late twenties, maybe a few years older.

Without much thought, I cupped her cheek, tracing my fingers along the pulse that fluttered with an erratic beat beneath it. I dipped my head. My lips tingled at the thought of contacting hers, to see if she tasted as good as she smelled.

A tiny gasp came from those lips as her head tilted back in my hand.

What in all the hell was I doing? I paused a hair's breadth away from kissing the strange girl who had accosted in the airport. She had clearly mistaken me for someone else, and I was about to take liberties I had no right to do in a very public place.

The thought doused my arousal, but the flush that spread from her neck to her cheeks as her joy transformed to embarrassment brought it back in an instant. Her chest rose and fell in a staccato rhythm.

I enjoyed every second of it: her eyes widening, pink lips parting as sweet breath brushed my lips. Something about me was clearly broken.

"I'm so-so sorry," she stuttered, backing out of the embrace she'd wound herself into. The girl checked over her shoulders with wide eyes, her hair flying at all angles.

"It's fine." I held up my hands, palms open. "It happened." Attempting to cover my ass with a smile, as if I hadn't just tried to kiss her in the middle of a crowded airport.

She blinked at me. "I'm sorry."

Sharp corners poked into my palm. A crinkling at waist level diverted my attention to the small package she pressed into my hands. I curled my fingers around it by reflex. In a flurry of honey-colored curls, she disappeared into the crowd that closed over her path.

I hefted the small bag, examining the shortbread cookies wrapped in cellophane. A tiny, yellow ribbon was tied at the top in a neat knot, and a little handmade tag sat to one side. A jaunty sprig of holly propped it up.

To Max, love Violet.

The crowd swelled, disguising her retreat. Carols cranked over the loudspeaker system, overriding the chatter of hundreds of people stuffed into a too-small space.

Plastic reindeer held me with their fixed stare as I pushed my way to where I thought she had headed, her scent dissipating into the crowd around us. I barely registered the man who appeared next to me, taking my bag from my shoulder. My driver introduced himself to deaf ears.

All I wanted was to find the honey-blonde curls of the woman who had ghosted into my life and disappeared.

****

I sat in the back of the silver sedan, sunlight glinting off the hood. We passed the giant LAX sign, decorated with snowflakes, and merged around airport traffic until we hit the highway. Ignoring the world fussing outside the car, I studied the crinkly bag of cookies, rubbing my thumb over the point of a fresh holly sprig.

"Everything all right, sir?"

I hadn't seen her again, though I'd searched every face as we left the terminal.

Violet.

Max was a very lucky man.

"Fine, Bernard."

"We'll be on the road for a while, sir."

I nodded, leaning back in my seat. The Mountain Training Center in Pickel Meadows I'd been stationed at before my deployment sat a solid six-hour drive north of LA in clear weather, the trip slower due to a freak snow season that had closed roads already cluttered with holiday traffic.

Bernard was full of enthusiastic information, happy to play tour guide to a jaded officer determined to return to his pragmatic military lifestyle with nothing better to occupy his time.

The drive gave me plenty of time to forget the girl I had met at the airport, though *met* might be pushing it. Her scent was etched in my senses, the feel of her still filling my hands, though all they held was a bag of cookies that crinkled in my palm. Adjusting my pants, I forced my attention away from the ghost of her.

Giving cookies to returning veterans in uniform at airports as a *thanks for your service* gesture had become something of a tradition. A beautiful and welcome touch; I had seen a young soldier return to his home soil careworn only to cry on a random biddy's shoulder as if she were his grandmother.

But this package was far more personal. The card was handwritten, and that hug meant she missed him something fierce.

I want hugs like that every day.

By the time we'd passed city limits, I was ensconced in the brief memory of her. Soft curls tumbled around her pink cheeks, eyes I could lose myself in for days. Weeks.

The gates of the base came up too fast. I fumbled for my pass, the bundle of cookies crinkling between my knees. The MP checked my ID, emerging from his tinsel-covered sentry box. I returned his salute with a half-assed effort. I hadn't thought about being back in the US; where I'd sleep, who I'd have to face, who wouldn't be part of my unit anymore.

For hours, I'd thought of nothing but her. The buttery scent of her that haunted me, the way she wrapped around my neck, how her sweet curves pressed to my body in a perfect fit. Hell, I might even *enjoy* reintegration if I had a woman like that around. I let my mind tick over as I collected my single utilitarian bag.

Thanking Bernard, I headed to the transit accommodation to collect a key, drifting back to my thoughts of the woman.

She'd confused me with someone else; there was no mistaking the uniform I wore. Did I resemble a man she knew? How many Max's could there be in the US Army?

Eight hours on home soil, and I hadn't thought about anything but her the entire time.

Violet.

Chapter Two

I sat in a familiar office filled with unfamiliar things. Someone else's work lay in my inbox. Scraps of paperwork filled the shredder beside my desk. All evidence that the world continued to turn in my absence. I had become a temporary participant in my own life.

The little bag of shortbread cookies sat on one corner, my single personal addition to the utilitarian room. I pressed my palms flat to the surface of the desk, inhaling, but even the smell of the place was different than I remembered.

A sense of unreality swamped me.

The window presented a view of the same patch of the parking lot and the same bare trees as before I had left. The car park stood empty at this time of year, with a few vehicles scattered around the lot from personnel remaining over the holiday season. With the base winding down for the year, the majority of soldiers returned to their own homes and families.

For those who had a place to celebrate the season.

For others, it presented an opportunity to get work done in the quiet days of the year. I had to admit it would make getting back into the flow of routine easier before everyone returned to their postings and new teams in the new year.

That gave me a few weeks to get my ass together before I had to deal with too many people on home soil.

With all I needed to catch up on while I'd been

away—who'd promoted into what position, which battalions I'd be managing—I pushed it all aside and focused on finding Max.

Except that it turned out there were six hundred and twenty-one variations of *Max* enlisted or otherwise in the US Army. None were stationed in my region of California.

What were the odds?

For the moment, I'd given it up as a bad job. But the image of Violet's purple-ringed eyes settled deep into me. The warmth of her body pressed against mine was fast developing into a craving I couldn't satisfy.

How could a woman I'd had contact with for so short a time have such a lasting effect on me?

I wasn't a family man. No one who took as many deployments as I had could ever have the luxury of a stable life. It was difficult to have a family when you would only ever be an absent husband or father in your own life.

Movement outside my window drew me back to the present. A lilac bubble car pulled up a few spaces from where I'd been dropped off.

That had been today?

I scrubbed a hand over my face, too-long bristles biting into my hand. I needed to shave, and a shower would be great. I'd taken the room key, not caring that it was below my entitlements. I wouldn't be staying in it long enough to care, anyway.

The faint purple car door opened. I stared at it. When no one emerged, I shook my head and returned to the small stack of papers I'd printed out. Words blurred into illegible lines the longer I stared at them.

I blinked dry and grainy eyes. A combination of lack

of sleep and hydration reminded me that my body wasn't eternally infallible. At some point, I would need to take care of myself, which drew my thoughts back to Violet, and the thought of having a home with a woman like her.

Or, hell, just her.

I shook my head to dispel the thoughts, and when they wouldn't dissipate, I pushed them far enough to the back of my mind to be able to focus on daily life.

Focus, Cage.

Hydration. Of course, my water bottle was nowhere in sight. Already swimming with inconsequential details of daily routine, I returned to the real reason I'd come straight into my office without sleeping off my jetlag.

Half spinning on my chair, I riffled through the desk drawers. The last call to deploy had left me with little time to prepare. A few hours to pack and get my ass onto the C17 back to the desert that had fast become more of a home than my own country.

The hard panel of the back of the drawer sat firm. I scratched at the wood facade for a minute. Maybe it had been found or moved? I scrabbled faster, trying to locate the corner I'd edged out of the false back. My heart hammered; I *knew* I should have put my meager possessions in storage. I slammed my fist against the back of the drawer hard enough to bruise.

I am a first-class idiot.

A thin piece of plywood landed on the back of my hand.

I blinked, huffing at my frustrations as I extracted the thin rectangular box. Tension I hadn't known I'd been holding in my shoulders relaxed beneath the familiar weight. The top flicked open with little resistance. I ran my fingers over the raised imprint on the round and star-shaped medals, down the colored ribbons attached to their bars at the bottom, metal glinting beneath fluorescent office lights. When the paperwork went through, there would be another two to add to my collection.

I smiled, closed the box, and returned it to where it had sat for the past two years.

Who puts their meager possessions in the back of an office drawer?

A man who had nowhere else to secure them.

I shoved the poor but accurate reflection of my life aside and dove into my work.

****

Hours later, I hovered stiff fingers over the keyboard. I couldn't feel my rear. Plenty of my desert hours had been spent in an office environment, but during my last tour, I'd been on the ground with my training brigades that were no longer in training. Returning to Pickel Meadows dredged up new meaning to paperwork as I printed off form after form to sign.

I balanced my pen between numb fingers over the last sheet of paper. The Record of Recommendation read the same as the last five times I had gone over it. I sighed and put the pen down before ink blotched all over the thing. A full promotion meant more responsibility and moving into a political arena, and away from a role focused predominantly on leadership.

I had zero interest in becoming a politician, but that was the next step on the career ladder. Acting rank had been awarded to me in the desert. It had seemed fun at the time, but now I knew just how heavy that rank sat.

The promotion was temporary until I signed my papers; all I had to do was fuck up. But no matter how many times I did, the bastards kept promoting me—which meant more years working a job that replaced my heart with a coalescent lump of guilt and self-loathing.

Sighing, I shoved the paper across the desk, pushing hair back from my face. I *really* needed a haircut. The paper fluttered to the other side of my desk, the pen following it, rolling languidly to the edge. It faltered, wavering.

A knock at the door drew my attention as the pen made a last-ditch effort and rolled off the desk.

I didn't move.

A clean-shaven soldier with sandy blond hair in a neat buzz cut stepped through my open doorway and caught it. He spun the pen between his fingers and tossed it back to me.

I snatched it out of the air.

"Nice reflexes, old man." The captain grinned at me.

His uniform fit him with greater ease than mine, though I'd changed into jeans and a collared shirt once I'd reached my office. I rolled my shoulders, conscious of the soft material, but I'd known Matt for too long to hide anything from him.

"Energy like that is indecent in here, Somerville," I grumbled, but I couldn't hold back the grin creeping across my face. The smile had an alien feel to it. I coughed into my hand, then gestured to the fresh pair of bars decorating his shoulders. "Nice rank."

Matthew Sommerville tapped the crumpled paper at the edge of my desk. "Could say the same to you."

That wasn't going to happen. Becoming a politician didn't suit me. I rolled my shoulders back, knots popping beneath mangled skin. "We'll see."

A clean, hard-working soldier, Matt should have

been promoted at the same rate as me. The difference between us was that Matt took nice, safe jobs that kept him behind a sensible desk while I opted for the riskier postings. That sort came with either a solid pass or a spectacular fail.

So far, I'd scored well. The circumstances of how I'd gotten here, however, didn't sit well with me.

"That bad, huh?" Matt eyed me, folding his arms over his chest. "Wanna talk about it?"

"Are you kidding?" I snorted, leaning forward to plant my elbows on the desk, studying the form, and made no move to sign it. "I'm not—"

"Hey, congratulations!" A shadow fell over us. "Who died to make you kin—uh, brigadier?"

I looked up in time to see Matt roll his eyes heavenward. My gaze sharpened as it took in another familiar face.

Soft and unlined, this new face suggested little seriousness and fewer worries. The faux hawk perched on top of his head where his military-regulation haircut should have been topped off an impression that hadn't changed since I'd last worked with him.

Something in his easy stance had me leaning back in my chair with my hands clasped behind my head. I bit back the urge to comment on the hair. Just. Maybe I was growing soft, but I couldn't be an asshole all the time.

It was Christmas, after all.

"Will McBride. You haven't changed a bit."

"Can't say the same for you." A shadow flickered behind his eyes.

My lips twitched at the absence of a *sir*, but he was Matt's troop, and I knew the captain would come down hard on him later, well out of a ranking officer's earshot.

Matt turned his sandy blond head between us, the lines around his eyes creased.

"That happens when you actually work for a living." I kept my face smooth, resisting the urge to leap from my chair and eject the soldier from my office with force.

With a preference to the lethal sort.

"So they say." Will ran his gaze over the room, an inspection that would have made any warrant officer proud.

Pity he'd never make rank that high.

"Careful who you're talking to," Matt murmured over his shoulder, one eyebrow cocked. He shook his head in a minute movement.

Will looked affronted at the dismissal.

I waved Matt's comment away. "I haven't been back long enough to bother with technicalities. I'm not on duty, anyway." I gestured to my jeans and a collared shirt.

"You know that's never true," Matt joked, though his expression and tone sat at odds with each other.

I held his gaze, his study bothering me more than it should. Words circulated in my head, none of which should be spoken at all, but never in Will's presence. I tapped the reclaimed pen on my keyboard, allowing myself the small expression of my growing anxiety.

Matt leaned on my desk. He positioned himself as an effective barrier between myself and Will.

"Never!" Will laughed far too loud in the cramped office, slapping his officer's back.

A grimace worked its way onto my face. I morphed it into something that missed the mark as a smile. "But I do have work to get through, so…" I gestured to the paperwork in the inbox that wasn't mine.

The young soldier's mouth opened, but he didn't get the chance to protest.

"See you in the O's mess later?" Matt gripped his troop's arm, creasing his uniform, and towed him back to the door.

"Fine." I'd have to socialize. It took too much effort to keep the sourness from my voice.

Matt paused at the door, then shook his head, grabbing the handle. "You want me to shut this?"

"Please." I gave a sharp nod, ignoring whatever he wanted to say. I'd hear it later on, anyway.

****

The officer's mess held a skeleton crew of ghosts. A few souls remained on base over Christmas, their repetitive days fading into a rigid routine that was more of an existence than a life. Unfamiliar faces stared at me across the bar.

Afternoon shadows merged with dusk outside the long window overlooking the base, casting the unadorned buildings into a haze of snow and failing light.

Matt turned from his place at the bar, waving me over, and pushed a beer my way.

"Have I been away that long?" I looked over the bar staff, all a good decade younger than me.

"Honestly?" Matt stared into his beer. "No. But...maybe you didn't notice some of the changes last time you got home."

"So it is that bad." I grinned, pushing the pretense for the sake of it.

Concern wrinkled the corners of Matt's eyes, and I knew I fell well shy of the bar.

"Maybe. You can come back from it." Matt looked

back at me, his eyes clear, guileless.

"Can I?" The bitter aftertaste of melancholy swamped me. I hunched over my beer, pressing the toe of my boot into the plush carpet.

"You can." Matt straightened.

Any other man might call me out for my lack of appreciation for my position in life. At thirty-nine, I'd been handed a brigadier general's promotion and a professional career that would take me as far as I wanted to go.

But no judgment came from Matt, who had been passed over in favor of me, many times.

I wished I could have had a dose of his chivalrous nature. Mine had eroded years ago beneath the grains of sand that coated the ghosts of my experience.

A hand landed on Matt's shoulder, a voice close to us murmuring.

I turned away to give him privacy while I indulged in my own private pity party. A waft of butterscotch brushed beneath my nose, the scent of her still haunting me. I shook my head to clear it, swiveling back to face my audience.

A stunning face surrounded by blonde curls that bobbed about sweet apple cheeks jarred me as I turned, conversation jumping in on top of a vision that created a sensory overload.

I stared into luminous, purple-ringed eyes. My mouth dropped open, and my brain jammed, though I was reasonably certain everyone could hear the mess of thoughts shouting above each other inside my head.

Matt spoke over the lot. "Cage, you remember Max?"

Chapter Three

Her honey-blonde curls bounced in a gentle dance, framing a sweetheart face. The movement accosted me with the butter and caramel scent that reminded me of a past I'd rather forget, of family.

Lost in those amazing haloed eyes, I wanted to remember what family felt like.

Matt's words registered in my distracted mind.

"Max?" I turned blindly toward his voice.

"Good to see you back, sir."

I winced, even though I should be used to it by now. Working out who used it with respect and who was a ladder climber had developed into a jaded view of the junior officers, forgetting I was once one.

The man who stood opposite me had true joy in his eyes.

"Rochusky." I envied his unbridled youth.

"Ahh, no one's called me that since you gave me my new name." The young officer bounced on the toes of his combat boots. "Sir, I'd like you to meet Violet."

The air beside me shifted, then evacuated from my lungs into a soundless void. My lips tingled once again at the memory of my reaction to her at the airport.

They stood together, the perfect couple. His hand rested with familiarity on the small of her back, her sparkling eyes, her generous lips turned up to his.

Here I was, a hardened, scarred veteran lusting after someone else's wife. The self-loathing cranked up a notch. For a single moment, I hated the animated officer. Forcing my smile to stay kind, I nodded. "Yes, we've...met."

"This is the man who got your cookies." She spoke over her shoulder, a shy smile gracing soft lips.

Violet's haloed eyes fixed on me.

I held her gaze just long enough for it to be borderline unacceptable, then let my attention wander along luscious curves I wanted to fit into my hands— preferably without clothing between us. By the time I made it back to her face, I was rock hard, and her cheeks were stained the same color as her lips.

"Glad they went to a good home." Rochusky grinned, raising his beer.

They did. Pity she didn't come with them.

"Would you like something to drink?" I asked out of courtesy, gesturing to her empty hands to give myself a reason to continue staring at the young officer's—*no wedding ring on her hand*—girlfriend.

"Oh," she started, looking up with wide eyes. "No. Thank you." She edged back a little.

I nodded, collecting my beer. The conversation stalled.

"Cage here is how I got my name." Rochusky shifted from foot to foot, a goofy look spreading over his face. He nudged Violet.

The sparkle I remembered returned to her.

"Really? You'll have to explain it to me. Half the family calls him Max now, but they won't share the joke with the rest of us." She shrugged in a good-natured fashion, rolling her eyes.

I sipped my beer, pretending my total lack of understanding of how keeping half a family out of an in-joke could be something I'd view with affection.

Matt shook his head and turned to lean back against the bar. "Here we go."

"Really? You gonna drag this up every time you see me for the next few years?" I grinned despite myself.

Damn kid's energy was contagious.

"For the next decade, maybe. You gotta retire one day, man." Matt sipped his beer, the corners of his mouth quirking.

I shook my head, laughing. "Nah, I'll die on the job. You're not getting rid of me so easily."

But as my gaze settled on Violet, I knew I could be telling myself a brigadier-general-sized lie.

"Cage decided I needed career assistance and attempted to mentor me." Rochusky grinned in reminiscence.

Violet gazed up at him in pure adoration, hanging on his words.

I wanted her hanging on *my* words.

Rochusky took another sip of his beer. A wide, gold band glinted on his finger.

My gaze narrowed to a thin pinpoint, and I began talking before I'd thought it through. "Max was the greenest cadet to arrive on base. I'd just gotten back from the desert, my first deployment over there, and got introduced to a soldier with my head full of jetlag. Too skinny to fit the uniform they'd given him at the store. Good haircut, though. Could see skin through that."

Matt snorted. "This guy"—he jerked his thumb sideways, continuing my story—"was so shattered he couldn't sit upright. Shouldn't have come back in for a few days, but you can't make Cage stay away when he doesn't want to. Rochusky came in, but the clerk fumbled his name. Cage was so out of it, he genuinely thought the kid's name was Rockatansky. Like *Mad Max*, the movie."

"Max stuck since then." Rochusky raised his beer.

I'd spent a few years mentoring the young soldier, then he'd fallen off the radar, which happened after a few postings. No wonder he hadn't come up when I had searched *Max* in the database. It was a name I'd given him but nothing official.

Except to half his family, apparently. Max patted my shoulder, placing his empty glass on the bar.

I hid my flinch as best I could at the unexpected contact, ignoring the movement in my peripherals.

"Shouldn't have had that. Gotta get back on duty soon. But hey, it's Christmas." Max shrugged, squeezing Violet's arm.

I tracked the movement with my eyes alone, but I didn't miss Matt's easy grin. We were all breaking rules around here today. Tonight. The window showed a darkened sky, the base already illuminated. Hell, I did need rest.

Rochusky straightened his shirt and sketched a salute. "Sir."

"Max." I placed my empty glass on the bar, completing the ritual.

"Are you okay to get back to your car? I can't leave with you tonight." The young soldier's face fell a little.

Violet leaned into him, chatting in soft tones, her hand on his sleeve.

I avoided their small, domesticated scene, studying an old, sepia picture of a soldier from a previous war decades ago that hung above the bar. Though he smiled, his eyes held a wealth of knowledge of things a man

119

shouldn't ever have to encounter.

But he had survived, could smile despite his experiences. I stared at the photo, wishing I could meet a man who'd come through the other side, and find out how he managed to have a life outside the military. If that was possible, after what too many of us had been put through.

"I'll—um, I'll be fine." Violet's voice brought me back.

Matt shifted beside me, his empty schooner thudding on the bar mat.

"I'll walk you back." I turned fast enough to give myself whiplash. The offer fell from my lips even as I cursed myself for a fool inside my head.

Matt stared at me, his lips twitching. With a nod, he collected his hat. "Well. Merry Christmas," he said to no one in particular.

Violet fidgeted while Max spoke in her ear.

It left me in a private hell of my own making. I waited until he finished, then drew him aside. "You remember that whole mentoring thing you mentioned earlier?"

Max stilled. "Yeah?"

I ignored the tone of hope buried beneath his words. "Be careful who you send your wife out with, especially in the evening. Fine that it's me, but still…" I let my words trail off, deliberately using the wrong term for their relationship.

I focused on the woman who'd consumed me in the few hours since I'd met her. To hell with duty. If I had someone like her waiting for me at home, that's where I'd be.

"Oh, no, she's not my wife." Max shook his head

with a smile.

"Oh?" Good to know my senses weren't that dulled by travel. I feigned a lack of interest. "Girlfriend, then."

"Not that either." Max reached in to hug me, though we'd never been that close.

I bit my tongue, using the pain to stifle my urge to shove him away—

Arms, too heavy beneath our desert cams, hung around my neck. What little exposed skin was coated in a sticky, warm fluid. The body leaning against me went slack. Pink sand slashed at my face, the hot desert wind filled with the tiny particles.

"—cousin, once removed on my mother's side." Max stepped back, eyes wary with concern aimed at me. He had that same purple ring as Violet, though it wasn't as vibrant. Hers glowed with a light all of their own.

"Cousin," I repeated dully, blinking away grits that didn't exist.

"All yours, sir. She hasn't stopped talking about you since the airport."

That brought me back. "You knew she ran into me?"

"I was on your flight, seated a bit behind you. Got held up in customs. Didn't wash my boots well enough. You were out of it, a fair bit. Even the stewardesses had trouble getting you to respond."

"I don't remember that." I ran a hand over my hair.

"Understandable, sir, after what happened." Rochusky hesitated. "Take care of her, yeah?"

He stepped back, not waiting for my answer, reaching out an arm. A head of golden curls slipped into his embrace. Max nodded to the rest of our small gathering, his stride long, with a touch of bounce, as he left the mess hall.

Indecent energy appeared to be the theme of the day.

I pressed my boots into the carpet, willing some of that energy back, but when I looked up, I didn't need it.

Violet gave me a tentative smile, her eyes sparkling. "Let's get you back to your car."

Maybe hope existed for an old grunt like me, after all.

****

Ice coated the pavement when we stepped outside the officer's mess. Violet kept up at my side, her quick steps covering half the distance of mine. She gave me directions to her car, though I already had an inkling where she'd parked it. A light tactical vehicle passed us, driving far too fast on the icy base roads.

I caught her elbow, even though she'd shown no sign of being off balance. Any reason to touch her became my new mission. Imagined warmth pulsed into my palm. The pretense of normality I couldn't afford to indulge in returned, knotted muscles tightening across my shoulders beneath my jacket.

Violet didn't pull away after the car passed, nestling into my side.

Somehow, even through the cold, her scent drifted up to me with each bouncing step, and I found myself matching her gait. I memorized the way every inch of her fit perfectly against me, casting about for small talk to fill the void.

"I ate the cookies. They were really good. Sorry." I jarred myself into speech to fill the silence, though it wasn't uncomfortable. I wasn't sorry at all, but it felt like the polite thing to say.

"Thanks." Violet sneaked a look up at me, her eyes bright. "Max thought it was funny." Even beneath the bright lights of the army base, her cheeks showed the rosy hue that stained them. She came up to my chest. Just tall enough to kiss, if I leaned down to her—

Or not.

What the hell is wrong with me? I can't have this.

I ran a hand over my head. I'd let her become an obsession, the first thing I'd latched on to back on US soil. It wasn't healthy. I glanced down to find her watching me, a small vee creasing her forehead where it dipped between soft eyebrows that weren't over manicured.

"Are you okay?" she asked, hesitant.

"Fine." I didn't smile, dropping the pretenses. "Just...tired." I let my hand fall from her elbow, welcoming the bitter chill that replaced her natural warmth.

Violet nodded, her rose-tinted lips pursing. "Chris will be the same. Max," she said with a soft smile.

I laughed. "I forgot he had another name."

"S'okay. He'll crash after his shift. He tries to stay up for a day longer to reset his clock or whatever." She flapped a hand in front of her face.

"You know a lot about him." I edged around the subject of her family with care, wary of wandering into enemy territory.

"Of course, I do. He's my cousin." She grinned as if that was all the explanation she needed. Tilting her head back, she looked up at me. Lines traced downward around her mouth at whatever she saw there. "You don't have anyone to go to, do you? That's why you're here." She gestured to the half-deserted base around us.

I blinked. "I hadn't realized I was so transparent."

"Not transparent." Her curls bobbed around her

shoulders as she shook her head. "Just…you're the opposite of him." She shrugged in a gentle apology.

Irritation bloomed in my chest. "What old, crabby, and careworn?" It came out as a harsh growl.

Violet stopped, facing me. "No." She mulled on the thought a moment.

I waited, expecting judgment to fall swift and vicious. "Well?"

"Distinguished, experienced, and…" She let the sentence die. The tip of her nose turned pink.

"And?" I prompted.

"And…a tiny bit badass. Just a little." Violet held up her fingers a smidge apart, the flush in her cheeks deepening, though she held my gaze with steady eyes.

"I don't think I've ever been called that." The irritation died back a notch. I resumed walking.

"Not to your face, anyway," she muttered at the ground as she fell into step beside me. Her boots scuffed at the thin layer of ice crackling underfoot. She brushed her hand against my fingers, sending sparks shooting up my arm.

"Probably not." The corner of my lips curled, unbidden.

A lilac car sat in the center of the parking lot beneath my office window. I held back a snort. "Yours?" I pointed at it in an obvious gesture.

Violet nodded, working her already full bottom lip between her teeth. It popped back, rose-red and swollen. She studied me with curious eyes, her head tilted.

Today was the day to be beneath the microscope. I didn't feel judgment from her, more a bright curiosity, though I was more than happy to return the favor. Her lashes were longer than I had thought, curling up in a

Marilyn-Monroe-esque doll-like fashion. That tempting bottom lip swelled in a sweet curve where she had sucked on it. I squeezed my fingers into a fist to prevent myself from touching her.

"Would you like to come to our place? For dinner. There's a family Christmas—well, it's a pre-Christmas thing. You'd be welcome." Violet stared up at me, tipping her head back enough to look into my eyes.

I resisted the urge to find out if her cheek was as soft as it looked. "I don't do families," I said, my chest too tight to allow much air inside my lungs as the dream evaporated. "Thanks." The platitude was meant to soften the blow, but it came out snappish, nonetheless. I turned away, wincing.

"Neither do I," Violet said behind me in a soft voice.

I swung back around.

She hadn't moved. Didn't move, as I paced back toward her, the crisp ground crackling underfoot.

Her chest rose a little faster, the pink in her cheeks a little deeper.

I stopped a breath away from her, inside her space. "I'm not the man you bring home for Christmas, Violet." I held her bright gaze, losing myself in it again, though the asshole factor had returned.

Just once more.

She was close enough for the warmth of her breath to whisper over my lips before the icy air whisked it away.

"I've never invited a man home for Christmas before."

Her words were soft enough that if I hadn't been watching her lips, those soft, red, pouty lips, move, I might have imagined it. But I watched them move.

She stared into my eyes, wide and open, as though she did this every day. Only a quick rise of her chest belied her outward calm.

Something in my chest tightened. "I don't do relationships, Violet." My gaze dropped to her lips, sweeping slowly back to her face to show her just what sort of relationship I *was* used to, though my heart disagreed with vehemence. Both were lies.

"Maybe I can change that," she murmured, her fingers brushing the back of my hand.

Lost in those eyes, I dipped my head, closing the space between us. Her breath warmed my lips, but she still didn't back away. Tiny puffs clouded the icy air between us. I brushed my lips over hers, a barely there touch that sent shocks burning to every nerve ending.

Her breath stuttered, the faintest sound from her throat that became a whisper between her lips.

Every inch of me tautened, demanding I push her back against the car and give in to the primal desire that had my body craving hers. I squeezed my fists tighter, leaving crescent-shaped indentations in my palms. The pain was a useful distraction.

If I didn't stop now, I'd have her upstairs in my bed. Part of me said that wasn't such a bad thing. But for the second time in one night, my mouth worked before my brain caught up. I blamed it on jet lag.

"All right."

"All right." She nodded, backing toward her car. Cold air drifted between us as she grabbed for the door handle behind her.

I huffed a short laugh, stepping forward.

Violet's eyes, already impossibly wide, flared, the purple ring around them vibrant. She stilled, her head tilted back, a rabbit frozen beneath my gaze.

I wanted to see her on edge, to set her pulse racing when she was around me. Blood roared from my head to my cock, removing the ability to think with any clarity. I swallowed hard.

"Don't I need to know where you're sending me? For Christmas," I clarified, closing the short distance in a single step. Unlocking my phone, I passed it to her.

Her fingers brushed against mine.

I jolted at the warmth of her skin as she fumbled my phone, closing my hands around hers.

Violet stared at me, frozen.

"Put the address in. Please," I added. "If you haven't changed your mind." This time, when I smiled, I managed a real one.

She tapped at my phone for a long minute, flicking through a few things.

I frowned but didn't speak until she passed it back. "Thanks."

"The address and date are in there. And I added my number in. Um, in case you get lost."

Oh, I was lost all right. Totally and utterly blown away by those eyes. The cold of the night fell away, replaced by the warm butterscotch scent of her.

You're acting like an infatuated schoolboy, not a hardened soldier in the prime of his career.

A stray curl bounced free of the mass surrounding her high, pink cheeks. I tangled it around my finger to give a light tug before tucking it back behind her ear. With the back of my hand, I grazed her cheek. Her skin was soft against my cracked and weather-worn knuckles.

Her breath drew a warm line across my palm, her body arching into my touch.

I fell into her eyes, leaning into her.

Too close—

The contact should have jarred me, but it didn't. I touched my mouth to the corner of her plump lips, inhaling her scent. Violet turned into the kiss with a sigh that should have sent me straight to hell. I drew back, fisting my free hand into the pocket of my jeans, anything to remove the temptation to pull her into me and devour her until those lips burned with my kisses.

It had been too long since I'd had a woman, longer still since I'd fallen for one, and the latter hadn't worked out so well.

Is that what I'm doing?

Inhaling her, I drew out the moment as Violet gave a soft sigh, her sweet breath gusting against my mouth. Not tasting her took every inch of my willpower. I distracted myself with another gentle tug on her curls, sweeping my lips over her cheek instead. One last, stolen moment to breathe her in.

A tiny noise slipped between her lips.

"I'll see you at Christmas." Stepping back before I broke any more of my own rules, I effectively closed down the option of taking her up to my room, if we even made it that far before I gave in to the base desire surging through me and made her mine. My body was on automatic, starved for love and affection after a self-inflicted ban.

Violet swallowed, her eyes never leaving mine. "Pre-Christmas," she rasped, tracing the path of my mouth over her skin with trembling fingers.

I wanted to wake up next to her every morning to hear that sexy, come-hither voice before I fucked her into oblivion. I wanted to take those fingers into my mouth and fuck her *now*.

Maintaining a civilized front, I nodded, waiting as she got into her car and drove back through the base gates.

I sucked icy air into my lungs. Determined to end the confusing day, I strode back to the barracks, but my mind had started to fire up. It filled with a muddled mix of long-dormant memories of the desert and a fantasy involving curves I'd never touched, purple-haloed eyes tormenting every waking moment.

The first vestiges of light brightened the cold night in a false dawn before I managed to fall asleep.

Chapter Four

I stood outside the address Violet had entered into my phone, clutching a festive gift bag containing a bottle of wine and chocolates. The wine was for the hostess; the chocolates were my backup plan in the event she didn't drink.

The tiny box in the pocket of my jeans sat awkwardly against my thigh.

Hell, did they even do gifts two days out from Christmas? Did people wait for the actual day when they ate together, or was this the last time they'd see each other this season?

I had no idea how these things worked. It was worse than going into a mission without full information, and I knew just how well *that* worked out.

I shuffled my feet onto the stoop, ostensibly to knock the snow off my boots that I wouldn't wear inside anyway. Closed doors and glowing houses filled the street behind me, frosted in a light coat of new snow.

I raised my fist, letting it hover over the stout door, its fresh green wreath wrapped in red velvet and adorned with pinecones. The tips of each flared with gold and silver, and I wondered if I didn't sense Violet's touch in them.

What am I doing here? I don't do family.

I stared at the door for a long moment, then dropped my closed fist and turned away.

The door clicked open behind me.

A light snowfall obscured my smile. Streetlamps glowed back at me as flakes drifted to cover my boots in fresh snow.

"Cage?"

I pivoted on my heel.

Violet stood in the doorway, surrounded by a halo from the light inside the house. The warmth of her smile reached me in the soft light, ushering me inside. I paused to kick snow off my boots and parked them on the rack inside the door.

Violet rose onto her toes, her lips brushing my cheek.

I inhaled the vanilla and caramel essence of her—or maybe it was something being cooked inside the house mingling in the frigid night air.

"That smells divine," I murmured into her hair, sliding an arm around her waist and pulling her into me too hard, enjoying the squeak she made far too much. "This isn't the usual thing for me," I warned, breaking the moment.

"I'm glad you came. I-I wasn't sure you would." She gasped, then giggled into my shoulder, wrapping her hands around my neck.

For a long moment, I was back in the airport, noise swirling around us while I held her in my arms.

Violet stepped back, a bright red flush creeping up her cheeks that clashed magnificently with her truly horrid ugly sweater. Reindeer or another mystical holiday creature pranced across the swell of her chest, the oversized thing falling to mid-thigh, her jeans showing curved calves beneath. Her feet were bare.

"Aren't you freezing?" I passed her the gift bag, shrugging out of my jacket. "Uh—that's for whoever. I wasn't sure whose house we're at." I hung my jacket on a hook by the door, shoving two fingers deep into my pocket in a facade of posing.

"It's my aunt's house. Max's mom. She's my mother's sister, and she's married to Max's cousin on the other side…" Violet grabbed my hand and towed me along a lit hall.

Like I was a normal person, in a normal house, with a normal family that I didn't have.

Even if Violet attempted to adopt me.

Did I want to be adopted? That gave me pause, though I strode along the hall after Violet despite my misgivings.

Warmth emanated from the floorboards, the inside of the house far warmer than I had expected. I started to sweat in my undershirt, resisting the urge to scratch. Strays usually had fleas, right?

The soles of my feet grew hot inside my socks. That wasn't normal. "Vi, is the floor heated?"

She glanced up at me, then down. "Oh. Yeah. Lose the socks. You don't need them."

I shoved my socks in my boots, then dashed to catch up with her before she rediscovered the family who populated the house.

"Vi—wait." I reached into my pocket, pressing the pad of my finger to the corner of the box at the bottom, the sharp pain grounding me. "I wanted to—"

The door at the end of the hall swung open. A woman with a baby on her hip in what looked like a red version of the ugly sweater Violet wore peered at me, then smiled.

I pasted a facsimile of a smile on my face, searching empty air for Violet with my free hand.

"I thought I heard voices. Come on in, Cage. We can serve up." She disappeared back through the door, which swung shut behind her.

"Timing," I muttered. "Were you waiting for me?" Guilt for hanging out at the door swamped me.

"No." Violet squeezed my fingers. "She's just getting organized. It's how she is."

I followed her through the doorway, still grasping at her ability to accept people for who they were and not try to improve them or fix them in some way, as she did her family and all their idiosyncrasies. The way she seemed to accept me.

I stopped in the doorway. Ugly sweaters were everywhere.

Men prowled the wood-covered island of the kitchen, bickering and poking at a baked ham while the woman from before covered it in slices of candied oranges, poking at reaching fingertips with a toothpick that had already skewered a cherry.

I began to salivate as a woman wearing Violet's exact sweater passed us with a small wave.

Violet waved back, holding a stunted conversation with the woman amidst the cacophony filling the kitchen.

"It's like everyone's Mark fucking Darcy," I muttered in her ear.

"I'm shocked you know who that is." Violet giggled into her hand and stepped into the kitchen. "Everyone, this is Cage."

A chorus of *Hey, Craig* rattled around the enclosed space.

I didn't bother to correct them, giving a small wave in response. A glass of whiskey was pressed into one

133

hand, and while I attempted to thank the bearer, I was ambushed with a very British-looking Christmas cracker in the other.

A man I didn't know in a red and white ugly sloth sweater yanked the other end and took a selfie at the same time.

I jerked my head back in reflex born of too many skirmishes. As the smoke cleared, I hoped he wouldn't study my expression later on.

"You guys, give him space." Two hands planted on my chest, propelling me backward into yet another room.

Something landed on my shoulder. I froze, my muscles bunching into tight knots. The rogue fingers patted my back for a moment, then were gone, but the panic swelling inside me remained.

Violet's gaze found mine. She grabbed my hand again, squeezing tight, her eyes tracking my face, but it wasn't pity or concern I saw there. Her eyes filled with understanding.

When my heart swelled a little, the tension in my shoulders lessened. Anything else would have drawn the irritation higher. I nodded, inhaling everything Christmas in a long breath, coming back to the hubbub of the room and the person behind me talking.

She released my hand with a small smile and backed away, disappearing into yet another room.

I was abandoned in a rabbit warren.

"—works with me at the base. This is the man who gave me my name."

I turned in time to be surrounded by a round of applause by a crowd who stood as tall as my waist. A second inspection confirmed they were children.

Several pairs of wide eyes stared at me in a mixture

of awe and adoration.

"Thanks, Max." A toddler attached to me at the knee. I shook my leg in an attempt to detach the small body, but he resisted my efforts.

"He does that." Max canted his head, gesturing to the fireplace. "Should we?"

"We should."

Leaning on the mantel, sipping our respective drinks, felt very much *normal*. Especially to a man whose memories of normalcy predated any age below double figures. I angled my legs between the toddler attached to my calf and the open flame.

Children ranging from babies in diapers to kids playing with a full-sized train set milled about the room at floor level.

"Are any of these yours?" I asked, to fill the silence.

"Uh—" Max hesitated, then pointed. "That one and—that one. I think."

I raised an eyebrow and said nothing. A cheer went up inside the kitchen. "What's that about?"

"Oh, they might have found Annie's diamond ring. My wife's. She lost it carving a diamond pattern on the baked ham earlier." He waved his hands in a *what do you expect* gesture.

I stared. "That's…fortunate."

The toddler detached from my leg, scooting across the floor with unprecedented speed. He accosted another toddler who looked blank as his cookie was liberated in a premeditated sideswipe.

I snorted. "Hell, it's worse than a war zone."

Max murmured his agreement over his drink. "How're you coming back from that?"

I could say the same to you. Wait. You didn't see any

active fire.

I didn't say it, couldn't say it, without ruining his confidence. My relaxed state vanished, returning to my on-edge patrol of the area.

A single word and I'm screwed.

Violet backed into the room, dancing with an older woman, a crown of tinsel perched on her graying head.

"The aunt, I assume."

Max scooted a sideways glance at me. "Yeah. Mom!" he called, waving the older woman over.

Too late, I recalled the relationship between them. Heat radiated from the center of my chest.

It's too hot in here. I'll ruin what she has. I need to get out.

"Missus, er—Max," I finished, drawing a blank.

Max didn't quite meet my eyes as he coughed into his hand.

"You must be Dominic. Merry Christmas. You're welcome here any time. My Max tells me you're quite the soldier. And Violet says you enjoyed her cooking." The older woman beamed up at me, dusting lint from my shoulder.

I forced a smile. "Is that what he says?" I recovered my manners. "He'll do well, Mrs. Rochusky. He's hardworking, has a good sense of humor, and takes orders well. But he also knows when to question them." I leaned forward, donning my work persona as I returned her hug. "He'll do well in the military, ma'am. You've done a fine job."

Oddly enough, in Max's case, it wasn't a lie. Everything I said about him rang true. The people surrounding me since I'd returned home were genuine, but now I needed to get away from them before the stain on my heart became a blight on theirs.

Chapter Five

Violet arrived by my side, a familiar toddler clinging to her hip.

"I know you." I tapped his nose with my fingertip. "You were attached to my leg before, mister. Now you're off hanging around all sorts of women."

Violet protested, raising a hand.

Said toddler raised his own in mimicry and toppled forward at me. The room filled with short cries as I caught him, lifting the toddler until we were nose-to-nose.

"Cage—" Max started, leaning forward with a hand half outstretched.

I ignored him. "You need to make sure you respect all the beautiful women around you, little man. You got that?" I pressed my nose to his. He blew a raspberry at me. I nodded solemnly, though my face was coated in a fine spray of his spit. "Especially this one." I aimed him at Violet. "Your aunt will cook you under the table while you're growing, little man. Make sure you appreciate that." I passed the toddler to Max while Violet beamed at me.

"I need to feed you." Her hand wound around my forearm, towing me away from the mantel.

"You're not adopting me, Violet. I'm not that man." I murmured the words just low enough for her to hear.

"And here I thought you were that stray who needed a good home," she mused, securing me a plate and began to fill it. She bumped her hip against mine in a casual but strangely intimate gesture. "Maybe you're adopting us."

The impression her generous curves made on my body sent a wave of heat rioting through me. I gripped the plate she passed me with white knuckles, glad to have something to do with my hands.

A plate full of roasted ham, nine brussels sprouts, four parsnips, two bread rolls, and a cinnamon bun later, I leaned back from the table.

Violet dozed against my shoulder, playing a game of tic-tac-toe on a napkin with an older cousin. Or niece.

I couldn't keep them all straight.

"I overate," she murmured. Tilting her head back, Violet yawned, covering her mouth with one hand, and nestled deeper into my shoulder with a groan.

I traced my fingertip over the gorgeous curves of her tummy and hips. "I get the feeling it's not possible to come here and *not* overeat."

Violet murmured her agreement. "You're better at this 'people' thing than you think. Max...might have mentioned something." She nudged me.

"Is that so? Max seems to say a little too much," I grumbled, tracing circles on her hip, staying well clear of her waistband. My hormones were as bad as a teenager's. "Or maybe I show too much. So I'm having Christmas with a woman I know nothing about. Except that you're a hell of a cook."

"Thanks." Violet stiffened against me.

"Tell me something that makes you *you*? You've got a head start on me, already. My secrets are out there," I coaxed. *Well, some of them.*

She shrugged, looking away from the table. "I'm just me. You know I cook. I have a big family."

"One of your own?" I'd been wrong on my first assessment. Violet must be in her early thirties. Well old enough to have been married and have children.

"No. I...this is my family." She gestured around us. "I don't really do the whole dating thing."

"Too much work?" I dug a little deeper, hoping.

"No," Violet said, her tone sharp. She tightened her grip on my hand. "I'm—scared." The stiffness returned to her frame, her admission slipping out.

"You don't need to be scared of me," I murmured, stroking the length of her throat with my fingertips.

Violet tilted her head back to look straight at me. "I remember what rejection feels like. Because of this." She gestured over her gorgeous, curved stomach and hips.

I cursed, knowing better than to dig when someone wasn't willing to open up. Interrogation *one-oh-one*. And I still couldn't get away from my work. Good topic of conversation, though.

"What about how you spend your time?" I grasped that thin straw and went with it.

"I'm a graphic designer. Everything from business logos and websites to car decals. The occasional bit of art." She perked up, giving me that tiny window into her protected lifestyle.

Almost as protected as my own.

A thought occurred to me. "The pinecones on the wreath. Did you paint those?"

Violet giggled. "Yes, with the nieces." She picked out three girls ranging from toddler to about eight years old. "It's, um, much neater now. We had a ball."

"I'll bet," I murmured, running my fingers over her hair, hoping she had forgiven me for prying.

She sighed, tilting her head back. The curve of her

cheek pressed into my palm, a perfect fit.

Thoughts that shouldn't be present at a family dinner rioted across my mind. I turned my attention to the almost empty table even as I slipped an arm around Violet's waist, settling her against my side.

Violet shifted, sinking deeper into me.

Though I would usually jump to help clean up, I soaked up the moment and let the world revolve around us.

****

A finger poked into my neck. I jumped, sand swirling around my helmet. A stench that shouldn't have been able to get in wafted inside my helmet. I grabbed at the body in front of me, fighting to open my eyes. A thin, high-pitched whistle filled my ears.

I knew this scene; I knew how it ended.

The body clutched against my chest was lightweight and tiny, smaller than it should have been. I took it to the ground anyway, rolling in a gentle, controlled fall while I waited for a fine spray of shrapnel to shred my back once again.

I pried my eyes open when my back remained whole, staring into the face of a toddler I'd last seen blowing a raspberry at me. He repeated the process, covering my face with a not-so-fine spray of baby saliva.

I laughed, covering my episode with a too-cute moment of normalcy as I crawled to my knees. The conversation that appeared to have halted resumed around the room.

Max caught my eye.

I offered his child back to him, a fine tremor passing from my hands to the small body wedged between them. Or at least, I thought it was his child. One of them.

Max turned the small human to face him, checking the tiny features with a nod and a slight smile.

For half a second, I didn't feel so bad. Then my two realities clashed. My stomach flip-flopped, the roasted dinner sitting heavy amidst my churning innards.

This was why I never came out in public, why I never tried to have a family of my own. It was safer to stay on base and keep working, covering a decade or more of trauma with a constant supply of inadequate Band-Aid fixes.

Max nodded over his infant's shoulder with a concerned gaze.

I breathed again until a hand curled around mine. A familiar touch in my very unfamiliar world.

"Come on," Violet murmured, leading the way into the hall.

I took one look at the pristine white walls and the red cedar floors in all their normalcy and agreed. "You're right. This isn't suitable for someone like me."

"You're being silly." Violet paused, planting her hands on her hips.

"I told you I wasn't made for this sort of thing. I warned you," I snapped, flicking one hand to indicate the hall and *all this.*

My words from the parking lot hung in the air between us. *I don't do relationships.* There was a damned fine reason for that, and it had kept both me and a lot of people safe over the years. From the fine line of frustration that dipped her brow, she remembered them, too.

"You're scared. You don't lead a *normal life* because you don't believe you can," she retorted.

"I can't." I clung to stubbornness like it was a lifebuoy.

"You can." Violet actually stomped a foot.

I laughed, and it wasn't a pretty sound. "I'm more comfortable in a war zone, giving orders I've followed too many times to count. And I won't send a soldier into the field without him knowing that I've got his back and that I'm right there with him." My chest rose and fell in tandem with hers. The self-loathing I had never voiced tumbled out to this girl who knew nothing of a soldier's life past what her glorified cousin endured. "I've spent more time sleeping on the ground, outside base limits, than I have inside them. I've lost more soldiers than you have family, Violet. And I've lost them right in front of me. I'm broken. This"—I waved at the empty hall again, the chatter and warmth an impossible distance away at the other end—"this isn't meant for someone like me."

"Because you don't deserve it." It wasn't a question. Violet stared back at me. "You're not alone, Cage. Others like you have made it work. It can work."

Yeah?" I grated, folding my arms. "Show me a man who has all this."

"I will." Violet blazed back at me, a beacon of warmth in the wasteland of my life.

"Fine." Her positivity was overwhelming and well misplaced. I shook my head. "I should go."

"No. That's not what I meant—"

"But it is what you want. I'm not—" *I'm not safe to be around.* I snapped the words off before I could finish them, leaving the thought brittle in the air between us. Admitting them would break me. "I'm not suitable for the company of a family like yours."

A beautiful family I can never have.

I paced the remaining length of the corridor without waiting for an answer, grabbing my jacket from its hook and stuffing too-hot feet into my boots.

"No. Cage, stop. Please."

I hated hearing her beg; she shouldn't ever need to demand anything from anyone. Least of all from me.

I looked at her sideways, the hall receding behind her, my vision tunneling down to pinpoint on her. "I've stopped." I swiveled, my feet already in my boots.

Violet stepped into my space, none of the tentativeness in her of the day at the officer's mess. Her warmth dominated the space, the richness of her scent curling around me. "Don't go. Please. I under—"

"Don't tell me you understand," I snarled. My dream world shattered. Shards of memory surrounded us, invisible but present in the small space.

Violet moved through the minefield of my life, unarmed. Unharmed.

"You don't need to go. We live with this. We have lived with this, and it's okay. We get it. I get it. I get you, Cage." She stepped into my arms. "And I'm not afraid of you."

They folded around her as though she'd always been there. I tugged her closer until her body lined up to mine. "Vi—"

She inhaled, her amethyst gaze fixed on mine.

Before she could spout out whatever speech she'd prepared that I didn't want to hear anyway, I kissed her.

Soft, full lips pressed against mine, her curves finding the perfect place to fit against my scarred body.

A sigh whispered between us, but I couldn't tell if it came from her or me. I slid my hands through her curls, cupping the back of her head, angling her the way I wanted.

She arched at my touch, pressing up on her toes to meet my kiss. A tiny sound halfway between a sigh and a whimper left her mouth.

Those so soft lips parted to allow me entrance, the taste of her filling my senses. A soft growl filled my chest as I pressed her back against the wall, wrapping my fist in her hair. She moaned when I tapped her feet apart, sliding my knee between her thighs.

Violet's fingers crept across my shirt, clenching the material between her fingers. Her body molded to mine, fitting into all the right places as I had known she would.

I tilted her head back, deepening the kiss with a sweep of my tongue.

"Cage," she whimpered, tugging at my shirt despite the conflict—the *need*—in her voice.

Her sweet whisper against my lips was a heady mixture of cinnamon and vanilla that swirled around us until I drowned in her scent. Every muscle tightened, my jeans painful and tight, as I sank my hands into her soft curves, groaning as my control frayed. Tracing upward, I curled my fingers into her hair, the way I'd been dying to, and tugged her head back. Deepening the kiss brought a groan from me as I hardened against her soft curves.

She gave in to the demands of my touch with ease, her long moan echoing mine. It brought her out of that brief daydream we'd lived.

A luxury.

"Cage!" she hissed in a frenzied whisper, her cheeks as red as they had been at the airport. "I want to, but—"

"Want to, but what?" I inhaled the scent of her, wrapped around me. Drunk on it.

"Cage, not…here." She sighed, leaning into me, her

145

lips beneath mine, pink and sweet. And so damn tempting.

"No, I suppose I can't." I released her from my arms, breathing long and deep.

Violet didn't.

Her chest rose and fell in the same tiny breaths as she had in the parking lot that night I walked her back to her car. The reindeer on her ugly sweater danced with the movement. I watched, mesmerized. There was nothing ugly about the stain in her cheeks, the way her body curved into jeans it shouldn't have been able to fit into.

"So beautiful." I swept a hand over my short hair. "No. I shouldn't," I agreed, again, my thoughts muddled and disjointed.

She stared at me, those soft lips parting.

Why was I agreeing with her? That body had something to do with it, but it was the feel of her in my arms, the way she smiled for others, for her family, that I knew I had to step away from.

I wanted her to be my family.

But someone so broken and stained shouldn't intrude on the peace and love of a life like hers. I'd had my interlude, my window into the life others enjoyed. Now I needed to leave.

Swallowing back the heartbreak I suspected would bombard me soon, I tugged my jacket on. Violet didn't deserve the stress she'd get from me. Not the episodes or the trauma I covered with months—*years*—in active deployment, far away from home. If I didn't break her heart now, it would happen sometime in the future. The very near future.

I wasn't someone you could love. "Merry Christmas, Violet." I yanked my jacket over my shoulders. It caught on my shirt, tearing at the scars and hardened muscle beneath.

She stared at me in silence, her luminous eyes wide.

I grabbed at the door handle. One last glance back proved it was a bad idea.

She hovered where I'd kissed her, round cheeks pinked, her honey curls bobbing over a Christmas scarf she'd managed to don at the door that matched her hideous Christmas sweater.

I left before heartbreak could eat me faster than I'd devoured her Christmas cookies.

Frigid air sucked into my lungs, squeezing until my heart hardened to its usual state, letting the bitter seeds of isolation envelop me.

Her family had so much love, were bound so tight together, and Violet thought I could be a part of that? A light snowfall dusted my cheeks, settling on my jacket. I ignored the cold seeping beneath my clothes, stealing the residual warmth of Violet's touch.

I stared at the wholesome faces through icicle-framed windows. The warmth of their family emanated onto the street, falling just shy of where I stood in the shadow outside its reach.

My broken life should never intrude on what she had, could never be allowed to ruin something so beautiful.

Pivoting on my heel, I strode away from the brightly lit house, my footsteps crunching along the snow-speckled pavement. A tingle on the back of my neck irritated me, the remnant of a wish that if I turned, I'd see Violet standing in the doorway, waiting for me to return.

I fixed my eyes on the invisible path before me and walked away without looking back.

Chapter Six

Someone had decorated my office in tinsel during my short absence. Possibly the same someone who had occupied it while I was deployed. The drawers were clean of the loose items that had filled them, though the small piece of plywood behind it sat firmly in place.

My inbox lay conspicuously free of paperwork, the desktop freshly wiped. A single piece of glittery paper fluttered to settle on one corner. I swiped it away with the back of my hand.

The tinsel was ostensibly a parting gift from the prior occupant that took all my restraint not to tear it down and wrap it around the person's neck who had decorated the office.

Removing the sheaf of papers I'd printed off the day before, from my laptop bag, I picked at the pile. I'd had full intentions to work on them last night, but life had gotten in the way, which brought on a snort. *Life*. I apparently had one.

I welcomed my own little pity party back, wallowing in my dark cloud as I signed the promotional papers. Why not? I swallowed past the rock in my throat. It wasn't like I had a better way to spend my future.

Shoving the form signed with my soul into my empty tray, I picked up the next one.

And the next.

****

A soft knock on my door broke me out of my

148

routine. I didn't look up, rereading the same paragraph and the same clause for the fifth time, though it might as well have been the fiftieth for all the sense the buzzwords made to me—contract law had never been my strength.

"Come in." I focused on the screen, but the words blurred.

An itch grew somewhere along my spine. I scratched at the back of my neck, tracing the thin lines etched there. A memory swirled at the edge of my consciousness. I banished it with a glance at my pile of work.

I need sleep.

Jetlag hadn't bothered me to this degree before; I had just arrived back on US soil, and already I struggled to play catch up. Nearly forty, and for the first time, I felt my age.

"What is it?" I laid my pen on the desk beside my paper and sighed, not bothering to hide the impatience I felt at myself and anyone else who accosted me today.

A package wrapped in clear wrapping crinkled at nose height, then lowered to the desk right in front of me. I peered into it, tracing the shape of the shortbread pieces inside. A hard lump filled my throat, though that wasn't what cut off my air.

"Merry Christmas, Cage." Her soft voice broke the strained silence in the small room.

I looked up fast enough to crick my neck.

Violet stood opposite me, her shy smile bringing light to my day that I hadn't known was lacking. She wore her usual jeans and boots, but this time, her sweater was a soft pink that framed her perfect curves.

A butterscotch aroma filled my office, though I couldn't tell if it came from her or the cookies.

"Violet." I rose, leaning on the tips of my fingers on my desk, and cleared my throat. "Merry—hell, Vi, I didn't expect to see you again."

"You didn't do anything wrong."

I jerked, pressing my fingers harder into the worn surface of the desk. "I'm not safe to be around. Not after—" I clenched my teeth together, unwilling to say it aloud.

"Merry Christmas, Cage."

I looked at her for a long moment, then back to the offering between us. "My mother used to make shortbread. Not at Christmas, and in all honesty, it had nothing on yours. But the kitchen had that buttery scent all year round."

The same scent I associate with you.

I spun on my heel to look out the window, but I just ended up staring at her little purple car again. Something fuzzy brushed my arm. I looked down at her head of honey-blonde curls beside me.

"How did you get on base?" I frowned.

"Oh." She looked up at me, a hint of guilt crossing her face. "My pass. I have one because of Max. We do a swap with the kids sometimes when Annie works."

Annie is Max's wife.

I had a vague recollection of the woman who'd lost her diamond in the ham the night before. My eyes closed. I gripped the windowsill, trying not to sway. More sleep was required.

"Right. So what are you doing here?"

Violet was silent for a long moment.

I brushed my fingers over hers. They flickered on the bag of cookies, dancing beneath my touch.

"I thought we might go Christmas shopping." She

didn't look up at me.

My world jerked, slowing around me. Voracious Christmas shoppers were on my list of never. Crowds didn't sit well with me. Hell, people didn't sit well with me.

"That's, uh, sweet. But I don't have anyone to buy for." A weak excuse, but a true one.

Violet lifted those bright eyes to meet mine. "You mean you can't deal with people jostling you, or the noise."

I stared out of the window, unable to focus on the car that I knew stood in the parking lot outside the window but couldn't see. The muscles across my shoulders tightened.

Not now. This can't happen right now.

The parking lot washed away to be replaced with a hazy pink mirage.

A hand gripped mine. Violet's fingers wound around my heavy calluses, her soft skin pressing and releasing as she tugged me away from the waking nightmare.

"I can't—I'm not suitable for—"

Not suitable for human consumption.

It made me sound like a dish, but the grain of truth in it hit home. Hard.

I wasn't suitable to be around anyone. Least of all, someone as perfect as Violet.

"You can do this."

"I can't." I gave her a knee-jerk reaction—a kid's game of yes and no—because it was all I had left.

"You can," she said, winding her fingers through mine. "I know you can because I know a man who has been through what you have. And he came back. He managed to make a life."

The feel of her anchored me.

Her bright eyes saw right through me, bolting me to the floor. To her.

Max has never seen what I've seen. You can't compare me to that.

I couldn't say it, couldn't break whatever trust or idol she'd made of her cousin. Yet again, my stained, shattered life began to encroach on hers, threatening to darken the love that lit her.

Violet smiled, reading me all too well. "And you'll meet him at Christmas." She tugged my hand, leading me to the door. "Come on, I found a little market that isn't too crowded. I've got you."

I let her lead me out of my office, grabbing my jacket from the door, my mind catching up. I would be spending Christmas with her. Hell, I hadn't even agreed to go with her, but Violet was a force of her own design.

I huffed a laugh as she led me along the rabbit warren of offices and down to her car, her hand never leaving mine. When we reached her car, Violet leaned up on her toes, brushing her lips across my cheek.

My heart pounded in my chest cavity as I tried not to respond, but by the time I'd won my silent war, she had released my hand and started the car.

Staring through the frosted glass, I let myself grasp at the glimmer of hope she offered.

The market Violet had discovered sat a few miles outside the base limits in a sleepy town that probably existed to feed base personnel when they were off duty. A broad strip of hessian cloth hung between two buildings, creating a sort of covered alleyway.

Stalls decorated with garlands, wreaths, and more

tinsel lay beneath its shadow. Handcrafts, art, and food covered the tables, treasures not yet given to their owners.

I recalled my own treasures, stuffed away inside a drawer in my office, an ache spreading across my chest.

Violet tugged me across to stalls filled with sweet aromas. Mingled with heavy perfumes and a constant chatter it created a dizzying mix. The sharp scent of fresh pine boughs hung above it all.

She entwined her fingers around mine as we walked.

I glanced down at her as she chatted, pointing out presents I had no one to give to. But instead of it being an alarming or jarring process, I sank into her world. I found myself discussing the finer points of basket weaving and how much her mother would love a beaded bracelet.

I was still caught up in my internal debate of whether she'd made the right call on a tasseled macrame potholder for her great aunt when she stopped in front of a selection of biscuits.

"You don't need these," I murmured in her ear, taking the opportunity to brush my fingers along the curve of her neck.

She shivered at the contact, turning to me with wide eyes. Then her hands went on her hips.

I knew I was in trouble.

"I don't need them?" she asked in a quiet voice that failed to disguise the edge beneath it.

My eyes traveled over her generous hips to the biscuit stand and my mind clunked into gear. "That's not what I meant." I raised both hands in a not-so-mock defense as she advanced on me. "I meant your cooking is so much better that you just don't need these. Although

I'm sure these are very nice," I added, weakly.

The woman behind the stall glared my way.

I turned back to Violet, hoping I hadn't earned a solid slap.

Violet's eyes sparkled at me above perfectly pursed lips. She let the torture go on for a long moment before she released a small snort of laughter.

"You have no idea." She linked her arm through mine, towing me along the row of stalls. "Do you?"

"None." I held her gaze as she tilted her head back, her eyes still sparkling. "Hopelessly inept on the social front, I'm afraid."

"How long has it been since you've had someone to share your life with?"

I broke her gaze, propelling us too fast down the row. "I'm surrounded by people all the time. I don't get a lot of time alone."

She stopped, planting herself in the middle of the row. People milled around her as the market grew busier.

"Cage?" she asked, uncertainty flickering in her eyes.

"I started taking deployments over ten years ago, Vi. I've been a nomad that long." I ran a hand over my fresh-shaven head with a sigh.

My first stop had been a proper shave and a haircut. Razored bristles bit into my palm. "You've been alone for that long," she corrected, then pressed a hand over her mouth.

I shrugged. "It's fine. It's the truth."

People jostled around us, the familiar knots tightening across my shoulders. I took Violet's elbow in a firm grip, tugging her with me down a side alley covered in leafy plants. A few people browsed the pop-up nursery, but the absence of the constant chatter of the main area allowed me to breathe.

Violet stepped into me, sliding her arms beneath my jacket and around my waist.

I took the comfort she offered, breathing in and counting. A cube formed behind my eyelids, and I breathed in a pattern around it, a regular rhythm that slowed my heartbeat. The knots in my back released in slow stages, but I counted every moment I didn't fall back into the desert a win.

Violet rested her head against my chest. I slid my fingers between her curls, cradling her to me. For a moment, the rest of the world fell away, and I finally found peace.

Chapter Seven

The cool of the shaded alley sent a shiver through me despite the warmth pressed against my front.

"Vi? We should move. It's freezing." I caught a curl and tugged at its springy coil.

"But you're so comfortable." Her voice muffled in my shirt, the words lost somewhere between us.

It took me a moment to work out her words. "I'm glad, honey, but still…are you going to pick a plant to go in the potholder?"

"That's not a bad idea." Violet emerged from my shirt, her face pink where the material had pressed to it.

I traced over the crease pressed into her cheek, then dropped my hand. "What would she like?" I asked, falling back into our conversation from before my mini-episode.

Shoving my hand into the pocket of my jeans, I ran my fingers over the shape of the box I hadn't given her yet that was still stashed there. A sharp corner bit into my fingers. I couldn't spend Christmas with her. Look what had happened last time I came near her family.

I stepped back, intent on putting space between us.

"Oh, no, you don't." Violet hooked my arm with her hand, tugging with determination.

"I'm not a fish, Vi. Stop. Look at me." I used a voice that had never failed on any troop.

"Not gonna work on me, badass. Lilies or maybe snowdrops. What do you think?" Violet raised an arched eyebrow that I wanted to kiss.

I huffed a breath that clouded the air between us. She was forgiving to the nth degree, and positive. Her rose-tinted view should have been too much for me to handle, but it wasn't.

And that easily, I was drawn back into her world of mundane Christmas things I'd never really done.

****

We walked back to the car with the pot of snowdrops dangling from Violet's shoulder. She set them on the backseat with care, surrounded by bags of cookies. I swore she could have made better herself, but I'd learned my lesson on that front.

"You've given me more in one day than I could have wished for in a lifetime, Vi." Tugging her around to face me, I dipped my head to brush my lips over her cheek.

She studied me with those incredible, purple-ringed eyes, diving deep into my soul.

"You're not getting out of Christmas, Dominic Cage," Violet declared, straightening as tall as her small height allowed.

She reached my shoulder. I grinned despite myself, ruffling her curls.

A tiny growl emitted from her lips.

"Hells, honey, but you're cute." I rested a hand on her hip, tracing the curves beneath her jeans with light fingertips.

"I'm cute?" That same, quiet voice as before.

This time, I expected it. "Damn right."

Violet wrapped her arms around my neck as she rose onto her toes, brushing her hands over my short hair. She pressed those soft lips against my mouth in a gentle touch and then not so gently, her frigid hands sliding beneath the collar of my jacket.

I yelped.

"Cute, my ass," she muttered, releasing me with a glare that her cheeky grin undermined.

"To be fair, it's a great ass." I grinned, rubbing at the cold spot on my neck.

Sniffing, she slid into the driver's seat.

****

Violet pulled up outside the transit accommodation, nibbling on her bottom lip as she stared at the bleak-looking building.

I dragged my gaze from her lip slipping in and out between her teeth to follow her gaze. "I know it's basic, but it's got everything I need," I hurried to reassure her. "Honestly, Vi, I don't spend any time in it, not now…" I wondered again at my own choices, pressing my lips together.

I hadn't filed the form yet, could race back to my office tonight and shred it. But I knew I wouldn't.

"You signed your promotion," she said, staring at the windshield.

"You saw that, huh?"

She nodded. "Yes. And Max mentioned you might get promoted after your last trip. Was it that bad?" Violet changed topics at speed.

"Steady on, honey. I can only follow one conversation at a time. Mere man, and all." I grinned, but it didn't reach my eyes, and I knew she saw it.

Violet's eyes flared. She slapped my arm. "Don't you do that. So it was that bad, then?" She searched my face with eyes full of questions.

I didn't want to answer any of them. My body tensed as I cupped her chin in my hands.

She rested there with a sigh. "Stop that."

"No." I kissed the corner of her mouth.

Her hands came up to cover mine. "Why?" she whispered, leaning back to look into my eyes.

"Because I don't want you to see the parts of me that will…" I drew her back to me.

"You're not going to scare me away, Cage." Her confidence floored me. Her innocence.

"You can't know that," I snapped, regretting it in an instant. I stroked her cheek with my thumb, leaning in to trail kisses along her jaw. "And…I'm too old to change."

She snorted. "Hogwash."

"It is?"

"Yup."

I nodded, dipping my head to kiss her properly. The buttery aroma from the cookies in her backseat mingled with her scent. I cupped the back of her head, pulling her up to me, kissing her deeper, slower. The sensation of her against me sent my head whirling.

Violet sighed, settling into my arms, her hands going on a little tour of their own as they trailed over my shirt, pressing against the muscle and scars I knew she could feel beneath the thin covering.

I stroked the rounded sides of her breasts, tracing beneath them. Her head tilted back when I tugged on a handful of curls, sweeping my tongue over the seam of her lips. I swallowed her sigh, drawing her closer.

She opened to me, her tongue stroking along mine, exploring.

"Come up," I murmured against her mouth, the sweet taste of her leaving me aching. Her body went rigid in my arms. "What? Vi?" I drew back just far enough to catch her gaze.

"I haven't—" Her eyes fell closed, she pressed her lips together tight, then opened her eyes looking right through me. "I haven't done anything like this. For a very long time. And you said—"

I stalled, my mouth half-open to say I was only inviting her up for a cup of tea, but that rang untrue, even in my head. Catching her hand instead, I raised it to my mouth to kiss her knuckles. Her grip on my fingers softened.

"I'll make you tea. You talk. If you want. I promise not to be too scary. Maybe a bit nosey." I gave her a quick grin, still holding her hand in mine. "Or I'll see you at Christmas."

"You promise?" She leaned forward, pressing her chin over our joined hands.

"I promise."

"Then I'll come up."

****

By the time we'd made it up the three flights of stairs, battled with the ancient door at the top, and found my room, I had begun to think this was a terrible idea. My key jammed in the lock, and the entire building was an enormous ice cube.

Violet's teeth chattered, her arms wrapped around herself.

"Give me a sec. I'll get this open and then—" The door flew back, hitting the doorstop and rebounding at me. I caught it. Just. "I'll get the heat on."

Violet ducked under my arm, edging into my room. Her keys and phone clacked against the small table set to one side of the bed. A single window drew the remnants of the day's light into the room.

I took in my accommodation with fresh eyes and

160

realized there wasn't room to swing a cat. "I'll get something off base. When I figure out what I'm doing." It hadn't occurred to me to care about which lodgings I secured, until right now.

When I've figured out if I'm staying.

Violet watched me from the other side of the room, her arms wrapped around her waist. In a different life, I might have chased her around the bed, pinned her to it, giggling, and kissed the hell out of her, ending up with us both naked and sweating despite the icy air. But I had the feeling she wouldn't appreciate that, just yet.

"Tea. I promised you tea." I flicked the kettle on, fiddling with the heating.

"You did." Violet perched on one corner of the bed, facing the TV, still chattering away.

"Here." I swore under my breath, kicking the unit, but all I accomplished was a bruised shin. Grabbing a blanket from the end of my bed, I tossed it to her. The soft cloth opened in flight, fluffing out to land square on her head. Bigger than I expected, it covered her head to toe.

"Help?" She came up, spluttering, from beneath it.

I grimaced. "Not my best toss."

"Are you going to quote movies at me all night?" Violet laughed, pulling the blanket around her shoulders, still perched on one end of the bed.

"Come here." I sighed, shaking my head.

Bundling my few, flat pillows together against the headboard, I snagged the end of her blanket, winding her toward me.

Violet's eyes flared, as they had in her car. Pink lips parted to show the tip of her tongue flicking over her teeth.

I stopped, then gave in to my baser instinct, hoisting her over my shoulder and plopping her back down on the bed where I'd collected the pillows.

"Cage!" She shrieked, wriggling as the kettle clicked off.

"Pick something." Resisting the urge to kiss her again, I tossed the remote onto her knees.

"What do you usually watch?" she asked, scrolling through the menu.

I dipped our teabags into the cups a little longer than necessary. "I don't *usually* watch anything at all," I confessed, sliding onto the bed.

She cuddled her mug, sipping the steaming tea. "That's so good. Wait. You don't watch anything at all?"

"Nope. I work, I get back, I have a cup of tea, and I crash, still thinking about what I need to do the next day. Then I get up and do it all again."

"What about weekends?" She watched me over the rim of her mug.

I fake-coughed into my fist. "What are weekends?"

"Cage." She elbowed me. "I am going to show you there is a world outside of your work. My New Year's resolution."

"Is that so?" I raised an eyebrow. "You just met me, and today you're planning my future? I'm not a puppy you can adopt from the pound."

"You're right. You're a mangy mutt who got lost and needs a little TLC. Maybe a lot."

"Gee, thanks." My control waned, and I dipped my head to kiss her.

Violet smothered a giggle, tilting her head back. The taste of her became familiar, her kisses less tentative than before as she pressed against me.

I wanted to take the cup out of her hands, flick off every light along the hall, and fall asleep with her in my arms. Hell, with Violet around, reintegration might actually be possible, for the first time in my life.

Keeping up the act of a normal facade drained energy from me. Violet appeared intent on putting that life right back, and my resolve to push her away weakened with every kiss.

I stretched an arm around her as she snuggled into my side, flicking through Netflix series I'd never heard of before.

Violet exposed me to a whole new world, as promised, picking something involving muscle-bound action men and girls in short skirts I had no interest in.

She stopped talking halfway through, leaning up to press her lips against mine, her touch tentative again. Tracing her fingertips along my jaw, she settled trembling hands against the collar of my shirt, playing with the button there.

I took the mugs from her, gathering her curls in my hand with care. Stroking along her neck, I brushed over her breast through her shirt. That earned me a soft moan. I pulled her closer against me, running my fingertips across the top of her breasts.

Violet mewled against my mouth, pressing her body against my chest. She skated her hands down the front of my shirt, resting over my stomach. Flicking at the join of material there, she slid two fingers against my skin, her touch warm.

She was all too easy to lose myself in, and I had no interest in rushing her. I sank my hands into her hair and did what I'd wanted earlier, kissing her until I was dizzy with it. Her moans and soft touches tested the limits of my control, but I had no intention of breaking my promise to her.

After a time, I broke the kiss. The movie had gone to credits long past; I fumbled to flick it off.

Violet grumbled a little as I pulled her onto my lap, her legs stretching the length of mine.

The weight of her against my body reminded me of the ache I had hidden from myself for too many years. I cradled her head against my chest, and within minutes, tiny purrs rumbled against my chest.

I drew her curls back from her face, tracing over her eyelashes. The lines of her face softened in her sleep. Yawning, I settled back as much as I could without disturbing her and flicked off the lights, glad of my small room, as it meant I didn't need to move away from her.

Real sleep found me beneath a cloud of butterscotch and honey.

****

The sun hadn't yet risen when I opened my eyes. An ache began in my back, reminding me why I hated sleeping on the hard sand. Hair that didn't belong to me splayed across my face. I scrubbed my cheeks, batting a curl away. I'd had a cat, once, but he was long gone. And dogs in the desert often were infected with rabies. By now, I'd become hardwired to avoid befriending them.

I caught a soft curl as it bounced against my cheek, winding it around my fingers, recognizing the new habit. Buttery vanilla notes filled my senses.

Grinning like an idiot, I ran my hands lightly over Violet's curves so I wouldn't wake her. We'd slept through the night together. Sans dinner, but that would be an easy fix. Violet seemed determined to alter my life, and she'd started off just fine. Change didn't come easily to me, but she had slipped into my meager existence, nestling in as though there'd always been a place reserved for her in it.

I couldn't remember the last time I'd slept with a woman—either slept, which happened with far less frequency than I liked, even on my own—or to have sex.

Stroking over her soft skin, I curved my hand around her cheek, running the pads of my fingers over her temple. She sighed in her sleep, settling deeper against my chest.

I leaned back and closed my eyes, a deep sense of satisfaction filling me.

Chapter Eight

Violet stretched on my lap, rolling to settle between my legs. Sunlight slanted across her face from the single window beside my bed. She yawned, pressing a kiss to my chest.

"Morning, beautiful," I murmured, sweeping mussed honey-blonde strands from her face. Her curls were still tangled around my fingers. I made no move to extract them.

"Morning." She smiled, her eyes all dozy.

I fell. Hard.

It's only been two days.

Well, three. But that wasn't the point.

"What is it?" Violet frowned. She swiped at her hair, succeeding only in piling it on top of her head. It tumbled back to where it had been before.

My shock gave way to a grin. "You're far too cute for my sanity."

"Mmmm. Maybe." She eyed me. "I snored, didn't I?"

"A little, yes, but—"

"I am so sorry," she groaned, burying her face in my chest.

"You're too cute." I curled my fingers beneath her chin.

"Mmhmm." She didn't look up when the bed shook. "What, Cage?"

"Sorry," I murmured. Smothering my laugh, I traced

166

a dimple in her chin with my thumb.

"You're not sorry." She let me tilt her head back, glaring at me for a second, her nose twitching. Holding my gaze with wide eyes, she tipped her chin down to lick my thumb, then nipped it.

"Damn, honey." I tightened my hand against her back, my body responding to her instantly.

An impish grin spread over her face, her eyes sparkling. The flush of her cheeks told another story as her tongue darted out again.

Wrapping my hands beneath her shoulders, I rolled us, sliding one hand down to press her hard against me. My knee slid between her jean-clad thighs, up, a little. Her gasp rewarded me, and I leaned down to kiss her.

"Cage," she murmured, wrapping her hand around the back of my neck, the pads of her fingers digging in, more than she had last night.

The hand I had tucked beneath her curves stilled, and I withdrew it to rest on her hip. Bracing my weight on my elbows, I looked down at her.

Violet nibbled on her bottom lip.

I dipped my head to tug it free with my tongue. "I'm not rushing you, honey. Now, or ever." I kissed her again when she gave me no reason to stop. "I promise."

"It's not that." Loose curls bounced around her face. She curled her hands around my shoulders, tugging to get closer.

"No?"

"I just—we just fell into each other."

Wishing I had something profound to say, I nodded, but my mind drew a blank. I gazed down at her, torn between wanting to kiss the hell out of her and gather her in my arms for the rest of the day.

It's happened too fast. There's no such thing as too fast. I love you.

I was thinking like a schoolboy. Even in my head, it all sounded stupid. I closed my mouth in the event nonsense slipped out of it. My chaotic thoughts wouldn't have made sense to either of us. I didn't believe in instalove. Hell, I didn't even believe in true love.

Just good, solid love would be enough for me, and it had been a very long time since I'd let anyone in.

Violet drew back from my kiss, running her fingers over my face as though memorizing it. Movement started outside the small transit room, drawing her attention.

"They're going to think we slept together, whoever I have to walk past. Won't they?" She stared at the closed door for a long moment, then back at me.

I pressed my lips together; she was right. Girls—and a few guys—left the accommodation throughout the year. It happened more often during the holiday season when soldiers had days of leave to cash in.

"Probably," I agreed, my mouth drying, but I had to ask. "Does that bother you?"

"No." Her eyes never left mine. She held still for a long moment, then shook her head. The admission came out as a whisper, her eyes widening. The purple of them deepened.

I claimed her mouth again, this time kissing her a little harder, a little wilder. Settling my weight against her, I sought entry between her lips, letting my control out inch by precious inch. The taste and feel of her surrounded me. She enveloped me as I ground against her, my tongue mimicking the motion of my hips.

Violet whimpered beneath me, her gorgeous, curved body moving with mine. She tucked her legs behind my knees. Tangling our limbs together, Violet arched into me, her body molding to mine with each movement.

Tiny whimpers caught in her throat.

"Are you okay?" I drew back, my gaze searching hers, but there was no distrust in them, no hesitancy. All I saw was my desire reflected back at me.

Violet nodded, tugging at the buttons of my shirt to slide her hands beneath the material, pressing her lips to my mouth. Her light touch became more exploratory as she picked at the buttons, flicking them open one by one.

I held perfectly still while she explored every ridge of muscle, every scar. The worst of it was on my back, but my stomach and chest had taken plenty of damage. I waited for the pity, the disgust that often followed from viewing my marred flesh, but it never came.

Her touch remained tentative the entire time, and when she slid her hands between us to cup me, my control frayed to the last inch.

"*Christ*, Vi," I growled, sliding my hands beneath her ass, kissing the hell out of her as a distraction for both of us. I caught her wrist, entwining my fingers through hers. "My control isn't that good."

"And here I thought it was all badass," she teased, leading my hand to the hem of her tee instead.

I traced the line of skin there. "I don't want to rush—"

"You're not." She released my hands to go on a rediscovery tour of her own.

I groaned, stroking the soft flesh of her stomach, sliding my hands beneath her top to cup her breasts.

Violet sighed, arching beneath me.

"Needy thing," I murmured, pushing the lacy cups down to free her nipples to my fingers.

She cried out when I tugged them, rolling the hard buds between forefinger and thumb.

I pressed harder against her, catching her hip in one hand.

"Cage," she moaned, her nails raking my stomach, then lower.

I caught both her hands in mine, pressing them above her head, and kissed her until she was writhing beneath me.

I kept to my promise, and Violet left my spartan accommodations still clothed, though a little mussed and more than a little flushed.

She kissed me again at her car with her hands linked behind my neck. When she pulled away, her lips were red and swollen. I held her tight against me, then released her with reluctance and a measure of determination in the event I dragged her back to my room and removed every inch of her clothing.

The last of her tentative touches disappeared.

"I have to finish up a few documents here, but I'll see you tomorrow. Okay?" I asked, suppressing a groan. "Honey, you are the perfect fit."

"You're coming to Christmas?" Doubt crept into her voice.

I held her away from me to look her full in the face. "I keep my promises. Vi?"

"I just thought you were maybe saying goodbye," she mumbled at her feet.

My chest caved. Dammit. I *knew* we'd gone too fast. She had sunk into my life as if she'd always been there and when she left, there'd be a very deep, Violet-shaped hole left in my heart.

"Is that what you want? A goodbye?" My fingers

curled beneath her chin, drawing her back to me.

"Cage—" she whispered, breaking off as she studied my face.

The ground moved beneath my feet as I realized I'd been lying to myself upstairs.

Instalove did exist.

I'd found it and lost it within a matter of days.

Work would cover the hole of loss in my chest. I had been filling holes with my career for years; I saw no reason to break that habit now. There were plenty of things I could occupy myself with for the next week before the base began to run at full capacity again.

"I said I'd love to have you at Christmas. You haven't met Mom yet. Or Nanna. Or Gramps. He'll adore you." Violet tapped my nose, a small smile curving the lips I'd spent an hour kissing, just like that schoolkid who went and fell fast and hard.

"What?"

She frowned, standing on her toes, but it didn't make that much difference. Violet puffed a cloud of icy air at me, pressing clenched fists against my chest.

My lips curled at her frustration.

"Cage. There's no goodbye. Promise." She pecked my lips, throwing my own words back at me, and fell back onto her heels.

I stilled, her initial response starting to make sense to me. "Are you still scared I'm going to reject you?" I asked, recalling the way she had stiffened when I'd started to ask her about relationships at the last dinner.

"Maybe," Violet whispered, her head tilted forward. Curls bounced around her cheeks, covering her face.

"I think we've proved I'm not into you just for sex, honey." I curled my fingers beneath her chin, and she let me draw her face up.

"You're just too good to be true." She smiled, turning her cheek into my palm.

"And you just need your eyes checked." I huffed a laugh, the ground solid beneath my feet again. I held her gaze, pressing a sweet kiss on those plump lips. "I *will* see you tonight."

Mumbling platitudes to myself more than to her, I held the door to her car open as she got in, watching as she drove away, her eyes bright, her usual mischief returning.

Clearly, the silly season was rubbing off on both of us.

****

I used the communal iron to press my shirt, which turned out to be a bad idea. A red stain, burned black at the edges, sat in the center, looking as though Rudolph had one too many and crashed all over my best cotton shirt.

Christmas appeared to be intent on ruining me this year.

I'd woken in the small room alone and cold. The heating hadn't been resurrected, though I doubted the lack of warmth had much to do with the patch of absence in my chest.

Violet sent me a few short videos of puppies tearing around wrapped in ribbons. A fifteen-second video of herself followed, her cheeks pink as she wished me a merry Christmas, though I'd see her in just a few hours.

I watched it a dozen times before I remembered to send something back. Chickening out, I wrote a quick message and found a revoltingly cute video of puppies in Santa hats to share, hoping it would be enough.

Then I spent the next hour worrying about it.

A gym session burned off my worries, my body relieved to be back into a routine I'd kept up in the desert. Work from before daybreak until ten or eleven at night, hit the gym, and get up and do it all over again.

Except for the hours spent on patrol or gate duty.

My warrant officer had argued it wasn't my job. I'd responded that if I expected soldiers under my command to do a job, then I would damn well do it, too.

He'd backed off but grumbled. None of us had gotten much sleep, though the routine kept me sane—almost—until I got home and ran into Violet.

After a few attempts at removing the stain, I gave it up as a bad job, pulling a long-sleeved black tee over my head. As I looked around my bare room, I knew things would change. Maybe I needed to hit pause on taking deployments and make a base for myself. A house filled with the cooking and love of a sweet girl to come home to at the end of each day didn't seem as distant a dream as it had forty-eight hours ago.

A new routine.

Still musing on my near future, I remembered my beanie and threw my jacket over it all. It took a few calls to find someone to drive me to the address Violet sent, this time paired with a baby reindeer video.

I added a car to my list of things to fill the void of my life and hoped we wouldn't end up adopting a Christmas-themed zoo.

Chapter Nine

The address Violet sent landed me on a street not so different from the aunt's house I'd met her at before. Streetlights came on early, but with the number of decorative lights twinkling around the town and houses, they were more decorative than anything else. Snow fluttered between where I stood and the house, its warm light reminded me of how I'd left the last event Violet had invited me to.

A resolution to not host a repeat performance tonight formed in my mind, though I had no real way of keeping to it.

Lights blazed in every window of the quiet neighborhood. An assortment of cars filled driveways, many parked along the curb. I nodded to my driver again. I hadn't caught his name, wrapped up in thoughts of Violet as we drove away from the base.

From my safe place.

My crutch to a poor excuse of an existence. I'd worked myself stupid and had all the promotions in the world to show for it, but the cost highlighted my scenario every holiday season. I'd made a point of spending them overseas.

Until someone with cute, round cheeks, a gorgeous smile, and better cooking had launched into my life in a blur of Christmas cheer. That whirlwind was Violet.

I crunched my way through the snow to stand beneath the light over her door and knocked.

Mistletoe dangled over the lintel. I tweaked the flower over my head, wondering if I would get the chance to kiss Violet beneath it. It disintegrated between my fingers for my efforts. Bruised petals fluttered to the ground as the door opened.

An older woman I'd never met peered up at me.

"Merry Christmas, ma'am. I'm Dominic. Cage," I added, in case Violet had only given one name for me. Had I got the address wrong? I slid my hand into my pocket, searching for my phone.

"Merry Christmas, Cage." The woman smiled, her face wrinkling into a display that took me back a step. A faint accent tinted her voice. "Welcome."

She stepped aside, holding the door for me.

I edged past her, not wanting to knock the little lady for six on my way to her Christmas dinner. "Nanna?" I asked, leaning down to hug her, surprising myself.

Something about the tiny woman screamed of family, a safe place, and home. She nodded, taking my jacket, and shooing me along a short hall that opened into a living area.

The same kids rolled on the floor as they had at the other house, the same crew of brothers, sisters, aunts, and uncles stuffed into their matching ugly sweaters.

I smiled, waving at their greetings, searching the room until—there.

Violet curled on the floor at the foot of an aged armchair, speaking to an elderly man seated beside the fireplace. A random toddler perched on her knee. A flush spread over her face as her thick lashes rose and her eyes found mine. The toddler slid off her lap into a pile on the floor in a mass of giggles.

A grin spread over my face. Joy fizzed in the air in

a combustible sense around her wherever she went, bringing light to the shadows of my life.

"Cage!" Her arms wrapped around my neck. Her lips pressed full against mine despite our audience.

"Merry Christmas," I murmured against her mouth, inhaling her.

Her face flushed, she tugged at her sweater. Red and white snowflakes clashed against a lurid magenta background. Violet's gaze followed mine, her cheeks flushing darker as she motioned me closer.

"It suits you." The grin was back; her good humor was infectious.

"It's my favorite sweater." Violet sucked her bottom lip between her teeth.

It took all I had not to suck it back. Curls framed her face, and I tucked one behind her ear, instead. "Shouldn't you be looking after, um—"

The toddler she'd been nursing tottered between us on his way to the kitchen.

"I want you to meet my grandfather. Gramps, this is Cage. Cage, Vince. I think you two might have just a little in common. Merry Christmas!" she called over her shoulder, hoisting another random child onto her hip who graced me with a gummy grin on their way to the kitchen.

Cloves, cinnamon, and something I couldn't quite pinpoint wafted through the door she'd exited from, her whirlwind form greeting me and leaving me in a moment.

A soft cough brought my attention back to the man seated in the armchair before the fire. Deep wrinkles covered a once angular face. A few strands of white hair complemented his olive skin.

"You're the soldier, eh?" He sized me up with an assessing eye.

"Merry Christmas." My limited phrase for today. My safety net.

I nodded, unsure if I should be saluting this man. Something about him reeked with familiarity. I leaned forward as a glass of golden liquid and ice appeared in my hand.

Violet returned to wherever she'd appeared from, leaving a flutter of honey curls in her wake.

I shook my head, grinning.

"She's become a fine lass," Vince said, tapping his fingers on the arm of his chair.

I swung back to him to find a wide grin spread across his face, and it clicked. "Your photo—it's hanging in the officer's mess at the base," I blurted.

"Still there, is it?" Vince gestured to a chair pushed against the wall.

"I thought you had to be dead to get your photo hung up in the mess." I hauled the chair back one-handed, settling next to him. The fire was hotter than I'd expected, and I ended up scooting back.

Vince chuckled. "I'm not dead yet, and a few tours to the tropics will strengthen your disposition."

"Only desert tours here, I'm afraid." I raised my glass, sipping the whiskey. It flowed down my throat, followed by a silky burn.

"Don't know much about the desert. But I do know what it's like to fight. To be bare in the open. Exposed. To have to wait."

I snorted, swirling the liquor in the tumbler. "Always waiting. Working on…"

"Nothing at all."

"Yeah."

I felt his gaze on me, but I didn't look up. I didn't want to see myself reflected in this old man's eyes.

"Not easy, coming back home. You know, they used to put us in a hospital when we came back home. To recuperate." The sarcasm in his voice was unmissable. "Told us not to speak a word and let the world think we returned home heroes."

I looked up, surprised to see the older man using air quotes. I began to count back, wondering which skirmish, which war he'd fought in.

The room emptied of children until one remained. She crawled between us, a pair of glittery fairy wings sparkling at her back.

"It's never easy coming home. If you have one." The emptiness, the meaningless career life I had hidden behind, threatened to overwhelm me.

"Every man needs a home, son. Every man needs someone to come home to, else one day he won't come home at all." Vince leaned back in his armchair, his eyes closed.

The glass turned between my hands, light flitting through it against the reflected flames of the open fire. Being caught between two worlds had never been easy. It had never been sustainable. I had to admit that. I'd never allowed myself to dream there might be another option. To wish I could have someone waiting for me, to have a home.

Fairy wings burst between my knees, a toddler appearing in a shower of glitter. Her wand tapped my nose, earning her a snort of laughter.

My heartbeat maintained its usual rhythm without startling. I scooped her up in one arm, flying her over the chair to the other side of the room.

She hit the ground running, disappearing out of the living room with a war cry.

I laughed again, surprising myself.

"Magic, they are." Vince yawned, settling his shoulders in his armchair.

"Would you like one?" I offered, holding up my glass.

He grimaced. "Blood pressure medication. Doc says I can't," Vince grumbled. "And the nightmares never go away. But I'll take a serving of the turkey the ladies are baking in there. Maybe some sprouts?" he asked, hopeful.

"Yes, sir." I stood with a grin.

"Something tells me I should be making my best salute." He stared into the fire. The fingers of his right hand flexed, but they stayed on the arm of his chair.

"It's me who should be saluting you." I shook my head, though he wasn't looking at me.

****

The kitchen buzzed with movement. People—far too many for the wide space—circled the room in a living wave. Everyone, it seemed, had their own opinion of how the roast should be cooked and what vegetables went on a plate in which order.

I leaned against the doorway, watching. The fairy toddler ran circles around my legs.

A cacophony rose as Annie withdrew the turkey from the oven, weaving between hands already grabbing for the bird. She batted them all away with a laugh that filled the room.

Festive scents overwhelmed me, my stomach growling. I realized I hadn't eaten anything since last night.

"Hungry?" Violet nudged my arm, then slipped beneath it.

"Always. I've lived on ration packs for the better part of a decade. There's a solid chance I can't deal with fare this good."

"Get in while you can," she advised, reaching across the kitchen to grab a corner of the roasted bird and a sprout leaf. "Oh, that's incredible. It never lasts long." Violet stuffed food between my lips.

I choked, half-laughing and trying to swallow at the same time. "You're right. That is amazing." I swiped at watering eyes, slipping my other arm around her.

"Told you. Sorry." She dabbed tears from the corners of my eyes.

"It's fine." I swept her apologies away. "Are we serving up? What can I do?"

Quite a lot, as it turned out. I carried dish after dish to the center of a long table—Nanna Hazel's, the woman who had greeted me at the door.

I snuck a portion of roasted bird and sprouts out to Vince, though he was snoring beside the fire when I placed the plate on a small table beside him. I finished my drink there while Vince snored away, wondering what it would be like to grow old, surrounded by a noisy family who made you abide by your doctor's orders.

I left my empty glass in the kitchen, pausing to watch the family interact.

Violet played with little miss fairy wings, tugging on the other end of a Christmas cracker until they were both red-faced with laughter. The thing popped with a familiar retort, showering them both with a rain of confetti. Crumpled circles of colored paper fell from

Violet's hair.

Dinner was a semi-silent affair. Violet sat at my side, stealing glances at me. The limited conversation involved stretched manners as the feast was devoured with no small degree of reverence.

"You people cook with amazing skill." I wiped my mouth and tucked my napkin beside my plate.

"You're coming back next year, then?" Max grinned at me from beside Annie. "For Christmas with us mad ba—people." He coughed into his hand, grinning at me over his wife's head.

I raised my hands in surrender, warding off an iced finger bun Hazel waved beneath my nose. "Actually"—I stretched an arm along the back of Violet's chair—"I thought I might have Christmas in my own home, next year. Maybe with select company." It was my turn to steal a sideways glance.

Violet fidgeted with a piece of tinsel beside her empty plate. "You're going to be here next Christmas?" She stared at her plate.

I curled my fingers beneath her chin, turning her face to mine. "I thought I might stay in the country for a bit. Seems there's a nice family who's adopted me."

She blinked. "You're staying home?"

"Yep."

"You're taking a desk job?" she asked. Her brow dipped in the middle as she processed my words.

"Yep."

"You're—"

"Yes, Violet." I grinned, collecting her hands in mine. "I thought I might get my own place and try this home thing for a bit. Will you help me sort it out?" I dropped the jokes, holding her hands clenched tight in mine.

She nodded, her eyes wide as I leaned in and kissed her in front of the entire table.

When I drew back, an iced finger bun sat in the middle of my plate.

Epilogue

I wrapped my arms around Violet's fantastically pink ugly sweater, tugging her back into me. Residual light from the house illuminated the few snowflakes dusting us with Christmas frosting. The yard was silent, except for us. She settled her back against my front with a soft sigh that was almost lost in the light snowfall neither of us seemed to mind.

"Did you mean what you said, about staying? Here?" Violet twisted in my arms to look up at me. A snowflake landed on her nose. She swatted at it, cross-eyed.

I huffed a laugh and pressed a kiss there. "Yes." I opened my mouth to say something more, but there was nothing left to say. I had a lifetime of wasted words and actions, and I didn't need to add any extra to the list.

"And you'd be happy with that? With not going back?" she asked, her tone dubious.

"I think I might." I leaned down to kiss her as snow drifted around us in tiny eddies. "Would you share that time with me?"

It had been over a decade since I'd asked a woman out, and I'd well forgotten how. I apologized for my lack of—well, anything, but she batted my excuses away.

"You need to mean it," she whispered. "It's been a long time since I trusted anyone, Cage. If you're saying you won't go back for now, then you need to mean it."

"Mean it." I mulled on her words for a moment,

breathing in the pure sparkle and joy that was all her. Slipping my hand into my pocket, I retrieved the small box that had been a constant presence for the last few days. "Merry Christmas, Vi."

She blinked at the box, then her eyes lifted to meet mine, but she made no move to take the offering. "I didn't get you anything."

I shrugged. "It's just something little."

"Okay." She threaded her fingers through mine and slipped the lid back with a soft sigh. "Cage. It's beautiful."

I tried to hide my smile and failed. "I thought it might suit you."

She slipped the fine chain from the box, the silver and rose hummingbird pendant glittering in the soft light.

I flicked the catch I'd practiced with, sliding the chain around her throat. The tiny bird settled against her skin.

"Thank you." She pressed a hand to it. Her eyes shining, Violet wound her arms around me as though she might never let me go.

I hoped she wouldn't. But there was a lot I wouldn't be able to work through on my own, without slipping back into my decade of bad habits.

Violet pressed her cheek to mine with a soft sigh, her breath warming me.

"I'm not going back, Vi. I want to stay here with you. But I'm going to need some help. The longest I've stayed anywhere was three years in the same damn tent in a desert being shot at. Can you top that?"

"Can I top it?" she echoed, tugging that plump bottom lip between her teeth. "I think we're good, Cage."

"We had a Pizza Hut."

"Oh, well, any of my ideas are squat next to that, then." She laughed, her eyes sparkling.

"Hey, I loved those pizzas," I protested.

Violet turned in my arms, tilting her head back. Her honey-blonde curls iced with snowflakes, she leaned up onto her toes to kiss me.

I caught her around her waist, reveling in her curves pressed against me.

"I'll make pizza every day for you," she promised against my lips.

I inhaled her, breathing in everything I already loved about her. "Make me stay home, Vi. Help me make a home and fill it with new memories." I nuzzled the sensitive spot between her shoulder and neck, tasting a snowflake that had made its way inside her coat.

"We'll make memories," she promised, wriggled in my arms, her giggles and mewls mixing together.

I tugged her against me and kissed her until her giggles subsided into soft sighs beneath the light snowfall that covered us in a Christmas frosting.

****

Four days, a car, and a cottage later, we had a home before the new year set in. I signed the remainder of my life away to a sales agent I didn't like, and renewed a car license I'd never used.

A car, which now sported a slim sticker on the back window—a long rectangle similar to a very colorful barcode—sat in the drive. The colors matched the medals of every campaign tour I'd done on foreign soil.

Violet had presented it to me the day I'd bought the car, having made it up herself. I'd asked her to research Vince's tours so I could display his colors beneath my own.

She had helped move my meager life into one room, declaring a need for actual furniture, so we did that, too.

"Are you going to arrange my driver, as well?" I asked. "Because I'm entitled to that, and the decorative troops get a little pissy if they don't get posted into a grumpy political position at least once in their career."

"Nope. I've sorted that, too!" Vi called from behind a box which stood well over her height.

"Wait, let me get that. What do you mean, you've sorted it?" I asked, suspicious.

"Well, I talked to Gramps. He knows a young soldier who's just transferred from Australia. The grandson of a man who saved his life, once. Thought he might be useful to you." She huffed, waddling from room to room beneath the weight of the box. "Where's this one going?"

I groaned. "There. Vi, thanks. Honestly. You've done so much, but I can't have some poor fool who just arrived in the country driving me around. We'd be two lost idiots together."

"It'll be fine! Don't stress it," she called, hauling the box back to where a library would be.

"I'm not stressing it," I fired back, my heart racing as I said the words.

"You'll be fine. He starts Monday."

"Mond—it's Sunday now," I yelled back, nodding to a pair of bulky men hefting a dining room table across the house.

I stood in the middle of my new life, empty-handed and totally useless.

But I had a life. A real one.

With a home and furniture and the things you dreamed about having when you were younger. But those years were well behind me.

I had a home and a woman to help me fill it. Insta-life to go with the instalove I had acquired by accident. And a small part of me was functional, thanks to Violet.

Violet emerged from the library, clutching a bottle of champagne. The tiny hummingbird pendant swayed at her throat.

"Happy New Year?" she asked, a question in her eyes.

I didn't reply, dropping my lips to hers and sealing a future together.

Oh, Gingersnap!

by

Sonja N. Griffing

Christmas Cookies

Dedication

To the OI Community
for their openness and bravery.
To Dan who gets me to the start
and to Wordcrafty and Dark & Storied Night
for seeing me through to the end.
And always to Grandma—my forever biggest fan.

Chapter One

Hospitals always smelled the same. Grace exhaled, expelling the acrid sanitizer and bleach smell from her lungs. With it clung the memories of endless hours staring at dimpled ceiling panels and counting holes. Empty of air, the hollowness in her chest filled with the deep-seated sense of loneliness that accompanied her with each new bone break and hospital visit.

She inhaled sharply and adjusted the neckline of her post-surgical gown. "Enough of that."

Using the bed remote, she rose to a sitting position and scanned her room. Behind the blessedly empty folding chairs her family had scattered like popcorn hung her patient whiteboard. *Grace Stewart, distal radius fracture*. Then, sandwiched between asterisks, *OSTEOGENESIS IMPERFECTA Type 1*. The brittle bone disease label she'd carried her entire life. From the way her muscles ached, she'd slept off most of her medications. If she pretended not to feel pain, Dr. Barnes might release her, giving her time to focus on her next work event.

Sneakers squeaked in the hallway, drawing her attention to the door. A male nurse steered a computer cart past, and Grace's older sister trailed after, eyes glued firmly on his backside. Grace coughed, and Harmony turned, flashing a Cheshire Cat grin. She staggered into the room, holding a shopping bag in one hand and fanning tendrils of red-gold curls from her freckled cheeks with the other.

"Oh my, Gracie! I know it's December, but I'm feeling a bit overheated. Between that nurse and the doctors here, it's like we're on the set of some medical drama called *Hotties General*." She plopped down on a nearby folding chair.

Grace flinched as phantom pains shot to her previous breaks. A twinge of jealousy flared at Harmony's carelessness. Even though Harmony also had type 1 OI, she hadn't been diagnosed until recently, when her own daughter started breaking bones. Grace couldn't imagine forgetting the way her sister often did.

"Hot doctors are a Seattle thing." Grace forced a casual shrug. "Because of popular television, we can only hire attractive medical professionals." She peered past Harmony. "Are you...um, alone?"

Harmony took a seated bow, her long curls almost sweeping the floor. "You're welcome. While you slept, I hustled Mom and our overbearing brothers to their cars with the usual post-surgery platitudes. Moira's dad picked her up, so I came back for some sister time."

The tension in Grace's spine eased. She loved her family, but they could be...smothering. And awkward. Before surgery, they'd expressed sympathy, giving advice on self-care. But when the medical talk ended, the conversation died.

"Admit it. You came to stare at that nurse's butt. Which is presumably what you were doing when your daughter released her inner artist on my wrist brace." She raised her arm, showing off a cluster of brand-new asymmetrical triangles. "Guess you can't trust a second grader with permanent markers when you're passed out on pain meds anymore."

"I blame her father." Harmony studied Moira's 'happy little trees.' "My ex promised her a bike for Christmas, and I got to be the bad guy who said, 'not yet.'"

Grace's stomach churned. Seeing her niece affected by Osteogenesis Imperfecta was one of the reasons she'd resolved never to have kids. She just didn't have it in her to be as diligent with other people if she passed on the gene or to make the important decisions her sister made for Moira every day.

"I'm sorry." Grace crisscrossed her legs and pasted on her most innocent smile. "Let's talk hot doctors, instead. It's Dr. Barnes, isn't it? How sad. You're barely thirty, and you've already given up on our generation."

"Eww." Harmony looked horrified. "He's like our uncle." She quirked a brow. "And you have *no* idea what our generation offers. Do you even notice the opposite gender anymore, or are you still married to your job?"

A vision of toned, sand-colored legs, broad shoulders, and rippling abs swam to Grace's mind. Followed by the squared chin and warm smile of a dark-haired man in a pool-drenched, brief-style swimsuit. The gym Neptune she'd been thirsting for the past few months. She shook her head to dispel the image, afraid she'd start to drool.

Harmony's lips twitched. "Don't answer that. Your red face gives you away."

"I'll tell you about my gym god if you tell me why you're all hot for Uncle Doctor."

"Gym god, huh?" Harmony pulled a hairbrush, perfume, a half-dozen lip glosses, and a tissue-wrapped bundle from her shopping bag, arranging them on the tray table. "You're gonna regret teasing me about Dr. Bones when the drugs wear off. Might as well look fabulous while you wallow in shame."

"Shame? You're the one who calls my world-class surgeon, Dr. Bones."

"He was Dr. Bones to us before you needed training bras."

Grace glanced down. At twenty-eight years old, she was scarcely *out* of training bras.

Harmony combed the tangles from Grace's hair and fluffed the ends. "Thank goodness for dry shampoo." With a satisfied grunt, she spritzed the air with rose-scented perfume. "You know Dr. Bones has been in lust with mom since forever?"

"Lust with Mom? Now who's being gross?"

"Grow up." Harmony unwrapped the tissue, revealing a pile of emerald green silk. "I brought you some pajamas."

Grace lifted her eyebrows. "These aren't the penguin flannels I requested."

"Sometimes, you need to get out of your head and embrace the unknown. These feel like a cloud, and the top has ties at the shoulders. For the cast and the IV stuck in the back of your hand." She shut the door and tugged off Grace's hospital gown, draping her in the soft silk.

Almost immediately, Grace's nipples puckered against the cold air and smooth fabric. "They didn't have anything in cotton?" She wouldn't admit it, but it felt good to be sort of normal again.

"Not in this shade of green. It makes your eyes pop."

"Does my mini-makeover have anything to do with hot doctors? If so, start with yourself. You're all talk and no action."

"What? No!" Harmony shook her head. "I picked him for you."

Grace narrowed her gaze. "Him, who?"

"The new Pediatric Orthopedic surgeon Bones is mentoring, Dr. Raphael Herrera. Or, as I think of him, Dr. Hottie. My tongue hit the floor when I met him in the lobby."

Grace opened her mouth to protest, and Harmony took advantage, slathering a sticky coral gloss across her lips. "Much better. Dr. Hottie's invariably going to be Moira's doctor, anyway. Still wouldn't mind ogling him, as a brother-in-law."

A knock drew their attention, and Dr. Barnes strode into the room. For a man in his late fifties, he had the swagger of an air force test pilot and an ageless look to match. His brown skin sported deep smile lines, and his only concessions to age were a shaved head and black plastic-framed glasses. Surprisingly, it wasn't painful to picture him with her mom.

"I heard the term, 'brother-in-law' as I walked in. Who's my favorite patient going to marry?" Dr. Barnes scanned the whiteboard before sweeping a penlight over Grace's eyes.

She blinked. "I'm cantankerous, Dr. Barnes. I doubt I'm your favorite."

He guffawed, shaking his head. "I say something one time…" He gently picked up her left arm. "If I told the hospital you were like family, they'd never let me fix you. When are you going to start calling me Charlie?"

She snorted. If only he knew Harmony already pegged him as their future stepdad. Dr. Barnes had been their father's surgeon until sudden cardiac arrest had taken him ten years earlier. After that, Dr. Barnes had become her doctor. When he'd rushed to the emergency department, promising to fix her wrist, Grace had felt cared for. She supposed her mom could do a lot worse than Dr. Charles Barnes.

He prodded her incision site, sending a jolt of electric pain up her arm. "Ow."

"Sorry." He settled her hand on the bed. "When do I learn the name of your mystery guy?"

Harmony coughed to cover her snicker, and Grace scowled. "This is how rumors start. I don't have a—"

Another firm knock rapped at the door. A tall man sauntered in, and Grace found she couldn't complete her sentence. Probably because her tongue had joined Harmony's on the floor. The new arrival was none other than the sexy swimsuit gym god himself. And he was wearing a white lab coat embroidered with the name, *Dr. Raphael Herrera.*

Chapter Two

Rafe stopped halfway across the hospital room and blinked. The woman sitting on the bed was *her*. The purple swim-capped water naiad from the gym. The one he'd wondered about. Dreamed about. And, until that moment, hadn't even imagined all that glorious red hair. Now, he didn't think he'd ever forget.

When her cheeks blazed with color, he knew she recognized him. Did her thoughts align with his? Possibly. She looked scandalized, as if he'd walked in wearing swim trunks. He held back his smile. Two could play at that game. With very little effort, he pictured her in her high-hipped, black one-piece. All lean muscle and—

"Grace." Charlie waved Rafe closer. "This is my colleague, Dr. Raphael Herrera. He's in pediatrics but sometimes rounds with me. In all likelihood, because I'm the most interesting person in his life. Rafe, this is Grace."

It stung that Charlie wasn't wrong. Rafe advanced to shake hands but stopped when her eyebrows rose. She wiggled the fingers on her hand strapped firmly with an IV bandage and a blood oxygen monitor. The other was in a splint. *Oh. Right.* He offered a tight smile. "Pleased to meet you."

His words had come out as some sort of primitive growl. When her eyes widened, an odd sense of relief and frustration warred inside him. In all the times he thought of this woman in bed, he'd never envisioned her on a hospital cot. Or as his mentor's patient. He cleared his throat.

A woman with strawberry blonde hair and a knowing smirk waved from a chair near the window. Rafe recognized her as someone Charlie had introduced as being like family. Harmony Stewart. The same last name on Grace's chart. He scrutinized the women, finding similar features, and it abruptly all made sense. With irony only the universe could devise, his mysterious, lap-swimming naiad was Charlie's VIP patient. Therefore, off-limits.

This bothered him more than it should have.

He tried to transform his desire into something more platonic, shaking off the feeling of missing out on something spectacular. "A pleasure to meet you officially, though I feel like I already know you."

When her brow furrowed, regret swamped him. What a thing to admit to a stranger. Either she'd think he'd been stalking her at the pool—which seemed mildly accurate—or she'd figure out he had more information about the Stewarts than he should. In truth, he'd known about her family since Charlie presented on Generational Osteogenesis Imperfecta at Rafe's first ortho conference.

"At least we're wearing clothes this time," Grace said.

He stopped breathing as less than platonic images flashed in his find.

Harmony gasped. "Spill it."

When Grace turned an improbable shade of red and looked ready to crawl under the covers, he forced himself into action. "From the gym. We have the same swim schedule." At least since he'd stumbled upon her and switched his workouts from early evening to pre-dawn.

"That explains it." Harmony and Charlie exchanged a look that illustrated how close his mentor was with the family, proving that hungering for Grace was ill-advised. He'd known it, but knowledge didn't prevent the sharp sting of his disappointment. As Charlie detailed Grace's surgery, care, and prognosis, Rafe stood back and tried to reconstruct the way he thought about Grace Stewart.

When he'd first seen her, he'd been blind to everything except her wide, full lips and long, athletic limbs. Eventually, he'd noticed the surgical scars that covered her body. Then, how easily she bruised. The pronounced curve of her back. How cautiously she exited the pool. He'd long suspected type 1 OI and wasn't sure how he felt now that he had proof.

In less than five minutes, Grace had morphed from a fantasy to a person. One he could no longer morally pursue. Not because he was a doctor, but because Charlie would surgically remove Rafe's testicles if he pulled his usual love-'em-and-leave-'em routine. And he wasn't looking for anything else. Ten years of intense medical training entitled him to some freedom.

"I need to go home." Grace's strident tone roused him from his musings.

She sat stiffly on the bed, resplendent in her mutinous bearing and emerald silk. She'd managed to cross one arm over her chest, and he winced. A brief check confirmed she hadn't yanked out her IV.

"You said the surgery was a success, and I have to organize a New Year's Eve party for the corporate tech execs at work. With the holidays next weekend, I'm barely going to have time."

Charlie frowned, displaying that stubborn glint Rafe had learned not to cross. "I want you to stay until we can wean you from the heaviest medications. One more day."

Grace opened her mouth, but Harmony cut her off. "I called your boss. He already hired me as a holiday temp, so I offered to take your events. He was extraordinarily agreeable when I informed him you broke your wrist at the team Christmas party."

"I slipped on ice."

"*At* the party. Say yes. Moira's at her dad's this week, and I'm going to need something to do besides worry."

Charlie gave Harmony an approving smile before turning to Grace. "At least stay until tomorrow night. Your mom invited me to Christmas dinner, and I have a dozen gifts to buy and wrap in as many days. I won't have time to patch you if you fall again."

Grace's glare softened, but she didn't drop her arm. Anyone could see Charlie and Harmony were colluding to keep her in the hospital, but Rafe couldn't figure out why. Then Charlie cast him an apprehensive glance, and Rafe understood. Those two match-making fiends were conspiring to throw him and Grace together.

Horrified understanding dawned on Grace's face. She looked to him for support, but he knew better than to say anything. If he showed any interest, Charlie would never give up. After a moment, her whole body sagged. "Fine."

Harmony perked up. "At least we'll get to see more of that hot nurse of yours."

Rafe scowled. Maybe he could have Nurse Collin transferred to another floor.

Grace yanked on a lock of her long hair, looking

both indignant and fragile. He wanted to hug her. Instead, he put his hands in his pockets and backed away. She watched his retreat before turning to her sister. "Well, I *am* going to need something to do if I'm stuck here."

"Atta girl." Harmony beamed.

His hands fisted. "You could help me."

They turned toward him, each wearing a different expression. Grace caution, Harmony expectation, and Charlie approval.

"Help you?" Grace sounded like she couldn't imagine him needing assistance with anything.

He wished. He could use support digging himself out of the hole he just jumped into. "I'm in charge of the Pediatric Holiday Cookie Bazaar on Friday. You mentioned you were an event organizer, and I'd appreciate your input."

Grace tilted her head, and he watched, fascinated, as dark red locks spilled over her shoulders. "Is this some sort of hazing ritual for the new guy?"

Charlie whooped and patted Rafe on the shoulder. "Hardly. Dr. No-Strings volunteered. He's a planner."

Rafe glared at his mentor.

"No strings? Like a puppet turned into a real boy?" Harmony asked.

"Something like that," he muttered, staring at Grace. "It's no big deal. I've lightened my schedule for this, and you wanted something to do. If you'd rather play, *I Spy Nurse Collin*, go right ahead."

When the trio blinked at him, he wondered if he'd lost his mind completely. Ten minutes earlier, he'd been a medical professional. Red hair and intelligent eyes had turned him considerably more primal.

203

Grace shrugged. "I'll help. I'm an events coordinator for the largest tech company in the world. I can handle a cookie party." She nodded toward her splinted wrist. "Even with one hand tied behind my back."

She was funny, too. A potential detractor from his two-year plan. He rubbed his hand over his face and strategized his exit.

As if on cue, Charlie's pager buzzed. "I've got to run. Rafe, show Grace the venue."

In a flash, he was gone, with Harmony, unsurprisingly, trailing after. Rafe narrowed his eyes. This was either fate or really bad luck. He was alone with the clever, beautiful woman he'd wanted for months. Tethered to her for the next four days. What could possibly go wrong?

Chapter Three

After Dr. Barnes and Harmony left, Dr. Hottie Swimsuit God Herrera stared at Grace as though he wanted to race from the room like an Olympic freestyler. Part of her wished he would. She needed a moment to process the reality where she was confined to a bed sporting post-surgery hair, and the stud muffin of her dreams was close friends with her family's favorite orthopedic surgeon.

Dr. Herrera scanned the machines next to her bed and nodded, almost resigned. "These bags are nearly empty. I'll grab a nurse to unhook you."

He turned on his heel and disappeared. Odds were fifty/fifty he'd come back. She half hoped he wouldn't. Despite Harmony's never-ending attempts at matchmaking, Grace had given up on relationships four years earlier. Not that she was thinking about Dr. Herrera in terms of 'relationship.' Her life partner would always be her nine to five.

Still, a rejection was a rejection. Something akin to disappointment wormed through her.

If he didn't come back, she'd just have to find something else to do. When the image of a certain swim-oriented doctor flashed to mind sans swimsuit, she grunted. Not *that* kind of 'do.' Irritated with herself, she swung her silk-clad legs over the bed and contemplated the wheelchair resting along the wall. The bright orange

Fall Risk stickers shone like beacons, reminding her that if falling wasn't the problem, hitting the ground was. With a sigh, she shoved off the bedrail, trying not to be horrified at the giant bruise growing under her IV.

"What do you think you're doing?" Dr. Herrera rushed into the room, voice booming, wearing the countenance of an irate avenging angel. He reached her and placed both hands on her waist, anchoring her before she'd taken a step.

Waves of heat and tingling awareness radiated from where his hands pressed against the thin fabric of her top. Comforting and electric. Her breath caught, and her gaze locked with his. His brown eyes bore into her, his body stock still. Except for his hands. Those tightened. His fingers firm yet gentle against her ribs.

"I—I was getting ready." Grace hardly recognized the breathy quality of her voice. She tried to move, but he held fast. "You disappeared."

His right eyebrow arched, and he stepped away, taking his heat with him. "I'm here now." He pushed the wheelchair in front of her. "Sit."

She straightened her shoulders, and Dr. Herrera gawked at her chest before looking away. She crossed her non-injured arm over the tiny ski jumps she called a bosom and seriously considered sororicide. "You're not my doctor."

A mocking half-smile transformed him from annoyingly hot to just annoying. "No, but I have initials a mile long after my name telling me I'm qualified to give medical advice." He chuckled. "What was your plan? To turn yourself in circles with one arm?"

She sniffed, ignoring his devastating smile. "You'd be surprised at my skill set."

"Urgh-mmm." He coughed, and she dropped her head into her hand. Why did every conversation with him sound like bedroom talk?

Thankfully, a nurse she didn't recognize chose that moment to relieve Grace of her IV and fit her with a sling. When she was gone, Dr. Herrera cleared his throat. "Ready?"

She hesitated. "I'm not dressed for a jaunt down the corridor."

"I noticed." He squeezed his eyes shut. "You're fine. Urgh. I mean, there's no dress code here." His jaw flushed pink. "Here." Rafe tossed her a blanket. "This might make you more comfortable."

"Thanks." Grace tucked herself inside. His unexpected consideration warmed her as much as the blanket. She studied him, for the first time noticing the figure-hugging black sweater under his lab coat. Worn jeans rested low on his hips, and he smelled like coffee and pine tar. Her mouth went dry.

Needing distance, she sank into the chair. "How far are you into the cookie party planning process?"

"The cookies have been assigned, including specific dietary need options. We have last year's decorations, and the room's reserved." He spread his hands and shrugged. "What have I missed, Ms. Stewart?"

"Don't call me that. I sound like someone's maiden aunt." Which never bothered her at work. From that pair of lips, though, it wasn't right.

"Aren't you someone's aunt?" He pointed to the scribbled artwork peeking out of her sling.

She tucked it under her blanket. "Call me Grace. And no offense to your planning acumen, but I'm sure I'll find something you're missing."

His warm gaze met hers. "I'm Rafe."

Rafe. It suited him. And it changed everything. The hospital fell away. The wheelchair. Their respective roles as doctor and patient. She was a scantily clad woman in proximity to a gorgeous man who couldn't seem to stop looking at her. If she wasn't sitting, her knees would've buckled because, for the first time in forever, she wanted something more than her career. And that was far scarier than broken bones.

Chapter Four

Rafe found it was easier to talk to Grace Stewart from behind. Er, when being in a rear position...Urgh! While pushing her in a wheelchair. As they'd traveled across the building, she'd undoubtedly shared great event ideas. Problem was, he'd been focused on her pillow-mussed hair, imagining what would happen if he tugged on the artfully tied bows of her pajamas.

"Rafe!" Grace's alarmed tone cut into his decidedly non-chaste thoughts. "The pillar!"

Just in time, he swerved away from the inconveniently placed post that, he reluctantly noted, most likely supported the floors above them. "Sorry. Surgeons don't usually push people down hallways."

She twisted around and lifted an eyebrow. "Isn't your job about precision?"

"Meh." He bent to rescue the corner of her blanket trailing on the floor. "More like half brute force and half precision. None of it involves navigating narrow passageways."

She scanned the hall, which was at least ten feet across. "Uh-huh."

He arranged the coverlet on her lap. "Everyone's a critic."

When she laughed, his desire gave way to something else: like. *Not good.* He couldn't like Grace Stewart. With her ties to Charlie, her red hair might as well be a stop sign. He turned into the pediatric ward faster than he should have, eliciting a yelp from Grace. When he expected a scolding, she stayed silent. A glance up, and he understood.

Walking into peds was a bit like opening a doorway into a new world. Boring neutrals gave way to the vibrant colors of a seascape. The aqua walls were dotted with bubbles, expressive cartoon sea life, painted ropes of seaweed, and bright reefs. All neatly tied together with a blue and green mosaic floor. Instantly, Rafe's tension fell away. In this wing, he knew who he was and what he wanted.

"I love it here," Grace said. "It's magic."

He continued down the corridor until they reached the aquarium-themed main waiting room. A handful of visitors, with drawn lips and tired eyes, were scattered on custom-built furniture. He wished them a good evening, knowing nothing could ever be quite right for people moored in stasis in the children's wing of a hospital.

"This is it." He dramatically spun the chair in the world's slowest 360. Grace rolled her eyes, but he caught the hint of a smile.

She slid a glance at a family sitting on a bench fashioned like coral. A dark look passed over her face, an odd sort of understanding. "I've been here before, you know." She exhaled slowly. "The last thing I associate with Christmas cookies is an Under the Sea theme."

He nodded. "On account of all the extra salt."

"And the sogginess."

They shared a moment, and a lightness filled him. One that said he wanted more of whatever this was. "Let me show you the tables and decorations."

For the next hour, they talked setup and details. He took notes on his phone and 'learned' a few things about himself. Namely, he had no clue how to run an event, his ideas were outdated, and the entire bazaar would have failed if she hadn't volunteered.

"I'm ambidextrous, by necessity," she held up her broken left wrist. "But my right arm gets tired." She fluttered her lashes like someone had dumped a container of sugar sprinkles into her eyes. She never would have made it on the stage. "I'll be more than happy to dictate what you'll write on the invites."

Ah. There was the request he'd been waiting for. "Why invites? There are flyers everywhere and emails have been sent."

"For the kids that are here. They're stranded in a hospital during the holidays. They don't get to see their houses decorated or select the tree, or whatever their family traditions are." Her eyes glittered. "Hospitals are lonely places."

He sucked in a breath. She'd learned that the hard way. According to her chart, this was her twenty-fifth break. Not extreme for someone with brittle bones but about twenty-five times more than the average person suffered.

"So, wouldn't it be nice," she continued, "to give them a handwritten invitation to let them know they are thought of? That they matter?"

Something shifted in Rafe's chest. That smidgeon of lightness became brightness. *Oh, crap. Oh, crap. Oh, crap.* Had he just fallen a little bit in love with Grace Stewart?

"That's—" He cleared his throat. "Good thinking, but the doctor handwriting joke is all too real. You'll need another helper."

She made a shooing motion. "Bah humbug. You restore mobility to people. You can darn well pen an invitation. Fortunately, I have templates. All you need to do is fill in the blanks. Sit pretty, write pretty. Easy as pie."

"Cookies," he corrected. Then, he grinned. "You think I'm pretty?"

Her face flushed. "Focus on what matters, Dr. Herrera. We've got a lot of work to do."

Ah, she didn't deny it. "Yes, ma'am. Are you sure you were never a drill sergeant?"

When she lost some animation, he could have kicked himself. Because brittle bones and the military weren't often synonymous. "Sorry."

She shrugged. "People accuse me of bossiness a lot. My therapist says it's because I need to have control over something."

He didn't know what to say. The fact that she was comfortable enough to share something so personal seemed important. The whole night seemed important. "What's next?"

Whatever it was, he was looking forward to it.

Chapter Five

Until that evening, Grace hadn't known a stroll in a wheelchair could feel like a roller coaster ride. She'd tried to maintain an emotional distance. After all, she'd been keeping men at arm's length in one form or another since first grade, when Greg Williams ended their friendship to play on the monkey bars with Heather Miller. And Greg had only been the first of many to let her down. But Rafe was different. Harder to resist. Even knowing they'd been thrown together by a pair of unlikely matchmakers, Grace found it easy to relax with him, to enjoy herself. The brief escape from her hospital bed was the biggest adventure she'd had all year.

Which, in retrospect, probably wasn't great.

With no excuse to prolong their outing, she directed Rafe to return her to her room. As he propelled her down the peds hallway, a small voice called to them from an open doorway.

"Dr. Rafe."

Rafe stopped hard, causing her to lurch forward. She automatically braced herself and swallowed a groan as a wave of pain shot through her left arm. Such a big mistake. It had clearly been too long since she'd dealt with a break. *Wait. Too long?* Like she wanted snapped bones more frequently?

"Dr. Rafe." The voice sounded marginally desperate. "Can I talk to you?"

Grace stiffened. She'd been lost in thoughts of Rafe and the party planning process. Hearing a child's voice reminded her where she was, a hospital wing teeming with tiny humans.

Rafe looked at her, as if asking permission, but his feet were already pointed toward the door. Hesitantly, she nodded.

"Hey, David. Can I bring company?" he asked.

"Yes, please!" The boy lisped each word like her nieces and nephews had when they'd lost their front teeth, and Grace found herself smiling.

Rafe wheeled her inside a room more barren than hers. No folding chairs, flowers, or teddy bears. A small child lay dwarfed by his hospital bed. A mop of dark-brown hair fell over his pale face, creating a sharp contrast in the low light. Two legs peeked from the blanket, one bare and skinny, the second wrapped in swirled red and white fiberglass that covered him from heel to knee.

The kid fairly glowed when he saw Rafe. "Thanks for the cast. It's like a candy cane!"

Rafe chuckled. "Of course. I told you I could do it."

The kid beamed, revealing the expected gap in his teeth. Grace instantly liked him. "I'm impressed." She held up her sling. "All I have is this boring splint until I'm ready for my real cast."

He grinned in her direction, and it hit her square in the chest. It was always harder when they liked her back.

"Dr. Rafe can do anything. Like a yellow and blue candy cane or even purple and pink." He eyed her, and his lips curled thoughtfully. "Maybe not pink. My foster mom, two moms ago, said pink doesn't go with red hair, even though her hair was orange. Only apples and

214

firetrucks are red. What's your name? Hers was Jennifer."

He'd impressively said that in one breath, his compact body perpetually bouncing along. Just like when she was little. Heaps of energy and nothing to do with it. "I'm Grace. And you're David?"

He nodded. "Is Dr. Rafe your doctor? He works on kids, and you look old. Like a mom."

The air whooshed out of her at the punch of his words. "Not a mom or a kid. Dr. Rafe is my…friend."

David sat upright. "Like your boyfriend? My mom, Jennifer, had a boyfriend. He smelled like pickles."

"Pickles?" Grace inhaled. "Dr. Rafe smells like Christmas. He's obviously not a boyfriend."

"Christmas?" Rafe asked, eyes twinkling.

Great. Now he knew she'd memorized his scent. "Pine soap," she mumbled.

David looked horrified at the mention of soap.

"Grace is helping me organize the Cookie Bazaar on Friday. She wants to stick Santa hats and beards on the fish drawings in the waiting room."

David's brow furrowed. "I never saw a fish with a beard in my whole life."

"Wow. All six years?" Rafe ruffled David's hair before checking his toes. "Sorry about such a big cast for your foot. Fixing your growth plate was important."

"Yeah, I know." David nodded sagely. "I got the big cast because I'm wiggly. And so I won't jump off couches anymore. Am I gonna be here for the party?"

"Yup. Since you gave us that scare during surgery, we're going to keep you until Saturday."

The enthusiasm drained from David like someone had removed a stopper, and it all came rushing out.

"Who's coming to get me?"

Grace's breath caught when Rafe looked away, bleakness contorting his features. Then, he pasted on a smile and tweaked David's nose. "I don't know, buddy, but I'll put in a good word. Let everybody know how amazing you are."

David looked far from comforted, with his trembling lower lip and fisted hands. The maternal instinct she'd been pushing down for a decade writhed and flip-flopped inside her chest. It was clear David was waiting for a new foster home. At least when she'd been a kid stuck in a hospital, she'd had a family to go home to.

A tendril of affection reached out of a crack in the wall of her heart and wrapped itself around the sad little boy.

She offered a smile. "What's your favorite cookie, David? I like snickerdoodles."

That was all it took. "Chocolate cookies with chocolate chips, chocolate frosting, and chocolate sprinkles." His whole body vibrated with excitement.

"Genius."

"Hey, what about me?" Rafe asked. "My favorite is gingersnaps."

She affected a flinch, and Rafe stiffened. "What's wrong? Are you in pain?"

"Absolutely. Try being a redhead with Osteogenesis Imperfecta, and see how much you like gingersnaps."

He shot her a rueful smile. "I see your point."

"I don't get it." David leaned precariously over the bed's safety rail."Like gingerbread people, right? I like them with icing and red-hot eyeballs. I haven't had one since I was a kid."

A bark of laughter escaped her. "That must have been a long time ago."

David nodded solemnly. "Forever."

Rafe scratched his chin. "I'm in charge of gingersnaps, which are a bit different. But I think I can manage to make a special one with frosting and cinnamon candy just for you. Deal?"

David high-fived Rafe. "Deal." He looked at her. "Are you gonna be there?"

She shook her head. It was easier to avoid large groups of children. Why torture herself with what she'd never have? "No. I have to design a different event for work. I hope you have fun."

David went still like his batteries had run out. "Okay." He pulled his sheet high on his chest. "I'm gonna sleep now. Thanks for the candy cane cast, Dr. Rafe."

"You're welcome. Sleep well, kiddo, and dream of chocolate rainbows."

David giggled and burrowed into his pillow.

Grace blinked back tears as Rafe smoothed the boy's hair and tucked him in. When he turned to her, his gentle smile flattened to a grim line as censure radiated from him. Without a word, he grabbed her chair and propelled her down the hallway. As he made his silent march to her room, her own indignation rose. She got to choose what she did with her time. She owed them nothing.

After he deposited her into bed, Rafe situated himself on the recliner, legs spread as he leaned on his knees. "Would it have killed you to say you'd come? Would it be so bad to attend *your* event to say hello to David? Are you antisocial or just anti-kid?"

Suddenly cold, she yanked her blanket over her bosom. "You don't know me," she whispered through gritted teeth, "and you clearly don't know your own mind. You're too invested in David to be reasonable. If you're so worried, maybe *you* should take him home."

Rafe reared back. "Don't be ridiculous. I care about *all* my patients."

"If that's what you need to tell yourself." She was out of line. Especially since she didn't know him, either. But he'd cut into a wound he couldn't understand. "I don't have the fortitude to hang out with kids while I work." Her voice lost its power.

Some of the anger leeched from Rafe's expression. "So, anti-kid." His disappointed tone sliced into her.

"*Not* anti-kid." She pulled the blanket tighter. "I won't have any of my own, so why invest the time?"

His brow furrowed. "Is this about having OI? Genetically, there's only a fifty percent chance. Regardless, treatments have advanced—"

"Stop."

Remarkably, his lips flattened.

"The only kids I'll ever love are in my family. I already have everybody I need in life." There, she'd laid it all out. No way would Dr. Hottie be interested now.

He folded his arms over his chest and leaned back. "My mom had me when she was fifteen. Ran away from home because she was too scared to tell her strict, traditional parents. It wasn't easy. And even though she had to do adult things, she never really grew up. One day, I realized *I* was the one supporting *her*."

Grace tilted her head, taking in his guarded posture and wondering what his point was.

"So you're wrong," he said. "I'm not looking to be

anyone's parent any time soon." He leaned forward. "I'm not looking for *any* kind of relationship that will tie me down."

She inhaled sharply. It didn't get clearer than that. After the party, they'd go back to ogling each other at the pool. No relationships. No ties. She'd focus on work, and Rafe could keep his freedom.

But then she looked him in the eye and knew something he hadn't figured out yet. He'd been lying. She knew it because she'd been lying, too.

Chapter Six

The next morning, Rafe dragged himself out of the pool and shivered as he adjusted from cold water to humid air. Breathing hard, he sucked in the chlorine fumes and scanned the Olympic-sized lap lanes, emptier now, without Grace. Which irritated him. He'd deliberately swum later to avoid the memory. Tossing on a shirt and shorts, he headed to the weight room, hoping to absorb some manly 'I don't give an eff' vibes and forget about her.

Right when his muscles were burning, and he'd finished his last rep, Charlie called.

"Grace insisted I take her off the pain meds late last night. I have to send her home."

Rafe lowered the dumbbell he'd been curling and disconnected his headset before bringing his cell to his ear. Something close to panic crept up his spine. "Why would she do that less than twenty-four hours post-op? She's got to be in a lot of pain."

Charlie's responding laugh was humorless. "She has OI, Rafe. She's known nothing but pain most of her life."

All the muscles Rafe had been working squished like jelly. He swore as a sudden urge hit him to find Grace and drape her in bubble wrap. "Just because you're used to pain doesn't make it hurt less."

When Charlie didn't respond, Rafe sighed and ran his hand through his sweaty hair. "Fine. Send her home.

I had the cookie bazaar mostly figured out, anyhow."

"Huh." Charlie sounded surprised. "She didn't have any fresh ideas?"

Rafe pictured the decorations and craft supplies he'd purchased the night before, at Grace's request, piled in the back of his SUV. He hoped they were returnable. There was no way he could make holiday magic with sequins and a glue gun. "A few, but I think we'll be okay with what we have."

"Cookies plopped on paper plates and a fifteen-year-old artificial tree?"

Disappointed frowns of kids flitted across Rafe's imagination. Tiny patients gaping at disordered heaps of baked desserts haphazardly spilling over uninspired disposable platters. "Shit."

A woman squatting with a barbell scowled in his direction while her trainer scrambled to keep her steady. Rafe turned away, catching his own reflection, wide-eyed and pale. He smoothed his tousled hair. "I can't mess this up."

"Then hurry back. Maybe you'll catch her." Rafe recognized Charlie's tone as the one he used with his more difficult patients.

"I don't need her." It was such a huge lie, Rafe wondered if lightning could strike through buildings. All he'd done since first laying eyes on Grace Stewart, was need her.

Charlie snorted. "Of course, you do."

"Don't go there," Rafe growled a warning.

"Whatever you say. The kids only care about the cookies anyway."

Put that way, Rafe had no reason to panic. So, why hadn't the pressure inside him eased?

Charlie said he was off to release Grace and hung up. Rafe had a sudden mental image of her wandering the hallways, ensnaring some other unsuspecting doctor with that flaming hair and those guarded eyes. He didn't like the thought. He'd stay away, though, even if his version of a party ended up traumatizing some kid's Christmases for life. Neither he nor Grace wanted a relationship. It *should* have been easy to keep his distance. But 'should' and 'was' rarely saw eye to eye.

"Dammit." He yanked his duffel from the bench and headed for the shower.

Half an hour later, he was standing in the attending physician's lounge at the hospital, clinging to packages stuffed with crafting materials and wondering what to do next. The Santa hat he couldn't fit in the bag kept sliding on his head and flopping over his eyes.

The door swung open, and Charlie walked in, then stilled. Amusement creased his cheeks.

"Ho, ho, ho. So, this is you managing the bazaar on your own?" He peeked in the bags. "Stocking up on velvet, feathered boas, and glitter?" He widened his eyes. "Considering a career change?"

"Hilarious."

"I try." Charlie's smile grew. "So, let me process this. You insist on doing things all by your bachelor self, yet you spend your days making crafts for a kid's party you volunteered to coordinate. You're a real playboy."

One of the bags slipped, and Rafe bobbled the packages. "Volunteering my time doesn't mean I want to settle down. I've earned my freedom."

Charlie plucked a bag from Rafe's arms, offsetting the balance. "True. Being basically on your own, you worked harder than most to get here. I respect that. But it doesn't mean you have to do the enjoying life part alone, too."

Hazel irises surrounded by a slightly blue-tinted sclera danced in Rafe's memory. Grace's wary gaze. He narrowed his eyes, not liking Charlie's knowing smirk. "I know what you're up to, and it won't work. I've planned two years of wild abandon before I tie myself down again."

Charlie roared with laughter, almost spilling some glimmery white tinsel. "I hear you. There's *no* responsibility being a surgeon or promising a lonely boy a custom Christmas cookie."

David. Rafe slid his gaze from Charlie's. Since Grace had suggested it, the idea of fostering a child had ping-ponged in his head. Enough that he'd filed paperwork that morning to become an emergency foster parent. Not for David. That didn't fit his two-year plan. But potentially somebody down the road. She'd introduced a possible future he'd never considered, and it was common sense to be prepared.

Rafe cleared his throat. "You checked on my patient?"

Charlie swiped Rafe's Santa hat and planted it on his shiny brown dome. "I'm still your mentor. Just doing my job." He glanced at his watch. "Speaking of, I'm needed at the clinic." He tossed his bag into an empty locker and strode out of the room.

"He...he took my hat."

Rafe stared at the mystery sparkly things and decided he needed Grace's help despite the potential risk. Hoping she hadn't left yet, he dumped his bag next to the other one and went to find her. He'd put himself through medical school. He could sure as hell avoid falling for a woman he'd just met.

Deciding to start at the party location, he headed to peds. On the way, he peeked in on some of his patients. As his pace increased, he told himself he was *not* specifically checking on David. Still, when he found the room empty, Rafe's heart stopped beating. But no. David's single backpack of belongings sat on the recliner. He brushed his hair from his face with unsteady fingers, cursing Grace for making him care so much.

As he was leaving, a nurse strode through the double doors from the waiting room, the sound of stilted laughter following her. He stopped, and the cafeteria worker pushing a lunch cart down the hall slammed into him.

"Sorry." Rafe felt all at once weightless. That laugh was Grace's.

Which meant she'd stayed.

He hurried to the waiting room, catching another laugh. A measured bark cut off almost as quickly as it started. Except this time, it lasted a fraction of a second longer, as if testing the bounds of her constraint. She perched on a clam-shaped sofa next to David's wheelchair, surrounded by piles of white paper and a blizzard's worth of scraps.

A strange sensation washed over him. Something achy. Twelve hours before, David and Grace were a patient and a stranger. Now, they were…more.

David listed so far toward Grace it was a wonder his wheelchair didn't topple. She leaned close, too, wearing a soft smile, affection oozing from every pore. A tight laugh escaped him. So much for her claim not to have room in her heart for kids. He didn't like being misled. Even though he'd decided not to pursue her, it mattered.

A lot. He also wondered if Grace realized the truth.

David grabbed a pair of scissors, and Grace repositioned his hands, twisting the paper to the best angles for snowflake cutting. The kid stared at Grace like she invented candy canes, and Rafe could see why. She was kind and beautiful. Jet-black jeans hugged her thighs, and her green blouse perfectly displayed her creamy skin and the proud tilt of her chin. Her sleeves split at the elbow, and every time she moved, the flowy fabric brushed paper off the table.

He strode forward and scooped a handful of scraps from the floor before dumping them into a small recycle bin.

"Dr. Rafe!" David's shout echoed off the glass-paned walls. "We're making snowflakes. For the cookie party." He all but bounced from his wheelchair as Grace discreetly pried the scissors from his hand. "They're not real snow. They're paper! I thought paper was only for school. Look what I made!"

He held up something that resembled Julius Caesar after a fateful mid-March meeting. "I drew candy canes to match my cast."

Ah. That explained the blood-red holes. Rafe settled next to Grace, focusing on David but feeling Grace's heat like an electric blanket with a frayed wire. "I wish I could make a snowflake like that."

David whooped. "You can. We have three scissors." Except, because of his two missing teeth, it sounded more like 'thithers.'

Grace smiled but tensed. Her easy demeanor gone. Rafe didn't like it. He wanted her to look at him with the same raw fondness she'd gifted David. Rafe swallowed. So much for distance. When exactly had he gone from wanting her body to craving her affection?

"Count me in," he said, and made a show of cracking his neck and rotating his shoulders. He winked at David and held out a hand to Grace, palm up. "Scissors," he demanded in his best surgeon voice. Genuine amusement lit her eyes. She promptly handed him a pair, blue handle facing out.

"Paper."

Grace complied, and David giggled.

Rafe held both items in the air. "Excellent work, Nurse Grace. Now…all I need is for you to tell me what to do."

She joined David's laughter, and if Rafe wasn't mistaken, her mirth lasted twice as long as it had before.

Chapter Seven

For the first time, Grace didn't want to race out of the hospital, leaving a cloud of antiseptic fumes and backless gowns in her wake. Cutting paper snowflakes with Rafe and David, specifically with only one working hand, wasn't precisely relaxing, but it didn't make her want to scale the walls either. She was having fun with her unexpected 'staff.'

No matter the task, Rafe jumped in, all laughter, competence, and warmth. David's enthusiasm and energy were boundless. His infectious personality cheered even the patient visitors, who staggered around with pinched lips and slumped posture. When his nurse took him to physical therapy, Grace wiped invisible sweat off her brow.

"Phew! I can't imagine having that much energy. I'm gonna go home and sleep for a week."

"You'd better not." Rafe shook a finger at her. "I need you."

I need you. Her only path forward with Rafe was friendship, but that didn't stop the shudder of pure desire that danced down her spine. She eased her collar from her neck and began hole punching snowflakes. "You've chosen the right career. You're a natural with kids. You even managed to keep David focused for almost three minutes when it started to flurry."

They turned toward the windows that overlooked

the Puget Sound. Fat, white flakes fluttered in the sky like dancing fairies. Having brittle bones meant snow was dangerous, but snowfall in Seattle was so rare, the rebel part of Grace loved it. She'd always seen more magic than hazard, which is, feasibly, why she'd wrecked her wrist.

Rafe shrugged as he straightened the room. "You're no slouch with kids, either."

This was getting too close to the conversation of the night before. Too intimate. After her heart had been shattered, along with a large percentage of her bones four years earlier, she wasn't interested. If only she could overcome this magnetic pull he had.

"Thanks," she said. "Being an aunt of five, I've established that kids are awesome as long as I can throw them back in the water when I'm done."

He laughed, and she went back to struggling with the hole punch. When she finished, she shook out her right hand and discovered Rafe pushing an old-fashioned carpet sweeper across the floor. "They pay people to do that, you know."

The look on his face could only be described as horrified. "Are you one of those people who expects others to clean up after them?"

She teetered between amused and annoyed. "No. Are you one of those people who has a dust-free apartment and irons their underwear?"

He smirked. "You want to discuss my underwear now?"

Danger. She marched over and snatched the cleaner from his hands. "Are you avoiding the question?"

"Yes."

Amusement won. "Fine. Keep your secrets. I'll have

you know, my house is tidy, and I don't expect others to wait on me. It threw me that a surgeon would clean, but I'm over it."

"Sorry. Touchy subject." He took back the sweeper and dumped the contents. "My mom worked as a maid for ten years. I always try to leave things as good as, or better than, I found them."

Interesting. Before she could comment, a familiar song from the 1970s floated into the air. Her mom's ringtone. She held up a finger and turned her back to Rafe.

"It's snowing," her mom said in lieu of a greeting. "James said he can pick you up when he gets the kids from school. Or I bet Michael could leave work. He has an SUV—"

"Mom, I can get home without my older brothers." She breathed deeply, striving for patience. "God invented rideshare apps for a reason."

Her mom exhaled a long-suffering sigh. "I just don't want you in another accident. Go now, so I won't worry. And text when you're home. Maybe James will come shovel your sidewalk."

Grace contemplated her sling. That idea wasn't so bad. "I'll be fine. I'll text later. Love you."

"I love you, too."

She hung up and stared out the window. All of a sudden, the swirling flakes seemed threatening. Every minute, more of it stuck to the wet Seattle streets. More ice. More pain. She turned to Rafe. "I need to leave before Snowmageddon hits." She presented her wrist. "The last thing I want is to break this again."

He crossed to her and caught her injured arm. "When bones break, they grow back stronger."

One of his fingers brushed her elbow. She shivered. "Excellent. With all the rods in my body and with enough bisphosphonate meds, I should have a skeleton of titanium in no time."

His smile was slow and rueful. "Do you really have to go?"

She decided his emotions weren't hard to read. First, his desire for her, then, his affection for David, and now, his disappointment. A foolish part of her hoped it was because he'd miss her company.

He sighed. "We only have a few days until the bazaar."

Of course, the cookies. It was the response she told herself she wanted. She disengaged her arm from his grasp and stored the paper snowflakes in her tote. "I'll print the invites tonight. If you purchased my requests, I'll work on the Santa hats and the coral Christmas tree."

Another slight hesitation. She could almost see the gears in his head spinning.

"You're right," he said. "We should both leave before the roads freeze over. I'm not strictly used to driving in snow after a lifetime in southern California."

"Ooh, Dr. Perfect has a flaw." Grace's cheeks turned on their insta-flame. Had she really just blurted that?

He took a few steps closer. "You think I'm perfect?"

She swallowed and offered a small chuckle. "Just like me. I can see us being great friends."

"I agree."

About her being perfect, or the friendship part?

His lips quirked into a sexy half-smile, as if he'd guessed her thoughts. "In the spirit of friendship, can I give you a lift home?"

She hesitated. This 'friends' thing seemed feasible

in a hospital, less so in the cozy confines of a car.

He pointed toward the exit. "I've got my purchases down the hall. Pick what you need, and I'll deliver you and your supplies home. It's the least I can do."

Grace stood and shouldered her tote. They were both adults. A little ride wouldn't hurt. She extended her right hand. "Deal."

He wrapped his fingers around hers, and the contact tickled her skin, sending goosebumps to her shoulder. Her gaze snapped to his, and she knew he felt it, too.

"Thanks," she said.

"Anything for a friend."

Anything? she wondered, realizing he had yet to let her go.

Chapter Eight

The snow fell fast and thick, forcing Rafe's attention on the road instead of the woman white-knuckling the armrest of his passenger seat. Grace's drawn face roughly resembled the pale flakes. He took his hand off the wheel and briefly squeezed her biceps.

"I'll get you home in one piece."

She glanced at her arm, as if his fingers still rested there, then shot him a tight smile. "It's not you." She sighed, focusing out her window. "I was in a car accident four years ago. I sometimes succumb to nervousness."

Thinking of the surgery scars he'd seen at the pool, his gut tightened. Even a fender bender could be catastrophic for someone with OI. "I'm sorry. That must have been…terrifying."

"I'd rather not talk about it."

"I'll be extra careful," he promised.

She nodded but didn't release her death grip on the upholstery.

As he navigated Grace's neighborhood, the last of the ambient sunlight faded into darkness. Around them, headlights and Christmas lights popped on, bathing the snow with a kaleidoscope of color. It was magical, yet Rafe's knuckles ached from clenching the steering wheel. He hit ice several times. On each slide, Grace squeezed her eyes shut and didn't breathe. When he finally pulled into the driveway of a mid-20th century rancher, she exhaled and pried her fingers from her seat.

"Thank you." She reached for the door handle.

He dropped his palm to her thigh to hold her in place, and she stilled. Awareness arced between them and he snatched his hand away before he did something stupid, like let his fingers dip toward the vee of her legs. "It's treacherous out there. Charlie would maim me if I let you fall walking to the front door."

She rolled her eyes and unbuckled her seatbelt. "Dr. Barnes isn't here." She inspected Rafe's feet. "At least I'm wearing running shoes. If my driveway wasn't flat, you'd glide into the street."

He frowned at his loafers. "We'll help each other."

Grace grunted but didn't try to leave. Taking that as permission, he exited the SUV and the frigid air blasted into him. A fat, wet flake landed between his hairline and the collar of his coat, and he shivered as the cold sank into his marrow. He scuttled around the front and opened Grace's door, extending his hand. Jaw tightened in obvious annoyance, she reached her elbow to him, which contorted her body, and made the whole exiting process awkward. Especially since she'd gone almost as limp as a toddler throwing a temper tantrum.

A mischievous smile hovered at her lips. "What? Am I hard to manage?"

He heaved her upright. "Who would ever dream of managing you?"

"Exactly."

She grinned, and a nearby streetlamp added sparkles to her eyes and revealed the faintest smattering of freckles on her nose. A gust of wind pressed him forward, and he wanted to sink into her warmth. She was…magnetic. As he stared, her smile flattened, and her eyes opened wider. Her fingers, where they clung to his shoulder, curled into his coat. Her casted arm rested heavily against his chest, magnifying the rapid beat of his heart. For a moment, the world was silent. Empty streets and whisper-soft snow. The two of them breathing, gazes locked.

"Grace." His voice was low, her name trapped in the cloud of his exhale. The faint scent of roses floated around them. How had he ever thought he could avoid this woman?

She tilted her face up. "Rafe. This isn't—"

A clump of snowflakes landed on her eye, then tumbled into her open mouth. Her words morphed into frantic spluttering, coupled with rapid blinks.

He wiped the snow away. The moment was gone, but the feelings it inspired lingered, as if frozen in the winter air. His inhale came in stutters as he tucked her arm into the crook of his elbow. "Let's get you indoors. I'll come back for the packages."

She directed his steps, and they made it to her porch with minimal sliding. While she let herself into the house and texted her mom, he gathered the bags. Without Grace's guidance, he almost landed flat on his ass. Twice. It was also possible he'd sacrificed a Santa ornament to her rhododendron.

He stepped through the open door and found Grace in the middle of her foyer, pointing to a small table. "Over there, please."

After setting down the packages, he blew on his fingers, leaning forward for warmth. Her entire house glowed with Christmas. Twinkle lights, garland, and red and green tchotchkes filled every nook. He chuckled. This was not a woman who lived only for her work. This was a woman who needed Mr. Right, not Mr. Right Now. He'd had no business enjoying that perfect snow-filled moment.

He backed outside as she inventoried the supplies. "I should head home before I need a sleigh." Indicating the bag, he added, "Don't stay up too late. I'll need you bright-eyed and bushy-tailed for party prep tomorrow."

"No promises." Grace grinned, and he couldn't help but do the same. He doubted even Mr. Right would be able to manage her. "Thank you. For driving so carefully. It would have sucked to have to shun you."

He knew she expected a smile, but the sad tilt to her lips stopped him. "Is that what happened to the guy who drove during your accident?"

She stepped onto the porch. "Not quite. Why do you think it was a guy?"

"Just a feeling."

"Let's just say I have a justifiable reason to avoid romantic entanglements."

Another warning. A sound one. Though he wasn't interested in a family now, he wanted one someday, and Grace had been clear she did not. Knowing that made him incredibly sad.

She looked past his shoulder and frowned. He turned to see why and understood at once. Snow clumps the size of small mammals buried everything, including the footprints they'd left on her walkway.

"You should stay."

He forgot to breathe.

"For safety. And to help with decorations," she added. "I don't want to be up all night."

He choked on his exhale, coughing swirling clouds into the cold. *Up all night*. He unzipped his coat, cooling his suddenly hot skin. Her gaze followed the path of his zipper, lingering at his waist and lower. When she bit her lip, he groaned.

"I...I can't stay here, Grace. I can't." He pointed back and forth between them. "Our chemistry is...explosive. Having you so close...it wouldn't be a good idea."

A faint click punctuated his sentence, and he was nearly blinded. Bright, white twinkle lights glowed from Grace's front door, windows, and porch pillars. It was like standing in a snowy fairyland.

Grace laughed, squinting at the brightness. "Either it's five o'clock and my timer works as programmed, or two thousand Christmas lights think you staying is an excellent idea."

His heart skipped a beat. "You know there's no future for us. We don't want the same things."

She shot him a searing glare. A little anger and a whole lot of desire. "I'm not talking about a future, Rafe. I'm talking about tonight."

Oh man, oh man, oh man. "Charlie said—"

She slashed her hand through the air. "Dr. Barnes is not invited to my bedroom. You are."

She had his attention now. Every part of him. "Who am I to argue with a snowstorm and two thousand Christmas lights?"

Still, he hesitated as she beckoned him inside. That moment outside his car affected him more than mere friendship. More than a sexual itch. He'd felt—

"Now or never, Herrera."

Never was no longer an option. Shaking off his concerns, he leapt out of the cold and into the heat. Ten seconds later, his coat and shoes were on the floor. Five

236

seconds after that, Grace was in his arms. When their lips touched, the residual chill from the winter air against her skin came as a shock. Or maybe it was the perfect softness of her mouth. He melted into her, and she moaned. Seeking more, he slipped his tongue against hers. That was where the heat was. Inside her. Where he needed to be. Several minutes later, that's exactly where he went.

Chapter Nine

Grace awoke to an ache in her left wrist and the tickle of warm breath fanning the back of her neck. Then other sensations intruded. The weight of a muscled arm wrapped around her waist. The press of hard thighs against her own. The kiss of flesh on flesh. A rather nice way to wake up on a cold winter day, if not for the rising tide of panic in her gut.

She'd had sex with Raphael Herrera. Lots and lots of mind-blowing sex. All night, because neither of them ever seemed to get enough. Even now, she wanted him. The pressure of his lips on hers. His fingers marking a trail on her skin. Slipping inside—

"Urgh!" Grace tried to bolt upright, but Rafe's arm tightened around her.

"What're you yelling about?" he murmured against the nape of her neck.

She shivered. "We slept together."

He chuckled, and goosebumps raced down her back. "It wasn't sleeping, and it's too late to take it back." His lips pressed against her earlobe. "Not that I'd take it back for anything less than ending hunger or establishing world peace."

Grace relaxed against him. "You set a high bar. I'm flattered."

"With good reason."

Kisses trailed along her shoulder, soft and hot.

238

They'd be engaging in round four of the horizontal mambo if she didn't stop him. This time when she pulled away, oh, so slowly, he allowed her escape. She sat up, clutching the duvet to her chest with her splinted arm. His heavy-lidded eyes flickered with amusement.

"I'm serious, Rafe. We said no relationships, and five minutes later, it was like we'd entered an orgasm contest."

He rolled to his back. The edge of the sheet clung to his hips, revealing far too much temptation. She slipped out of bed and slid into a button-up flannel nightshirt.

Rafe propped himself against her pillows. "It was just sex, Grace."

She snorted, finding the buttons difficult to close with one functioning hand. "I don't know what kind of sex you normally have, but there was nothing 'just' about that."

His responding smile was open, sensual. "No, it was phenomenal. All I'm saying is, we know what we want." He frowned. "Or rather, don't want. So why can't we just…enjoy each other for a while?"

Grace gave up on her buttons and tugged her fingers through her hair to tame it. "Enjoy each other?"

He winked, and some of her panic subsided. It wasn't as if she'd been celibate since Peter walked out four years ago. She'd had flings and ended them neatly. What Rafe suggested was possible, though she suspected it would be difficult. Even the memory of him made her want to come. She'd also never enjoyed another person's company quite as much.

She padded across the room toward her slippers. "I don't know, Rafe. It doesn't seem like a sensible idea."

He swung his legs over her bed, and she had a hard

time looking away from his tanned toes on her cream-colored carpet. She took her time, inspecting his toned calves and smooth swimmer's chest. Did he shave, or was that natural? When she reached his face, one side of his mouth tipped in amusement.

"If you keep looking at me that way, whether or not this is wise will be entirely irrelevant."

The low rumble of his voice made her shiver. "You're proving my point. All I can think about is next time." She rolled her eyes. "And the time after that."

Rafe flashed a quick grin before rubbing his hand across the stubble of his morning beard. "We both know our own minds." A curious light brightened his eyes. "That is unless you're now thinking longer term?"

His blank face gave away nothing, and maybe she only imagined the tiny edge of hope in his tone. Or she was projecting secret thoughts she'd yet to consider.

"You're right. I'd have to be stupid to turn you away from my bed."

The gleam in his eyes faded, even as he smiled. "Excellent, because I really like being in it." He reached forward and buttoned up the front of her pajamas.

The gesture was so sweet; she gave in. Whatever feelings she had for Rafe, when it was all said and done, wouldn't matter. Even if he chose to temporarily forgo his freedom, he would someday want kids, and that part of her would never change. She didn't want to pass on her condition or the chronic pain that came with it or saddle a family with the uncertainty of waiting for the next big break. So, maybe they really could just have a little fun together. The decision lifted a weight off her.

She tossed his pants at him. "Guest bathroom's down the hall. There are extra toothbrushes. I'll make breakfast if you check the road conditions."

Grace hurried through her own bathroom routine, then headed to the kitchen to pull out vegetables for an omelet. Not that she knew if he liked eggs, or veggies, or even the low-acid coffee she'd brewed. Somehow, not knowing made her feel better. Their closeness had to be an aftereffect of total body satisfaction.

She laid a cutting board on the island counter and contemplated a more pressing problem: slicing the red pepper. She could hold one end with her splinted arm, but she wasn't sure she trusted herself with a sharp knife in her non-dominant hand.

"Need help?" Rafe strode into the room, hair dripping, and smelling like the French milled soap in her guest bathroom. She wished she'd thought to shower.

He lifted a pepper from the counter. "Why don't I slice these while you shower? Is a veggie omelet okay? They're my favorite." The coffee pot beeped, and he brightened. "You made coffee. I can't function without it."

The bottom dropped out of her stomach. "Th-thanks."

She hightailed it to the bathroom, stopping only to wrap her lower arm in plastic. She showered hurriedly, the entire time chanting, "It's only lust, it's only lust." So they liked the same breakfast, and he appeared to be able to read her mind. Big deal. They might not have anything else in common. Except swimming, and Dr. Barnes, and work ethic, and—

"Urgh!" Her echoed grunt was her word of the day. She shut off the water and stepped carefully on the mat. *Huh.* Her brow furrowed. This was the first time since they'd arrived at her house that she'd been acutely cautious. Usually, when she had sex, her brain worked overtime. Did her partner weigh enough to crack her ribs? Was there too much pressure on her hip joints? Which positions would be least likely to cause damage?

She dried her legs and scanned for new bruises. When her limbs proved unaltered, she removed the towel and examined her back and chest. Nothing new. And Rafe had touched every inch of her. Kissed and caressed her. She inhaled sharply. *He'd* been the careful one all night. He'd taken on that burden, giving her the gift of one night outside her head.

Then, her heart did a stupid thing. It shifted.

"Urgh..." She toweled off briskly and wrangled her body into clothes as she talked herself down. "He's an orthopedic surgeon, he was just...doing his job."

She'd calmed herself by the time she returned to the kitchen. When she reached the table, she froze. Rafe had laid out their meal, including paper towels folded into napkins. Hot coffee steamed from her mug. For some reason, tears stung her eyes. "It's only lust."

Rafe walked in holding two glasses of—of course—milk. "Did you say something?"

"Um," she blinked. "It's only...just...amazing that you cooked for me. I feel spoiled."

He pushed in her chair as she sat. "Beats hospital food."

He had no idea. "Speaking of hospitals, what time should we head over?"

"Tomorrow."

"Tomorrow?" she squeaked. Really, there was no other word for it.

Rafe nodded, then dumped a forkful of omelet into his mouth, smiling teasingly. He took a solid minute to chew. By the time he swallowed, her napkin resembled the continents of a paper shredder.

"Explain."

"Only the main roads have been plowed, and there's ice all over the city. Small hills, like the one you live on, are skating rinks. My appointments are canceled, and my surgeries rescheduled. It will melt by tomorrow. I'd like to stay here if you don't mind."

Grace didn't mind, though she should have. Still…she folded her arms, wincing at the pressure at her break. "What about the cookie bazaar? We only have today, tomorrow, and part of Friday."

Rafe wiggled his eyebrows and spread his arms. "I'm all yours. Do with me what you will."

Her cheeks flushed immediately.

"Tsk, tsk, Ms. Stewart." He smirked. "We have actual work to do."

She stood and grabbed her plate and silverware. "You think you're funny. I'm going to have you do so many crafts, you'll be dreaming in glitter."

When she tried to walk past, his arm snaked out, and he hauled her gently onto his lap. Without jarring her injury, he leaned down and kissed her. She kept her eyes open, realizing it was their first daylight kiss. As his lips ignited her, she studied the contours of his face. The way his still-damp hair fell over his forehead. Her chest tightened, and her lids fluttered shut. It was amazing, really, how familiar he already seemed.

After a minute, he inched away, wearing a loopy smile. "I feel like I've been kissing you my entire life."

"Oh." She bolted from his lap and stacked their plates, heading toward the sink. Lifting the faucet handle, she filled the basin with hot water and lemon-scented soap, strategizing how she'd wash the omelet pan. She refused to let Rafe take over. In less than a day, he'd already filled every corner of her life.

"Where do you want to start?" She rinsed their plates and arranged them in the dishwasher.

"I had something in mind for today, but I don't think you'll like it."

She eyed him and soaked the pan in the sink. "What won't I like? I brainstormed everything, so I'm pretty sure I like it all."

He stood and gathered their empty coffee mugs before padding over. "Not everything."

He looked far too amused as he rinsed the mugs and started scrubbing the pan. She racked her brain, gasping when the answer hit her. *The cookies.* "No. No way." She backed away from the counter. "I am *not* helping you make gingersnaps. They're my nemeses."

He situated the pan in the drying rack and turned to her, eyes twinkling with amusement. "You can't blame the dessert because you have red hair and a tendency to snap your bones. Gingersnaps and I…we have a history, too."

After drying his hands on her Christmas dishtowel, he withdrew his cell from his pocket and pulled up a picture of a magazine recipe. It was obviously well-used, covered in creases, grease stains, and clumps of dried flour. "Gingersnaps are the first thing my mom learned to make after she left home. She saw the photo and thought baking these would make her a better mother. It became our thing. It's also the *only* thing I know how to bake." He blinked and managed to look adorable.

Wow. He had no shame. She squinted at the recipe, pretending his story hadn't touched her heart. "I don't have some of these ingredients."

"I do." He returned the phone to his pocket. "In the back of my SUV. I picked them up yesterday."

"I have a thousand other things to do, you know."

He maneuvered her against him, and dishwater soaked from his shirt into hers. "If you help me, *I* can be one of the things you do."

The juncture between her thighs throbbed with memory. "Fine, but on one condition."

"Name it."

She tried to think of something to annoy him. "I get to make David's special cookie."

Instead of protesting, his eyes softened. When he placed a tender kiss on her lips, she wondered if baking with Rafe wasn't going to be the most dangerous thing of all.

Chapter Ten

"About time I tracked you down," Charlie's voice boomed across the waiting room. "You been avoiding me?"

Rafe jumped and tore his attention from the window. All traces of snow were long gone, though more was predicted for Christmas. The mercurial Seattle weather perfectly mirrored the tennis match that had become his brain versus his emotions.

"Why would I avoid you?" He couldn't meet Charlie's eye. Of course, he'd been avoiding his mentor. Charlie's intention was for Rafe to date Grace, not for Rafe to discover how many times he could make love to her in forty-eight hours. He cleared his throat. "Cookie Bazaar's tomorrow. Thought I'd check on the progress."

Charlie quirked an eyebrow, causing his forehead to wrinkle clear up to the top of his bald head. "What progress?"

Fair point. The only discernible difference was the series of twinkle lights that crawled up the walls and snaked around the windows and pillars. "Grace assures me it will all come together. After being her," he raised some finger quotes, "'assistant' for the past three days, I believe her. She's quite a force."

"Hmm." Charlie scanned the lights before flaying Rafe with a narrowed-eyed glare. "You two been spending a lot of time together?"

Only every minute Rafe wasn't working. He swallowed and leaned against a pillar, hoping to project some degree of nonchalance. By the way Charlie's lips flattened, Rafe didn't think he'd pulled it off. "Of course. We have an event to engineer. Besides, you and Harmony essentially locked us in a room and threw away the key."

Bad choice of words. Charlie was full-on scowling now. "Just so *you* know, I'm dating Olivia. Grace's mom." His sternness melted at Olivia's name.

"Congratulations." Rafe and Grace had spent many minutes debating the possibility. "Grace wasn't sure it would happen, but I was rooting for you."

Charlie tilted his head, his mien watchful. "You and Grace are close."

It wasn't a question, and Rafe couldn't have denied it. He and Grace had shared nearly everything between pillow whispers and couch cuddles.

"I find myself in a position I hadn't anticipated." Charlie became fascinated with his professionally manicured fingernails. "Grace is like family to me, and you're…"

Rafe tensed.

"Like a son."

Oh. Rafe swallowed over the knot in his throat. Having never had anything close to a father, the feeling was…overwhelming.

"So, you see my problem," Charlie continued. "I can't allow Grace to be another mile marker on your path of freedom."

Rafe stiffened as indignation flooded him. "It's not like that. I'm falling in love with her."

He froze. Blinked. Where had that come from?

Charlie grunted, squinting over the rim of his glasses. "What about your two-year plan?"

"What two-year plan?"

By the end of his first night in Grace's bed, Rafe had realized only an idiot would put limitations on a relationship with her. By the time she'd collapsed on top of him the second night, any delusions about controlling his feelings toward her had flown out the window.

Charlie's frown deepened. "And there's the other side of my dilemma. Olivia says Grace keeps people at a distance. I don't want to see either of you hurt."

Rafe nodded. "I'll be careful." He shook Charlie's hand. "I appreciate it. All of it."

Some of Rafe's emotion must have shown because, all of a sudden, Charlie didn't seem to know where to look. Within seconds, he was gone, and Rafe found himself leaning against the central pillar, contemplating Charlie's claim that he and Rafe were family. He chuckled. "That brings my grand total of family members to three."

Charlie's warning about Grace swallowed any joy he would've experienced. Why *did* she refuse to attend the cookie bazaar? He retrieved his phone from his lab coat, determined to extract an answer. When she answered on the first ring, his heart gave a tiny somersault.

"I have news," she said. "Harmony, Moira, and I are coming to the cookie party. We delivered decorations earlier, and David cornered us. He was quite persistent. I'm telling you, he's gonna do great in sales or politics someday."

That was easy. "So, I can stop asking you?"

"Yes. I guess I need to figure out how to finagle my

new cast through that ridiculous sweater you brought home."

He stilled. Had she realized what she said? "Christmas sweaters are supposed to be ugly." He stopped to clear his throat. "Besides, they go with our theme." When he'd stumbled upon His and Hers sweaters sporting a shark in a Santa hat at the hospital gift shop the day before, it had been like a sign from the cosmos. "Maybe I called for a different reason."

Her sharp exhale crackled like phone static. "Why else would you call?"

His grin wouldn't stop. She'd said 'home.' She was coming to the party. Charlie had been wrong. "Maybe I just missed you."

There was a pause, then a soft sigh. "I don't see how. We've spent fifty percent of our time together since we met."

It wasn't enough. "You've been keeping track?"

"I'm very organized."

"I know."

Rafe realized his face hurt from smiling. Who'd have known, after a lifetime of careful planning and intention, that when he jumped off a cliff, he'd enjoy the fall? "I should be done about four o'clock. Meet me here, and we can add another half a day to our tally."

"I'm looking forward to it." Her voice was a low purr as she hung up.

Rafe inhaled. In the middle of an underwater wonderland, he was buoyant. To this point, his life had been a series of blurred montages interspersed with blinding moments of detailed clarity. The moments that stuck. Graduation, losing his virginity, diagnosing a rare disease. He'd either been too busy or hadn't bothered paying attention to the rest. Yet, he recalled every minute with Grace. He'd crammed more significant memories into the past few days than he had in thirty years of living. And he wanted more.

"Dr. Herrera."

Rafe pushed off the pillar, focusing his attention on the hospital social worker as she walked toward him. When she smiled at the jellyfish chandelier dripping with twinkle lights and the snowflakes he, Grace, and David had cut, something very much like pride puffed up his chest. Grace should have been able to sign her name to her designs much like David had scribbled his on her new cast the day before.

"Is there something I can help you with, Mrs. Jenkins?"

The social worker's smile lines became deep brackets around tight lips. She swatted a loose gray hair from her forehead and adjusted her pink cat's eye glasses. "I need to talk to you about David Larese."

Rafe's fists tightened. His everything tightened. "Shall we talk in your office?"

She nodded, and he followed her through a maze of corridors until she seated him across from her at her desk. He drummed his fingers against his thighs. "What's going on with David?"

Mrs. Jenkins typed something on her keyboard and opened a file, frowning at the screen. She clicked a few buttons and a few more. By the time the printer whirred, a knot had formed in Rafe's gut. "According to his chart, David is scheduled to be discharged Saturday morning."

He nodded slowly, pushing back his nervous energy. He could almost feel himself detaching into doctor mode. "Yes, barring further complications. His most recent scans show the bone healing nicely, and the clots he formed after surgery are gone."

She grabbed the paper from the printer and passed it across the desk. "With the holidays and his record of, uh, excessive energy, we were unable to find a foster family for David. I need you to sign this release stating he's healthy enough for group foster care."

He bolted upright. "When?"

She cast him a wary look. "David's here on the government's dime. You know how it works. Someone will retrieve him as soon as you sign."

Rafe scrutinized the form. He'd signed dozens of these before. In pediatrics, it couldn't be avoided. But this one felt different. This one said he'd be the one to shuffle David back into the system. David. The kid who'd spent every possible moment at his and Grace's side making work a fun adventure. The kid who'd been treated like a shuttlecock between foster homes since he was three and still offered love and acceptance wherever he went. The knot in Rafe's gut got tighter.

"What are the chances he could be assigned in the next few days? His iron levels are still bordering on low. We could keep him longer."

"Dr. Herrera, his other doctors have cleared him." She slid a pen across the desk.

"Okay." Rafe leaned forward. "How about I sign tomorrow night? That way he can go to the party. He practically planned it."

The social worker shook her head. "It's better if he goes before the weekend. With Christmas a week away, he's going to need adjustment time before the routines switch up. I know you're new, but at *this* hospital, we work together for the best outcome for our pediatric patients."

What was wrong with him? The social worker was right. David was just another kid with the cards stacked against him. He wasn't any more or less special than anyone else. Except Rafe couldn't pick up the pen.

"Dr. Herrera." Mrs. Jenkins's voice was firm. "If you don't sign this, Dr. Barnes will."

Charlie wouldn't understand why Rafe hesitated. He didn't even know. Except, when he pictured David, he also pictured Grace. He saw the three of them joking about paper snowflakes and arguing over decorations. Every interaction not a burden, but a joy. Mostly, he remembered tucking David into his hospital bed and promising to put in a good word for a new family. And Rafe had been so caught up in Grace, so worried about *not* being attached, he'd failed David.

"What if I take him?" The words were out of Rafe's mouth before he thought them. His surgical detachment, long gone. He moved the pen back across the desk. Hell, he'd already filed the paperwork and could probably convince Charlie to not only be a reference, but to lean on the right people for quick approval. And why not add another member to his growing family? He'd already jumped ship on his carefully constructed plan, and this new twist felt right. He met the social worker's gaze. "What if *I* fostered David?"

Chapter Eleven

Grace sat at her kitchen table and shook her fingers, hoping to dislodge the sticky strip of red glitter tape she'd been trying to attach, one-handed, to a paper sea star. The tape embedded itself in her hair. Not surprising. Since Rafe had been in her life, none of her extremities worked right. Either still liquid from the way she came apart beneath him or shaking like crazy because she might be making the biggest mistake of her life.

"I need help." Grace waved the tangled mess Harmony's direction.

Her sister glanced up from the undersea Christmas tree she was assembling—a series of paper towel and toilet paper tubes constructed to look like coral. She'd pulled into Grace's driveway ten minutes after Rafe left for work and still hadn't said anything about the pair of mugs sitting on Grace's kitchen table. Either she didn't think Grace would have a man stay the night, or she was marking time for the right moment to pounce.

Harmony's jaw fell open. A glob of pink paint smudged her cheek. "Um, did my baby sister just ask for help?" She ducked under the table and peered around the breakfast nook, lingering briefly on the mugs. "Unless I'm missing something…" Long pause. "There's no one else here, so…"

Grace huffed out a breath. "I've asked for help before."

"When?"

"Today."

Harmony shook her head. "I'm here because I miss Moira and because you planned that New Year's Eve bash too well. Try again."

Grace searched her memories. "Second grade! I asked you to carry my science project board."

Harmony hooted, blowing a small pile of glitter on Grace's carpet. Grace winced. She'd have sparkly socks for the next six months.

"I carried that from your desk to the hallway. And only because you were cradling your first-place trophy." She stood and walked toward Grace. "You've always done everything on your own. It only got worse after...Peter?"

Grace's lips twitched. Harmony's fishing expedition for the identity of Grace's mystery lover was as amusing as it was distressing. Even after four years, she wanted to simultaneously cry and kick something when she heard her ex-fiancé's name. "Not even close." When Harmony smirked, Grace realized she'd given too much away. "My independence has nothing to do with Peter."

"Uh-huh," Harmony propped herself against the table, hands on hips, one pale eyebrow raised. "So, you don't need anybody?"

Rafe blazed into Grace's mind. His taut chest as he hovered above her. The firm press of his lips, of his hips, against hers. His slightly lopsided smile as he buried himself in her body. Grace shifted and shook her head. "Exactly. I don't *need* anybody."

Harmony dimmed.

Grace sighed. "Except you." She held up her tangled red-on-red glittery mess. "I'm stuck."

"Yes, you are, little sis." With careful fingers, Harmony untangled the tape and tossed it aside.

Harmony's gentleness chafed. As if Grace needed to be coddled despite being a capable confident woman.

"I'm sleeping with Raphael Herrera," she blurted.

Harmony froze, and Grace wasn't sure if she should be offended by the look of shock on her sister's face.

"Dr. Hottie?" Harmony propped her feet on the edge of Grace's chair. "This is better than I imagined. A fling with *Dr. Hottie*. Oh God, please tell me, is *he* better than I imagined?"

Grace's embarrassment sparked a four-alarm fire on her face. She pressed her palm to her cheek. "You could never imagine the things that man can do with his hands."

Harmony fanned her face. "I need to find myself a surgeon. STAT." Her demeanor went all dreamy, and Grace was afraid to imagine what her sister was fantasizing. After a moment, she turned her attention back to Grace. "Is this really a fling, or is there more going on? I saw the dishes. You don't usually do sleepovers."

Grace shrugged. "What else could it be?" Though the term, 'fling,' didn't sit right. Rafe meant...more. Hence the edge of panic she'd been pushing down since that first night.

Harmony jumped off her perch and pressed the back of her hand to Grace's forehead. "Are you ill? Rafael Herrera is not someone you sleep with and toss aside." She held up her hand, tapping each finger as she spoke. "He's smart. He's hot. He's a doctor. He comes recommended by someone we trust. And," she ticked her last finger, "he's hot."

Grace pursed her lips.

"It bears repeating." Harmony's eyelids lowered as she frowned. "I know work consumes you, but not to the point you'd discard the perfect man."

Grace slumped in her chair, mainly to increase distance from Harmony. "He's not perfect."

Harmony hoisted a brow.

"He avoids commitment."

"He slept over," Harmony said.

Twice, but Grace wouldn't mention that. "He spends a lot of time fixing his hair and has an unhealthy obsession with international soccer."

Silence.

"Rafe's going to want a family, and he's not going to get that from me."

"Oh. This again."

Harmony rested against the back of the couch and crossed her arms and ankles. Grace didn't fault her for the protective stance. Over the years, Grace had been clear about not wanting to pass on her bone condition. Since Harmony had passed the Osteogenesis Imperfecta gene to Moira, it was a topic the family avoided.

"You still think your niece is a mistake because she has OI."

"No!" Grace jumped out of her chair, stumbling slightly when her sling threw her off balance. "Don't insult me. You know I love her. This is about how *I* want to live."

Harmony exhaled, causing her bangs to dance across her forehead. "Alone?"

A chill crept into Grace's lungs, making it hard to breathe, but she nodded.

"It doesn't have to be that way. Not wanting to give

birth doesn't mean you can't have a family."

"I know that."

"Do you really?"

"Of course!" Grace glared, angry she'd lost her temper first.

It was a sort of contest with the Stewarts, and Grace rarely failed. Ever since she was five and broke her arm tripping off the school bus, she'd gotten far too skilled at withholding emotion. Brushing off each body ache and snap of her bones while ignoring the tiny breaks in her relationships. For some reason, David's toothless smile dashed across her thoughts. The kid with no family who let everyone in. She wished she could be more like him.

Harmony's fierce glare softened at Grace's outburst. "What is this really about?"

This is when Grace would have normally ended the conversation with, 'your OI is so mild, you'd never understand.' Except, she was tired of not letting people try. "Peter and I didn't drift apart after the accident. We broke up."

Harmony sat next to Grace. "Why?"

Grace closed her eyes, picturing Peter's pale face as he'd backed out of her hospital room and out of her life. "I never told him about my condition. He couldn't understand why he'd walked away with a few scrapes, and I had two broken legs, a broken back, and a fractured collarbone. He looked so guilty; I couldn't keep it from him any longer."

Grace trusted Harmony could figure out the rest of the story. After all, her husband had moved out when Moira was born with OI and Harmony was diagnosed. "He left you." Harmony's tone was as bleak as her expression. "Why do you think you hadn't told him?"

Grace arranged the Christmas-colored sea stars into piles according to size. "I think it started when kids stopped inviting me to adventure-themed birthday parties and only got worse when my prom date deposited me at home before heading out with the rest of our friends. In college, the guys I dated treated me like glass, or worse, a ticking time bomb. With Peter, I thought maybe this once, I can be me instead of 'that girl with Osteogenesis Imperfecta.'" She stared at her left hand, her engagement ring tan line long faded. "Look how that worked out."

Harmony twirled a strawberry blonde curl and squished her face in thought. "Maybe you need to keep looking until someone sees you first."

Rafe's warm smile danced in Grace's mind. She buried the image. "It won't happen. Sooner or later, it would grow old. Nobody wants to take care of somebody else in perpetuity."

Harmony straightened. "I do."

Grace was an idiot. "Moira's different. She's family."

"Couldn't you have a family, too?"

The vise-like grip on Grace's heart was instantaneous. It wasn't as if she hadn't asked herself that question dozens of times. "I don't think I'm strong enough."

Harmony jerked like she'd been electrocuted. "What are you talking about? You're the strongest person I know. You don't let OI control you, and you certainly don't apologize for being who you are."

Grace passed her sister one of the doughnuts she'd brought with her. "I accepted myself years ago. It's just hard when I expect the same from other people, and they let me down." She rested her cheek against the table. "It doesn't matter how strong I feel if nobody sees me that way. I thought Peter did until the afternoon I went from being the woman of his dreams to an unwanted burden."

Harmony tore into her maple bar without breaking eye contact. "Peter failed you, not the other way around."

The cool tabletop seeped into Grace's cheek, matching the chill she felt under her skin. "I see how you and mom struggle, watching your children experience the pain that comes with OI. I don't want to put a husband through that. Or kids."

"It doesn't work that way." Harmony ran her maple-scented fingers through Grace's hair. "When somebody loves you, they love all of you."

Grace contemplated her sister's words. She recognized the love between parents and children. It was the kind of love her mom and dad had shared that she wanted to understand. The idea of even one more person seeing her only as a carrier for her condition would be too much. "I'm too breakable."

Harmony's fingers stilled. "Oh, sweetie."

Grace sat upright. "Except for family, every person I've let in has left me. I know you understand. How difficult it is; the fear they feel being around me. Similar to my dread, knowing, at any moment, I'm going to have to pick myself up and move on again. It's exhausting."

Harmony nodded but stayed silent.

"I may be capable, and I may love myself, but there isn't a human on this planet who wouldn't be affected by the sting of constant rejection. And before you give me another platitude, it's not just about protecting my heart."

Grace walked to the coral tree and hot glued a random painted tube to the structure. "Love won't change the inevitable. I'd get hurt. It would make my children's lives harder. Who knows? Maybe the person I marry would no longer see me, but only the inconvenience and cost accompanying OI. How do you recover from that? I think…I think it would break me more than anything has before."

At this point, Grace could barely see through her tears. She set the hot glue gun on the table as Harmony approached cautiously, mascara running in a thick black line through the paint on her cheek, snot dripping, eyes leaking.

They were a mess.

A bubble of laughter tickled its way up Grace's throat, escaping in a puff of air.

Harmony's lips twitched, and their tears turned into giggles, then full-blown guffaws.

They traded the table for the sofa and the decorations for mimosas. When Grace's thoughts were fuzzy and her heart sat higher in her chest, she leaned against her sister's shoulder. "Thanks for listening."

Harmony rested her head on Grace's. "Thank you for trusting me enough to share."

"This is the best Christmas present I ever got," Grace said.

Harmony took Grace's empty glass. "That's the champagne talking."

Grace settled low on the sofa, pillowing her head on Harmony's lap. "No. If you could wrap this conversation and stick it under my tree, it would be all I need."

Harmony frowned. "I want so much more for you. Are you sure you and Dr. Hottie won't work out? He's a doctor. He'd take care of you. It might be worth a talk. He might even agree to adopt some kids."

The alcohol in Grace's stomach soured. *Some kids?* She got cold sweats just thinking about one. "He's going to want everything, and I'm not willing to give him everything."

"Even for that body?" Harmony wiggled her eyebrows, making Grace smile. "You might change your mind, you know."

Grace pictured Rafe's eyes, the way he stared at her like she was the sun and the moon and the stars. She imagined that look fading and being replaced with resentment. "I'm not going to change my mind."

Her sister's eyes reflected Grace's regret as she once again combed her fingers through Grace's hair. "Then, you'd better enjoy him while you can."

Chapter Twelve

Rafe couldn't repress his smug smile when the gingersnap platter was the first emptied. Technically, *he'd* taken the last one, but that didn't stop him from catching Grace's eye across the crowded room and making a big show of eating it. She pantomimed gagging, and he chuckled, loving that she took moments to be silly.

David tugged on his hand, pulling Rafe's attention. "You smile at Grace a lot. I had a foster brother who smiled at our babysitter like that. He was in lo-ove."

Rafe glanced around, making sure people were engrossed in conversation or cookie eating, before crouching by the wheelchair. "So what happened with them?"

David rolled his eyes and threw his head back energetically. "The babysitter got a boyfriend her own age. Marcus ripped up all her notes and said he'd never love anybody again. But then, before I went to another family, he got a crush on another girl. 'Cept this time, he just went around sighing." David's thin eyebrows squished together. "I don't know what happened next 'cause I never saw Marcus after that."

There was that pang again. The one Rafe got when he thought about David's life. He ruffled the kid's hair. "Sighing's unquestionably a step of falling in love. If you ever see me sighing about Grace, you'll know I'm in trouble. Until that happens, how about a chocolate-on-chocolate cookie?"

They dodged through clumps of people, every few seconds stopping to admire the decorations. The magic Grace had created in less than a week. The Christmas tree-shaped coral stood sentinel over a ring of tables draped in paper sea kelp wisps that moved like tentacles as people walked by. Every surface was paper snowflakes, Santa beards, or Christmas colors. Rafe's personal favorite was the clam-shaped MerSanta throne. Nestled under blue wave twinkle lights and sporting paper puff sea anemones, it featured quite possibly the only seasonal Santa willing to don a sparkly, red mermaid tail.

"Did you see the candy canes?" David asked for the millionth time.

Rafe nodded.

"Those were my idea," David said between bites of cookie, spitting chocolate crumbs all directions. "Grace said to pick one thing, and I thought of my cast. Now everybody gets candy canes!"

He beamed, and Rafe realized he'd let David share that story a million more times if it brought that much joy with each retelling. Mrs. Jenkins had helped Rafe speed through the foster parenting hoops, but he hadn't heard back from social services yet. Regardless, he felt connected to David. Not that David knew Rafe's intentions. Not that anybody knew.

A murky cloud of guilt settled on him. He didn't like keeping secrets. Not from Grace. He worked the room with David, occasionally speaking with patrons and patient families, keenly aware that he needed to be having a different conversation. But representing the hospital meant occasionally kowtowing. He managed it for thirty minutes.

He found Grace with Moira and Harmony, standing in line to visit the King Triton of Santas.

"Hello," he said as they approached the trio of Stewart females. His gaze immediately went to Grace before sliding past Moira to Harmony's amused smirk. "I need to speak with Grace." He indicated David. "Would you two mind hanging out with my friend here for a few minutes?"

Grace held up a finger. "Pictures first. Come join us."

Moira scowled at her aunt. "They're cutting!"

"No, it's okay," David said. "We're the decorating co...com...coomty...?"

"Committee?" Rafe supplied.

"Yes!" David leaned forward in his chair and nodded sagely at Moira. "The decorating committee. We did all the work, so we get to cut in any line."

Moira pursed her lips and nodded. "Okay. But I want to be on the committee, too."

She and David high-fived just as the seahorse elves called for Harmony and Moira. After that, a slew of different arrangements ultimately led to a photo of the original 'Decorating Committee.' As Rafe stood next to Grace and David, it struck him that this might be the *first* Christmas photo of the three of them. That there could be more in their future. His body jerked as a thought jolted through him. He *wanted* there to be more. All his life, it had only been him and his mom. Now he had Charlie and, hopefully, David. Maybe Grace. He wrapped his arm around her waist and held her closer.

When the photoshoot was over, Harmony waved

them off. "I've got this. But you'd better come back for clean up."

Rafe grabbed Grace's hand and led her toward a service hallway off the main waiting room. Each step he took tightened the tension in his muscles. The cookies he'd eaten sat like boulders in the pit of his stomach. He swung the doors open and studied the medical equipment lining the wall. Triage carts, wheelchairs, IV pumps, and ventilators. Not an ideal location, but it was past time to tell her about David. Though, he wasn't sure how to find the words when he couldn't even explain it to himself. He released Grace's hand and wiped his clammy palms on his slacks. He cringed when she did the same.

She propped her fist on her hip, obscuring the tail of the Christmas shark. Her sling covered the rest of it. "What's up? You've been mysterious since yesterday, and now you're dragging me down corridors." She tilted her head. "I'd think you were breaking up with me, except we're not in a relationship, so that can't be it."

Rafe straightened. That dart had hit dead center. "I'd really like to hear your definition of relationship someday."

Grace's lips tightened. "Fine. I guess what we have can technically be called a relationship. But—"

He kissed her. Not to shut her up, but because he wanted to. He always wanted to. "I have no desire to break up with you," he whispered against her lips. He could feel her smile and smell the peppermint on her breath. Obviously, a fan of David's candy canes.

She nuzzled his neck, and he wondered why she protested as much as she did. Maybe it was the feeling of control she needed. That, he understood. He'd lost all rationality when he'd agreed to stay at her house, and he'd certainly been snowballing since. He kissed her hair, inhaling the sweet fruity scent of her shampoo. As long as she didn't actually leave, he didn't mind that she pretended not to care. At least for now.

After a heartbeat, she shifted away. "So, tell me why you had to whisk me away from the fête of the year."

"You're so modest."

"You're stalling."

Rafe exhaled, allowing his shoulders to drop. "I applied for an emergency foster care license."

She blinked. "Excuse me?"

"For David." He splayed his fingers in supplication, hoping she'd understand what he still did not. "They couldn't place him. He was going into group foster care. For Christmas."

Her face went stark white as she took a step back.

His heart stuttered.

"I thought you didn't want commitment." She narrowed her eyes. "I thought you wanted 'freedom from responsibility.'"

So had he. "I changed my mind." He ran his hand through his hair. "*You* changed my mind."

She took another step back. This wasn't going well. He was literally scaring her down the hallway.

"I've known you less than a week, Rafe. What you choose to do with your life has nothing to do with m-me."

He would have believed she meant it if her voice hadn't caught. "Yes," he agreed, careful not to step toward her. Not that he would have been successful. His legs trembled like he'd done a hundred squats. "But I enjoy having you in my life. I'd like it to continue. If I get David, if they approve me, things will be different, but I don't want that to mess with what I think we could have." He held his breath and waited.

Grace's fist dropped as she studied him. "I like what we have, too." She chuckled. "And I like David." She walked toward him, and Rafe allowed himself hope. "But I meant what I said. I don't want kids, and I don't do relationships. If he comes home with you, we have to end it."

His jaw clenched with anger and disappointment. "Are you asking me to choose?"

"No." She placed her hand over his fist. "I just can't be a part of it."

He forced his hand to relax and cupped her chin. "Why not? I'm not asking you to have more kids. I'm not even asking for us to be a family. I hardly even know what that means. I'm only asking you to stay in my life a little longer, and maybe David's, too. Then we can just…see."

She hooded her eyes, and he wondered what she was thinking. What parts of herself she still held back.

"Is this about what Peter did to you?"

"If only I could blame it all on him." She sank into a nearby wheelchair, reminding him of that first night they'd met. "I break easily." Her voice was small, almost lost in the festive noise from the other side of the double doors.

He shoved his hands in his pockets so he wouldn't reach out to her. "I'm an orthopedic surgeon, Grace. If anyone can understand your condition, it's me."

She shook her head, and he didn't like how pale she was, how rigidly she held herself. "I mean, it's easy for people to break me. So I've learned not to let them." She swept her hand over her body. "All my life, I've either been excluded or ghosted once others decide I'm a liability. After enough people break your heart, you realize bones aren't what you need to protect."

He lowered himself into a wheelchair beside her. "I'm sorry. If those idiots couldn't accept your OI, it's their loss. Your condition will never factor into our relationship."

"Relationship." Grace pursed her lips. "Well, it *should* factor into whatever we call it. But I believe you'll try. It's why I forced you to sleep with me."

He smiled. Humor was easy. "That was an act of nature."

"Can't fight nature."

"Nope."

The party sounds faded as he stared into her eyes. "I get why you're scared." He wound his fingers through her low ponytail. "I don't personally understand what you've gone through, but I'm scared, too. Last week I was a single freewheeling surgeon, and today I'm a sort of boyfriend/sex toy and potential foster dad."

"Well, if you want to put labels on it." She faced him, eyes serious. "This isn't what we agreed to."

"No, it's not."

"And David..." She sighed. "I'm not sure I can handle kids."

"Just keep doing what you have been, and you'll be fine." She leaned away, and he surrendered her hair as a foreboding tingle started at the base of his spine. "No pressure, Grace."

He didn't mean it. Why else would his next breath hinge on her capitulation? He gave it one last try. "As long as you want me around, I'll be around. If you take the risk, I'll take it with you."

She scrunched her nose, and he wished he could hear her internal debate. Slowly, a small smile danced across her lips. "This is irrational. I've known you five days."

There was acceptance in her tone. He exhaled as relief and joy filled his chest. "Not true. You've wanted me for months."

She nodded solemnly, but a wicked gleam lit her eyes.

Sweet Christmas, how he adored her. "So, we'll play it by ear? With or without David?"

He didn't move until she nodded. "I'm gonna try, Rafe."

It wasn't perfect, but it was a start. He jumped from his chair and pulled her into standing. Pulled her as close as he could. "Let's seal it with a kiss."

Her lips felt like the moment he'd performed his first solo surgery. Exciting and new and right. He would have kissed her forever if the double doors hadn't opened, bringing in murmured voices, holiday music, and the soft snick of sneakers on linoleum. He stepped away from Grace and met the smiling visage of Mrs. Jenkins. His heart stuttered.

"I hope you made up your spare bedroom," she said. "Because you got conditional approval. David goes home with you tomorrow."

Oh, shit. It was really happening. He wrapped his fingers around Grace's and squeezed while beaming a quick prayer to the universe. What had he gotten himself into?

Chapter Thirteen

Only years of experience guided Grace through the rest of the cookie bazaar. She refilled platters, chatted with guests, and worked as an occasional handler for Santa. All of it with a zombie-like proficiency. More often than not, she watched Rafe and David. They bantered like they'd been acquainted for years, instead of weeks.

They looked like a family. One she'd been invited to join.

Fortunately, every time her insides tightened with panic, someone needed her assistance. She'd forget the edge of uncertainty that made her fingers shake and her vision darken. Until David's sweet giggle reeled her in. Until Rafe's smooth baritone worked like a siren's call.

When the party ended, Grace felt stretched thin, equally nervous and hopeful. Within minutes, almost everyone had gone home or back to work. She said goodbye to her mom, who'd shown up as Charlie's date, and pretended interest in a planter when they kissed farewell. Rafe and Harmony started stacking empty platters, while Moira and David sat near the windows with their heads together, looking like they were plotting a global takeover.

Grace took the opportunity to breathe into her diaphragm. To change her focus to what came next.

Dr. Barnes approached and nudged his glasses

higher on his nose. "This was the best cookie bash I've attended. The kids will be talking about it for months."

"You're welcome," Rafe joked, smiling as he dumped biodegradable plates into a compost container. Grace's heart tripped. He looked so…happy.

"You should be thanking me for introducing you two." Dr. Barnes said to Rafe, eyes twinkling.

"Believe me, I do."

Grace shook her head, hoping nobody guessed what she and Rafe had been up to all week. She started peeling Santa hats off the central pillar.

"Have you blocked off your calendar for next year's party, Gracie?" Harmony asked, a little too innocently.

"Rafe would be so lucky," Grace responded.

"Undoubtedly." He strolled past her, dropping a kiss on her cheek, before detaching twinkle lights from the temporary hooks they'd installed. Warmth spread over her entire body. This close, it was hard to remember her reservations. Or the fear she'd prove she wasn't capable of the relationship he wanted.

They worked mostly in silence, joking occasionally, as they restored the room. Every minute or two, ominous tittering would erupt from Moira and David's corner. An evening of cookies, cocoa, and candy canes made their conversation almost manic. It made Grace uneasy. But maybe because she was so used to worrying about Moira's OI.

"Seriously," she shook her head. "Pediatricians sponsor this event, and you never thought to hold it after lunch instead of right before bed?"

Rafe and Dr. Barnes blinked at each other as they rolled up strings of lights, as if it had never occurred to them to change the timing. She laughed. "You need more female doctors."

Rafe offered her a half-smile. "No, we need more parents."

Grace froze. Was he implying she was maternal? That he already saw her as a mom? She searched for David and found him and Moira playing a game that involved snatching paper 'sea anemones' from the pile near the pillar and tossing them back and forth. Moira had claimed an unused wheelchair, and the kids kept rolling backward, widening the distance. David looked as happy as Rafe. Had been grinning non-stop since the social worker and Rafe had told him his idol would be the one taking him home. David's joy erased the nervous tension in Grace's muscles. Was that what it meant to be a parent? To allow someone else's emotions to take precedence over your own?

"What's up?" Harmony's question made Grace jump.

"Everything's moving so fast."

"Huh." Harmony pointed as Moira lobbed a paper ball at David's head. "So you're saying it's too soon to point out those two would make fantastic cousins?"

Grace scowled.

"It *is* fast," Harmony said. "But you and Rafe click. Everyone can see it." She picked up the bin Grace had just finished packing and deposited it next to the others. "If a future with Rafe is something you can't see, or don't think you'd ever want to see, back out now. It's not about you and Rafe anymore. But," she balled her fists on her hips, "if it feels like something you want, even just a little bit, you've gotta try."

The problem was, Rafe felt right, and David felt…like a beautiful and terrifying bonus. Grace grabbed Harmony's hand. "I don't think I'd recover this time. I mean, yes, ultimately, but that doesn't make it easier to put myself out there."

Harmony gently squeezed Grace's fingers and scoffed. "Easier? You've never done anything the easy way."

Grace smiled. "You know what I mean."

"Are you giving this a real shot, Gracie?"

"I'm still here, aren't I?"

Harmony's brows rose as high as her smile was wide. "Yes, you are. And I'll always be here if you need me." She glanced around the room. "Except now. Looks like the guys need help lugging this stuff to storage. You keep the kids alive."

Grace nodded and held up her sling. "At least this keeps me from doing the grunt work."

When Rafe, Dr. Barnes, and Harmony were gone, Grace turned her attention to the children. Except, they weren't in their corner. And they'd gone quiet. Goosebumps skittered up her arm. She scanned the room, spotting Moira and David lined up against the far wall in their wheelchairs. Their hands were on the wheels, and their gazes locked ahead, eyes narrowed, faces set. Two peas in a pod. Grace smiled. They really would make great cousins.

Someday.

Maybe.

Then David started counting down from three, and Grace's heart stopped beating. By the time he'd reached zero, she was already running toward them. But not fast enough. They shot forward, howling with glee, as their chairs rolled across the waxed linoleum, eyes on each other. Grace knew neither of them saw the pillar. They were going to hit it, and she could only get to one of them.

"David!" she shouted and sped toward Moira.

David looked forward, eyes rounding when he saw the pillar. He leaned sideways, and his chair started to topple as Moira careened forward. With her good arm, Grace scooped Moira out of the chair as it crashed into the pillar. David hit the ground with a loud thump, followed by a wail. Then, Grace was falling, tucking Moira against her chest. The pain, when the back of her head hit the floor, was intense, though not as bad as the jolt to her wrist and the sharp sting in her ribs where Moira landed.

Grace's vision dimmed, and her ears rang. Moira's wiggles sent jolts of agony. David's sobs got louder. "Are…you…okay?" she asked Moira, each breath a red-hot poker in her side.

"I—I think so." Moira shifted against her, testing each limb as only those prone to breaks could. She rolled off Grace, and the ache in Grace's ribs decreased enough to do her own bone check. They mostly felt intact. She noted a series of lumps under her and realized she'd managed to land on the pile of paper balls.

"Are you hurt, Auntie Gracie?" Big tears rolled down Moira's cheeks. Her tight red curls sprang in every direction. "I'm sorry I raced the wheelchair."

"I'm…fine." And it was mostly true. She'd long since learned how to fall to avoid damage.

Moira offered a watery smile then scrambled to David. He was on his side, the wheelchair resting on his casted leg. Moira couldn't lift it. Grace stretched her neck, peering around the pillar to see David's face. His panicked eyes broke her heart. She tried to sit up, but the pain in her ribs and her bulky cast made it hard to roll over.

"Are you okay, David?" she managed. He nodded. Tears poured down his small face. "I'm stuck." His voice took on a frantic edge and he started bucking on the ground. "I'm stuck! I'm stuck! Help me! Grace! Help me!"

Each shout was a dagger a hundred times more painful than her ribs. This was it. The nightmare moment she'd never allowed herself to put into words. Swallowing her pain, she rolled and managed to get to her knees. If she could just stand. Just get to him.

"What's going on here?" The question overpowered David's cries. A nurse stood in the doorway, eyes widening as she took in the scene.

Before Grace could respond, Rafe charged into the room, face pale. "David!"

He shot forward and set the wheelchair upright before disappearing behind the pillar. Every few seconds, his hands would flash into her line of sight as he checked David for injuries. She could see the tremble in Rafe's fingertips, even as his voice remained calm.

She was well hidden behind the pillar. Which was ideal. She wouldn't be able to look at Rafe. Not after this remarkable failure. She took a deep breath and rocked back into standing. Dizzy, she leaned against the pillar, hand to her throbbing head.

Harmony sailed into the room and beelined to Moira, doing the same body check Rafe was doing to David. Grace remained unseen. Which was expected. It wasn't like she could help. For an hour, she'd forgotten. Convinced herself that OI wouldn't leave her alone again. She shifted closer to David, and Rafe finally saw her. His brows raised in surprise.

"What happened?"

Grace didn't know how to respond and physically couldn't. That single step had sent her brain pulsing. Through squinted eyes, she saw that David was back in his chair. His sobs had stopped.

"Is he okay?" she managed.

"He's fine."

Relief washed through her. David was okay, whereas Grace had been…shattered. "They decided to race wheelchairs."

Rafe sucked in a deep breath, closing his eyes as the muscles in his jaw tightened. "Well, that wasn't a good idea." She felt chided. "It's a miracle nobody got hurt."

I'm hurt, she thought. But his attention was back on David. She sagged against the pillar, hating that she was jealous of a six-year-old. Hating that all she wanted was Rafe's arms around her. But they had no future. Not after this. She squeezed her eyes shut and mentally rebuilt the walls around her heart. The last week had been a gift she'd known better than to accept.

After an agonizing deep breath, she opened her eyes. "I'm sorry, Rafe. Please don't be angry. I did what I could to stop them." She tried to shrug and winced. "It wasn't enough."

He adjusted David in the wheelchair. "I'm only mad at myself for not being here."

"*I* was here."

He looked her way then, focusing on her for the first time. She could only imagine what he saw. Disheveled clothes, wild hair. Certainly, she wasn't standing straight. His brow furrowed.

"Grace." He surged toward her, but David's hand

276

snaked out and caught Rafe's. Rafe looked down, his surprise evident. And he stayed. As he should have.

She lifted her uninjured arm as high as her ribs would allow. "I tried, Rafe. And I'm done."

She saw the moment her words registered. His brow flattened. His mouth, which had fallen open, zipped into a thin line. How quickly his surprise and hurt shuttered. How effortlessly he'd accepted it. Dr. Barnes strode into the room, ignoring everyone but her. When he reached her, face full of concern and affection, the tears she'd been holding back threatened to fall.

"Charlie." She collapsed against him, the pain in her side a mere whisper compared to everything else. His arms wrapped lightly around her, and she inhaled the spicy citrus of his cologne. How familiar it was. "I want to go home."

"Grace, please." Rafe dislodged David's hand and moved toward them, but Charlie shook his head.

"You see to your patients, and I'll see to mine." Charlie glared at the rest of the gawkers, nurses, and orderlies that had stopped to witness the worst moment of her life. "The rest of you, get back to work." They scattered. Even Rafe crossed to check on Moira.

"Are you hurt?" Charlie whispered.

Grace nodded. She was beyond hurt. "I think I broke some ribs."

He sat her in Moira's empty wheelchair. "It'll be okay, Grace. You're going to be fine."

Rafe watched from across the room, his expression unreadable. "I'll call you," he said.

She didn't believe him. And even if he did, she wouldn't answer. Eventually, Rafe would realize she couldn't be part of a family with kids. She was a liability, and he needed to forget about her. Maybe someday she'd forget about him, too.

"Let's go," she said to Charlie. As he wheeled her out the double doors, Grace didn't allow herself to look back.

Chapter Fourteen

"You're in love."

Rafe looked up from his yogurt and granola, meeting David's golden-brown gaze across the table. "What?"

"You were sighing again." David's spoon clattered in his empty cereal bowl as he flopped on the tabletop like a seal. Rafe chuckled. The past six days living together had proven David did nothing by half measures. "You said sighing was one of the steps of falling in love. Right after smiling. You never said any other steps, so you've gotta be in love."

Rafe blinked. "I wasn't sighing."

"Come on. I wasn't born yesterday." David rolled his eyes and swung his feet to the floor. Rafe winced when David's new walking cast thumped against the linoleum. He hoped the downstairs neighbors didn't report them to the condo's Homeowners Association. He needed the building's gym now that he couldn't drop everything to work out when the mood hit.

David drained his orange juice and slammed the plastic tumbler on the table. "You've been sighing since the cookie night. And more since I put our picture on the fridge."

Against his will, Rafe looked at the picture, then flickered away again. Not fast enough to avoid the inevitable gut punch of regret. It was bad enough David had talked non-stop about Grace for almost a week, but it had been physically painful to print and display the picture from the cookie bazaar. He looked so blissfully naïve, like before he'd figured out his mom was not much more than a child herself, and he'd have to make his own way in life.

Speaking of which…Rafe glanced at his watch. "We have seven hours until we pick up my mom at the airport." Not much time to pull himself together. "What do you wanna do until then?"

David narrowed his eyes, and Rafe grasped that the poor kid was torn between his current line of questioning and his interest in the closest thing he had to a grandmother. While David thought, Rafe took another bite of his yogurt. Wishing it was a veggie omelet. Wishing he was sharing it with Grace. The granola lodged in his throat. Coughing, he gulped his coffee, only to spit it all back into the mug when it scalded his mouth.

David's tiny hand patted his shoulder. "You're a mess, Dr. Rafe."

A bubble of amusement tried to break out of the tightness in his chest. "When are you going to call me Rafe?"

David's eyes darted away as he shrugged. It wasn't hard to fill in the answer: when David was sure he was going to stay.

Rafe covered David's hand. He might have lost Grace, but he had no intention of losing David, too. "Maybe by next Christmas, huh?"

"You mean tomorrow?" David eyeballed the Fraser fir Rafe had delivered, along with an assortment of Christmas decorations, the day after David had come home with him. The tree's base was buried by fragrant sap and a pile of gifts.

"Nah." Rafe gathered his and David's dishes. "That's a lot to expect in less than a week. I mean next Christmas."

David ducked his head and tromped to the dishwasher. "Is Grace the person you love?"

Rafe imagined himself prepping for surgery. It was easier to think of Grace when he summoned his professional detachment. Since he'd taken paternity leave, he'd found it increasingly harder to slip into 'Dr. Mode'. Or maybe he missed Grace more every day. He rinsed the dishes, and David positioned them in the dishwasher. "I spent a week with Grace. I hardly think that's enough time to fall in love."

"But…" David looked up, eyes stricken. "Never mind."

This was definitely not nothing. After drying his hands, Rafe squatted to David's level. "Want to tell me what you're thinking?"

Shaking his head, David added a dishwashing tab and closed the door. "It's just…"

"Yes?" Years of training kept Rafe's tone even.

David turned to him. "If you can't love someone in a week, does that mean you don't love me?"

Rafe rocked back on his heels, lost his balance, and landed on his butt. David giggled, then held out a hand, apparently thinking his six-year-old self strong enough to lift Rafe from the floor. Instead, Rafe invited David down and squeezed him in a side hug. "How are you so smart?"

"I'm in first grade."

Rafe couldn't argue with that logic. "I didn't need a week to know that I love you, David. It only took a minute."

David's lips trembled for a second before a beatific smile escaped. There was enough light in it to break through the gray fog that had surrounded Rafe since Grace left.

Still grinning, David scooted away. "So, after a week, you could love Grace, too?"

In spite of himself, Rafe smiled back. "You never give up."

David shrugged. "Why should I?"

Why indeed? "Is there a reason you keep bringing up Grace?"

David plucked at the graying edges of his cast. "I like her. She let me pick candy canes. She didn't yell, even when I crashed the wheelchair, and she smiles at me all the time."

Rafe swallowed and stared at the picture on the fridge. "She does have a nice smile."

It was genuine. Joyful. Before everything had gone wrong. He was certain she carried guilt over the accident, and he hadn't made it easier. But maybe it wasn't too late. At the very least, he owed her a conversation.

He stood and hoisted David to his feet. "I made a mistake with Grace. I'm not sure my feelings are going to matter much."

David paled. "Were you mad that Grace saved Moira instead of me? 'Cause we talked about that. I didn't even get hurt 'cept that bruise."

"That's not it." Rafe didn't fault Grace's decision. Moira had OI and had been in more danger. He faulted his own. Grace had risked her safety for the children, and he hadn't considered her health until too late. Now, he understood her warnings and reservations. Having a partner with OI took conscious effort, and he wanted to take the time to learn.

David retrieved his crutch from the kitchen counter and tucked it under his arm. "Can we go to Grace's mom's house for Christmas tomorrow with Dr. Barnes? Maybe we can tell Grace we're sorry, and she could come over."

The scheme could either lead to heaven or a quick road to hell. He may have fallen fast, but he'd fallen hard, and he wasn't sure his heart could handle another rejection from Grace. He'd sent a dozen apology texts and phone messages, and she'd only responded with a single text: *Thanks for a fun week. Send David my love.* A fun week. Like he'd been merely a plaything to pass the time. If she'd been trying to hurt him, she'd succeeded.

Rafe ruffled David's hair. "She knows you're sorry, kiddo. I promise. Go brush your teeth and get dressed."

"Why?"

David's favorite question. And a thought-provoking one. They'd already agreed to spend Christmas Eve watching movies and eating frozen leftover cookies. But David's wisdom had, once again, reigned superior. Why should Rafe give up? He didn't have more to lose. If this sick, empty feeling combined with smiles and sighs was love, he really had no choice but to try one more time. "We have some last-minute shopping to do."

"Hmm." David narrowed his eyes at the tree. "I don't think I need more presents." Then he lit up, and Rafe's whole body expanded with its warmth. "Are we gonna see Grace tomorrow?"

"Yup." Rafe crossed his fingers. "I hope it works out."

"It will, Rafe." David nodded sagely as he thumped his way to the bathroom.

Rafe.

He knew he was smiling like a fool. And perhaps he was. Maybe everything would work out, and this would be his *first* best Christmas. Just in case, he crossed the fingers on his other hand.

Chapter Fifteen

Grace ignored the knock on her bedroom door, then pulled her quilt over her head when her mom walked in anyway. "Go away. I'm recuperating."

Her mom flipped the blankets back. The glare from the sun on the fresh snow outside created a red-gold hair halo around her mom's freckled face. "With you hiding under your covers, surrounded by band posters and swim ribbons, it's like we've gone back in time, and you're moping over a boy again."

Grace side-eyed her mom. Dressed in chic slacks and a designer Christmas sweater, she looked utterly innocent. Grace knew better. Her mom had no doubt heard what transpired after the party. Olivia Stewart's greatest gift was meddling in her children's business.

"I have two broken ribs, and the nieces and nephews had us up at six. I need a few minutes."

"You'll be fine." Her mom sat inches from Grace's toes. "Charlie says your ribs are only slightly cracked."

Grace couldn't believe it. "Wh—Did you—My ribs—" Was this the same woman who panicked when Grace popped her knuckles? "Even slightly damaged ribs hurt, you know." She sat up, dramatically wincing at every tiny twinge. "It's Christmas. Where's your compassion?"

"I have three hours to prepare a meal for sixteen people. I'm tapped out."

"Make my siblings help." Then Grace did some mental math. "Sixteen people?"

"Harmony and the boys are working on side dishes. I need you on salad detail."

Grace frowned, the three extra people a smaller issue than her mom's behavior. "It will take me twenty minutes to chop a carrot. I know my limitations."

"I thought you wanted me to stop babying you. You're an independent woman, and I need to treat you accordingly."

"Independence doesn't live up to the hype." Tears filled her eyes, and she blinked them away. "Like I said, I *know* my limitations."

In a breath, Grace found herself cradled against her mom's chest. "It sounds as though you've been doing a lot of thinking."

Grace nodded, inhaling her mom's cotton candy perfume and steadying herself against the beat of her heart. "There's nothing like hiding in your childhood bedroom for a week to help you see how far you *haven't* gone in life."

"Pish-posh. You're accomplished, and you know it. This is about Rafe. Maybe if you tell me what went wrong, we can fix it."

"I thought you were done babying me."

Her mom squeezed her. "Old habits die hard, but I promise to try."

"I want to change too, but…" Grace sucked in a lungful of air. "I'm too broken."

"No, you're just wounded. Everyone knows broken things heal stronger."

And because that echoed what Rafe had said, and because she missed him so much, the dam burst. She told her mom about the distance she'd kept people at. Her fears of rejection. The moment she'd broken Rafe's trust.

"I've been unfair to him, but I was hurting. I didn't recognize that he was just doing his job." A familiar murky sickness twisted in Grace's gut. It did every time she remembered how she'd thought worse of him for not coddling her like her family did. For going straight to his patient. "I'm so selfish." She shuddered, thinking of the nasty text she'd sent and the way she'd been avoiding his calls. "I owe him an apology."

"And maybe a serving of grace?"

Grace's lips twitched. "I see what you did there. Yes, I'll give him a call."

Her mom stood. "No need." She clapped twice. "This is going to make tonight's seating arrangement so much easier."

Grace jumped from the bed, ignoring her protesting ribs. "You invited Rafe to Christmas!"

Her mom dismantled her perfect bun and rearranged her hair. "And David. And Rafe's mom, Valeria."

Grace sagged against her dresser. "His mom?"

"Yes. After you two talk, the day's going to look much better."

Her mom was halfway out the door before Grace was able to gather enough thoughts to form a single word. "Wait."

Her mom paused and turned, pale eyebrows raised expectantly.

"It's not about Rafe." Grace grabbed a teddy bear from a pile on her dresser. "I accept that I need to apologize, but we don't have a future." She squeezed the worn stuffed animal. "I can't give him what he wants."

"What does he want, Gracie?" Her mom's eyes were

soft.

"A family." She needed her mom to understand, so she wouldn't feel like she was making a terrible mistake. "I can't be a mother."

Her mom plucked the bear from Grace's arm. "What are you talking about?"

"I couldn't help David. I couldn't take care of him. I can't keep my kids safe." This was the truth she'd been unable to articulate until she'd been lying powerless on the floor. The real reason she'd shied away from the thought of children.

"You kept Moira safe."

Grace didn't have a response for that.

"Is this why you pushed Rafe away? Why you haven't returned his calls?"

"How did you—?" Dumb question. "Charlie has a big mouth."

"Charlie loves Rafe." Her mom kissed Grace's forehead. "I think you love him, too."

Grace nodded. There was no use denying it. Her heart had flipped the moment he'd walked into her hospital room, and then it had jumped around the entire week, never quite resting where it had before.

"You are a smart, compassionate, and loving person. You can be anything you want." She sat Grace on the bed like she was a small child. "The fact that this hurts so bad tells me you want it, but you've somehow convinced yourself it can't happen."

That *was* the problem, because Grace did want it. Rafe. David. Everything. She just didn't know how to make it work.

"You and Rafe are good for each other," her mom said. "Build on that. Together, the little things won't matter."

"You mean the little things like watching a child get hurt?" She tried to cross her arms, but the cast and her ribs made it impossible. "I get it, Mom. I'm a good person. Truth is, I like me. Even the OI part. That doesn't mean I'm meant to be a wife or a parent."

"Did you ever suffer because of your dad? He had four children and OI. Did he ever fail you when you needed him?"

Grace blinked. "Of course not. And Dad had *you*."

Her mom winked. "A worthwhile partner makes everything easier."

Grace groaned. She'd run right into that trap.

"Your dad had the same fears as you, Gracie, but he didn't let that stop him from having a family. I'm going to tell you a secret." Her mom leaned so close Grace could smell the coffee on her breath. "We are *all* scared of the unimaginable. You have to decide if the reward is worth the risk."

She straightened and smoothed her pants. "I wouldn't trade a minute of the time I've had with you, including hospital visits. And your father wouldn't have changed a single decision that led to our family." She kissed Grace's head. "Now, I'm way behind schedule. Come out when you're ready."

Then, Grace was alone, her heart bleeding and mind whirring. She gathered her cell from her nightstand and scrolled through Rafe's texts. She'd been dismissive, and he hadn't given up. He was coming to dinner. He was fighting for her. He deserved so much more than she'd given him.

A sob tore through her, and the sound disappeared swiftly, sucked into the walls, flooring, and bedding that were the hallmarks of her past. She'd been fighting, too. For a lifetime. Fighting to stay safe and whole. For independence. Why couldn't her next fight be for Rafe? For David?

She opened the picture from the cookie bazaar. David grinned from his wheelchair, her fingertips resting against his neck. She remembered the downy softness of his hair. The way he'd grounded her. On her side stood Rafe, his arm wrapped around her waist. Although his face was forward, his eyes were on her, his smile soft.

She wanted him. Them. All of it. This time when she broke, she didn't try to stop it. She'd heard that cracks let the light in, so she allowed herself to shatter. To splinter. Her fear, her sadness, her disillusionment poured from the fissures in her heart. Then, she let in hope. And love. And courage. It might take a while, and she would stumble, but she knew when she was rebuilt, she would be stronger and full of light.

Chapter Sixteen

Charlie answered Olivia Stewart's door with a happy smile, and Rafe was grateful his *de facto* dad was on his side. He followed Charlie through the house, acutely aware he might see Grace at any moment. Each second she didn't appear, the box weighed heavier in his arms. In the kitchen, he nodded and smiled through endless introductions—Grace's family, his mom, David. Still, she didn't appear.

Someone offered to take the box. "No!"

The room, which was already quiet with the first awkward exchanges of new acquaintances, fell silent. Rafe's mom sent him the Mom Glare, and everyone else watched with coiled anticipation, the air crackling with curiosity and expectation. He hadn't considered that they'd all know his and Grace's story or would have an opinion on its outcome. It wasn't as though he'd spent a lot of time around a large family.

He rested the box on the counter and wiped his palms on his jeans, smiling at the eight pairs of eyes that watched him. "We brought presents. David wrapped them."

The eyes shifted from Rafe to the gifts. Wine for each adult, and packages for the kids that resembled holiday-themed lumps with tape tails.

"You shouldn't have," said one of the men. His teasing tone was what Rafe imagined an older brother's would be.

"Grace!" David's happy shout pulled Rafe's attention to the living room. Pulled his feet there as well.

She and David hugged in front of the Christmas tree. The bright lights cast a rainbow aura, and all Rafe could see was the two of them. Smiling at each other. Loving each other. The box almost slipped from his grasp. He swallowed. "Grace."

She stilled, straightened the hem of her holly berry t-shirt. "Merry Christmas, Rafe."

He became aware of his own shallow breath, noticing even the kids were silent witnesses. Then a buzzer went off, and Olivia Stewart giggled. "Oh my! Dinner is almost ready, and we have so much to do." When no one moved, she cleared her throat. "Well, if nobody wants to eat…"

In an instant, chatter resumed, chairs scraped across floors, cupboards opened and closed, and the kids went back to playing. Only David, Grace, and Rafe remained.

David tugged on Grace's arm. "We made you a present."

Her gaze tore from Rafe's as she smiled down at David. "Made it? I can't wait."

She settled on a sofa, and David curled up next to her, both their casts hanging over the cushions. Rafe didn't feel that brave. He sank into an armchair across from them, chest so tight, the process was uncomfortable. He drank in Grace, frowning at her red-rimmed eyes. He hated that she'd been crying. But her smile was genuine, and there was a subtle difference in the way she held herself. Shoulders lower, spine rounded, posture open.

Something inside her had changed. The thought

terrified him as much as it gave him hope. Eyes never leaving her, he removed her gift from the box and slid it across the coffee table.

"We made you a gingerbread house," David said, bouncing in his seat. "It took all day. I put candy canes *everywhere*! And look!" He pointed to a gingerbread person trio with red-hot cinnamon dot eyes and dripping with icing. "I made us. You, me, and Rafe!"

Rafe watched as she inspected every detail, from the lopsided walls to the drips of icing that never stayed quite straight. She lingered over the gingerbread family but didn't comment. He wished she'd look at him. Maybe then he'd know if he had a chance.

As if reading his thoughts, she glanced up, and he stopped breathing. There was nothing in her eyes except possibility. "I thought you only baked gingersnaps."

He forced himself not to smile, not to cross over and kiss her. "I'm learning new things. Gingerbread is strong. Like you."

She nibbled on her lip. "It still breaks."

"I'm here for that, too. For all of it."

Her smile was slow, but when it came, so brilliant, he had to blink at the sting in his eyes.

"Check inside," David commanded, prying off the roof.

Grace peered in the house and hesitated before pulling out the oblong jeweler's box.

Rafe cleared his throat. "It's from me and David."

When she had a hard time with the lid, David took over. "Don't worry. You can open the one next year."

He popped the case, revealing the gold chain and locket nestled inside. "Just like in that singing orphan movie." David's chest puffed up. "Rafe and I are like…Daddy Richbucks."

She chuckled and examined the necklace. "It's beautiful." She let it dangle from her fingers. The shiny surface threw color around the room.

Job done, David pried a candy cane from the roof and wiggled to the floor. "Me and Rafe figure we'll just take new pictures every year at the cookie party." He clomped away, and Rafe and Grace were alone. Well, as alone as possible in a house with sixteen people.

"Open it."

She pressed the button and used her thumbnail to maneuver the tiny, hinged insert that revealed the tri-fold charm. Rafe examined her face, wanting to catch her reaction when she saw the pictures inside. He and David on either side, Grace right smack dab in the middle of their shared heart.

Everything seemed to balance on the edge of this moment. The tip forward into something new and exciting, or the breathless backward plunge into emptiness.

When she froze, he stood and settled into David's vacated spot. Close enough to smell the fruity scent of her shampoo. To absorb her heat. "There's a lot I want to say, but the most important is, I love you."

She gasped but didn't speak.

"I know it's only been a few weeks, but I don't want to go back to a life you're not a part of. David, too. He's around forever if I can manage it." He pointed to the locket clutched in her hand. "This is what's in my heart, Grace. What's in yours?"

He forced his body to stay relaxed. He'd said what he needed to. The rest was up to her.

Her brows knit, and her lower lip trembled briefly.

"How are you okay with all of this change so fast? My head is spinning. My whole life is spinning. Why do you sound so calm?"

"I spent my whole life working toward goals." Needing to touch her, he wound his fingers in her hair. "When I met you, my plans didn't seem as important." He chuckled at the memory. "I fought it, of course. For about a day. I stopped listening to my head and started doing what my heart wanted. Then, everything avalanched, and honestly, I've never been surer of anything."

She released her hair from his grip, eyes watery. "That easy, huh?"

"Nothing's easy, but you're worth the effort." He scooped the locket from her fingers. "Let me."

She turned, and he opened the clasp, bringing his arms around her. "I'm sorry about what happened the night of the bazaar. I switched into automatic pilot, and I am so regretful I didn't stop to check on you." He said this next to the shell of her ear and was encouraged by her resulting shiver.

"I know," she sagged against his chest, and he closed his eyes to savor it. "I was afraid you'd seen my body's limitations and decided I was too much work. It felt like every other time when people rejected me because of my condition."

He trailed his finger down her arm, watching goosebumps form on her pale skin. "I know I'm going to make mistakes, but OI is part of you, and I want all of you."

She turned and kissed him lightly. Once. Twice. "I'm sorry this hasn't been as easy for me," she whispered against his lips. "I'm sorry about that text and for not calling you back. I wasn't ready."

"And now?" He held her gaze and held his breath.

Her lips lifted, and her nose scrunched, not quite obscuring her freckles. "And now, I am. Or at least the closest I've ever been."

He gathered her to his chest, needing her weight as an anchor. "And David?"

"We'll work through it. I need some mental adjusting, and I'm going to need your help, but I'm happy with David. I love him." She pressed a firmer kiss to Rafe's lips. Soft and sweet and sure. "And I love you." She smirked. "I've loved you since the first time I saw you in that barely-there swimsuit."

He laughed. The rumble started deep in his chest, messing up the rhythms of his heart. He palmed the locket where it rested against the vee of her T-shirt. Allowed his fingers to linger on her soft skin as he pressed it against her chest. "Two weeks ago, I didn't even know your name, and now all I think about is how soon I can convince you to change it to mine."

She sighed loudly. "You're making plans again. Maybe you'll become a Stewart."

He couldn't stop his happiness from bubbling over. "We'll discuss it. We have time to figure it all out."

"A lifetime." And there were stars in her eyes that had nothing to do with twinkle lights.

Then, her mouth was on his, and he could feel the promise of her kiss seeping into every part of him. He'd never be convinced it wasn't possible. Or that the universe hadn't caused the snowstorm that brought them together. Or that Charlie hadn't had this in mind from the second he'd asked Rafe to consider a job in Seattle.

Something light smacked him in the head, and he

pulled away in time to see the partially sucked-on hook of a candy cane fall into his lap. "Dinner's ready," David said. "I thought you'd never stop kissing."

Rafe blinked, immediately understanding the hint of irony most parents had when they talked about the 'joys' of children. Grace looked over his shoulder. Her face paled, then flushed.

"There are fourteen people staring at us right now, aren't there?" he asked.

She nodded. "They're all smiling."

"Even David?" he asked, cupping her cheek.

"Especially David."

"Let's go, love birds," Harmony yelled. "I'm hungry."

He stood, helping Grace to his side, and faced the people that were to be his family. He was unsure of how it had all happened but was very glad it had. He entwined his fingers with Grace's. "You ready for this?" he asked.

She smiled at him. Dazzling. Bold. Confident. "Let's get started."

Thank you for purchasing
this publication of The Wild Rose Press, Inc.

For questions or more information
contact us at
info@thewildrosepress.com.

The Wild Rose Press, Inc.
www.thewildrosepress.com

CPSIA information can be obtained
at www.ICGtesting.com
Printed in the USA
LVHW010903160622
721261LV00013B/268